To Jenny,

TWISTED
BRANCHES

All the best,

Black Shuck Books
www.blackshuckbooks.co.uk

First published in Great Britain in 2023 by
Black Shuck Books
Kent, UK

Set in Caslon
Titles set in Baskerville Old Face
Cover art and interior design © WHITEspace, 2023
www.white-space.uk

978-1-913038-87-8

Twisted Branches

by

Rachel Knightley

BLACK
SHUCK
BOOKS

*For my mother, for always trusting me to discover
the power of my own stories.*

Contents

~

Letter

[2021]

Take two slices of the thinnest cucumber. Cut with the sharpest knife available, ever so slightly aslant, so their reach is longer than seems quite natural.

Lay one of the slices on the grey-streaked white marble chopping-board (the white board, not the brown one; Adam, I am looking at you. Dead as I no doubt am, I am looking at you, my youngest darling. A bread-board is not a chopping-board, Adam. If the board in your hands is made of wood then it is a bread-board and your matrilineal line deserves better than to be rotating in our respective graves. Put it down and pick up the white one. Don't be too sure I'm not watching. Especially in the kitchen).

Spread the first of the two cucumber slices with cream cheese. You'll find it on the bottom shelf of the fridge towards the left, unless Gerald has moved it – and he almost certainly has, so you may as well look on the top shelf first.

It occurs to me only now that the top shelf of the fridge-freezer is the one corner of the house I've never seen. Your father is six foot five and has no idea how anyone can be otherwise; I married a man with no concept of how tall he is. I'm contemplating moving a chair over there when I've finished writing to the pair of you, simply to *have* seen it. The one mystery left of this house; seen and ignored by the rest of you every day. Perhaps that's what I was always painting: what I couldn't see. There is no such thing as dull when it comes to other people: the normalcy of other perspectives, so unsettlingly different from one's own. Particularly those closest – physically closest, at any rate: it was never for me to say who any of you consider truly closest to you, though perhaps I may guess.

There is no need to answer, even if you could – she is gone. As, presumably, am I.

Sprinkle dry-roasted peanuts over the cream cheese. The nuts must be dry-roasted, however confidently Vincent will say it doesn't matter. Vincent saying it doesn't matter has nothing to do with the peanuts, any more than it has ever had to do with anything else but Vincent. Things not mattering works very well for Vincent, drenched as he is in the kind of thoughtless ease that opens doors and melts walls simply by smiling at them and who, therefore, does not know what he is missing: that there is a deeper, more complicated world he is skirting over. Perhaps that is for the best. It is of no use and certainly no joy to know where other paths would have ended.

But you are right, in your way, Vincent; just as your little brother is right that you "can" use a bread-board to chop vegetables: nothing really matters if you care little enough. But what is also true, my darlings, is that *everything* matters, when looked at in the right way, through the right pair of eyes; everything matters and goes on mattering – and that is a truth far more disturbing.

The individual peanuts will need to be poked into order, or they shan't stay where you put them. Pick up any stragglers, poke them back where they were, sprinkle a few more over anywhere you see space. You can eat the escapees; they are fair game, though don't put that on the recipe card. The one important thing is to keep the first ones jammed in. Extras are expendable.

This part always puts me in mind of making a hedgehog cake at school – not out of a hedgehog, you understand; I believe it was marshmallow sponge cake and chocolate fingers for spines although at all these decades' distance I couldn't swear to the cake-mix. Thanks to Vincent, by which I suppose I must mean thanks to Veronica as there is increasingly little difference (I'll say this for Veronica: Veronica knows everything matters, if only because it all orbits her: I may never have said so but you've found your match there, Vincent) I understand we have vegan chocolate fingers in the biscuit tin. That will have to do.

I don't know why it suddenly should matter, why I need you to have known my night-time snack of choice or that chocolate fingers always reminded me of hedgehogs. I assume that my reason is correct, that my story is relevant; we'll never know now, of course. If Gerald has taken this letter from where I am going to put it in the one remaining locking draw of your grandmother's desk, it will be at the time I asked him to do so. If you're reading this, we all know what that means. I trust your father absolutely, in all things unrelated to refrigerator shelf height.

Now for the second slice of cucumber. You will have cut it the same width and length as the first, and you might choose to cover it with just as much cream cheese. A few peanuts will escape again when you press the halves together (remember, Adam, not the bread-board, please. I cannot bear to think of green juice leaking like so much spilt blood into those beautiful grooves) but extras, as I say, are expendable if the principals are packed in close enough. There's no point planning exact quantities at this stage in the recipe. This house – and particularly the kitchen – rebels against too much control as aggressively as the world beyond it does. Just stick the important things back in whenever they try to fall out. Extra spines never hurt anyone. Even when they're meant to. And you know how rarely I really hurt anyone and only, ever, to protect you.

Perhaps you think I was mad. Perhaps we all think that of the choices of others. But all this private nonsense, the peanuts and cream cheese and half-memories of chocolate hedgehogs, these are the things I couldn't bear to think I'm dragging with me into the darkness.

Now, at this point comes the first bite. I won't overshadow that with my experience. I'll leave the moment to you. Perhaps you'll hate it. Perhaps you'll never have thought me mad until you taste this. Not everything we love is likeable, certainly not to others, and in that I will have been no different from anyone else. My true secrets were accidental. I was the late-night painter, you the heavy sleepers. In daylight and dark, I saw more in this house than you ever did, more to defend from the world – and more to defend the world from. All my stories, the ones I carry tightest, happened here. And words were not enough to hold them, in the end. Painting is so very much safer. In words you take a side, declare a perspective, expose who is right and who wrong, what is real and what imaginary, as if it is ever that simple.

Paint a picture, and you whisper no such secrets, make no such promises. You attribute no thoughts, and can have none attributed to you; only colours. Observation before interpretation. Everything in one snapshot, with nothing of which you are unaware slipping out through your version of a story and into the world, to be seen by all but yourself. Who would not prefer the simple, unarguable truth and safety of a snapshot? Can you blame me for picking up a paintbrush and never writing another word?

It feels strangely sad now that none of you ever saw me make these peanut-and cream-cheese circles, drink my late-night coffee blacker than the night beyond the open curtains, our fir trees, earth and sky forming one death-blank canvas while inside I sit in the shadow of each new white one, the moths circling the lamp I tilt towards my canvas, and watch them driven mad by my beams of misdirected light. While you all go on sleeping and I turn each blank void in turn to something so much more complicated, something of my own design.

Never mind the cream cheese and peanuts. Vincent is right: most things do not matter. Only know that I loved you, my darlings. Whatever else may come, if you are too much like me and never do quite know what else is real, know that this was.

Tangled Roots

[2022]

They're standing alone in the middle of the wood but she takes the call. Nobody calls anyone this time on New Year's Day, and she never answers an unidentified number anyway. But she takes this one, and she might as well have left that house in her phone memory, because there's nothing unknown about that number. Maybe that house – that time, the list of family mobiles scribbled in archaically neat emerald fountain pen, blu-tacked to the edge of both computer screens in that forest-green study, packed with the scent of ink and watercolours that as she presses the green button and shuts her eyes she can practically see him calling from – maybe she knew something more than the number. Maybe she knew something else entirely.

'Kerry-Alice?' He says in the way only *they* ever did, as if she has a perfectly sensible name. As if the two words belong together, as if there is nothing strange or unrealistic in the coupling of tones, that they come as naturally together as the twist of roots she sits down on now before her legs have a chance to shake.

'Hi.' She tries to double-bluff herself into putting nothing but the friendliness she truly feels – always truly felt – for that voice into her own, and not the years of questions behind it. But there's only one reason he would be calling. If it were anything else, he wouldn't be allowed to.

'Kerry-Alice. Hi. Look, I'm sorry to be calling with bad news…'

Effie is dead. She knows this means Effie is dead. Her wood disappears around her, a blurred kaleidoscope of brown and green. She sees the house he's calling from so clearly that she feels but does not see Daniel take her hand, settle himself cross-legged in front of her, knees to knees on the sloping pile of tangled roots. She grips his hand, not in thanks necessarily but to help keep the tears out of her voice. She knows everything she needs to, knew as soon as the phone rang. Still she asks, 'What happened?'

'Well the important thing is it wasn't Covid. She got through all that fine. You know Mum, that was important to her...'

He trails off and she doesn't leap in. Just listens to his silence, until more words come. When they do, she doesn't speed or stall him with sounds of agreement or sympathy. She'd known, she supposes now, the one way her exile would end. That she would see their faces again only when the central one was gone.

Does he know how it ended? Why she's not been back? Does he understand she didn't choose to leave them? That it wasn't him she betrayed? The house phone was really the business phone. He hadn't called from his mobile. Did he wonder about the risk of letting her think the person whose death he'd phoned with news of was calling her after five years' – unexplained, she had no doubt, Effie never explained anything – absence?

'...which meant she knew her time was limited, that was the thing. And she'd always said that if it came to it, well, you know. She... that she wanted to choose.'

'Oh God.'

'Yeah. Look, the funeral... it's... Well, that's the problem really. The funeral, it's just family, she was very clear on that...'

'Of course.'

'And it's not that I didn't think of you as... that we...that I...'

'Of course.' She rescues him from having to tell her what they both already know. Effie wouldn't have wanted her there. Not the final version of Effie. Not the one she'd last seen, and sees now in this blurred and empty glade, ever-present worry lines smoothed, in the last moments she saw them, by that mask of perfect anger.

'But if you'd like to come by the house?'

Her eyes refocus on the wood around her. The trees are clearer, sharper. A woodlouse runs over the trunk above the knot in the branch she finds she's pressed her hand to. She'd know this place no less for her eyes being blurred, the scent of earth and air recycling itself over and over so that in all her life nothing seems to have changed here while at the same time everything has, everything is always recycling itself over and over, coming back in different forms if you wait long enough.

'I mean, the thing is, we'll be selling it. The house.'

'Oh. God.'

'Eventually. We need to empty it first. Comparatively at least. I mean space sells, doesn't it? Emptiness. That and the smell of bread. And coffee. People want to project on a blank canvas, don't they.'

'Yes. Yes, they do.'

'Yeah, well.' The beginnings of a laugh. 'They certainly couldn't do that in its usual state.'

'No. No, I suppose they couldn't.' That house would never know how to be empty. It was the fullest place she'd ever known. Easels, paintings, expectations, sons, students, rivals. Effie. Effie. Effie. Tears burn the backs of her eyes as she mentally walks the parquet floor of the painting studio downstairs, stands at the French windows looking out into the overgrown garden; the black-grey ghosts of Aubergine and Cauliflower appearing in briefly snatched sightings, all bright eyes, sharp ears and flicking tails, darting into and out of sight.

Daniel's other hand is on hers. She's grateful. That he doesn't ask what is happening, demand knowledge. Just waits. Trusts that whatever needs to be done she is already doing it, and doing it well. The borrowed reality of Daniel's belief in her is strong in her hands; she can prove that family wrong one last time, even if she can't prove anything to the one person she aches to show how wrong, how vilely wrong, she is. Was. How like that irreplaceable, terrifying bitch to find any possible way to hurt them all; to make, to score, one last interminable point. To find one more way of not just cutting off her nose to spite her face but leaving her family to mop up the pieces, the collateral of tears and blood as likely theirs as her own.

When they've picked the time and made arrangements and ended the call and the mobile is still pressed to her cheek she tells Daniel, 'Effie's dead.'

'Fuck,' he says and then, not letting go of her hand, 'Are we still breaking up?'

She nods, and smiles, and squeezes his fingers in the silence, listening to the familiar rustle and whisper of her own private wood. It occurs to her for the first time in decades how lucky she is for it to be normal to say "my wood", the way other people said "my kitchen" or "my living room" or "my shed", can see afresh how her life gloriously disobeys the London rules she hadn't noticed herself internalise, that you could be rich in space and time without the money that bought them. For her to walk from her back door to her wood was no longer than walking the length of what floors had been revealed to her of Effie's house, from the painting studio to as high as she'd ever reached, one floor, half-way up the spiral of landings. She feels her face breaking into an unfamiliar, inappropriate smile.

It was a corpse that brought them together. It was fitting that another corpse had signalled there was no way back.

So why did she feel so much like it was all beginning again?

The Moth, Part One

[1993]

'We look like we belong up there,' her reflection whispers into the ear of mine, from where she's pressed to my side as I gaze up comfortably into my own eyes. 'Don't we?'

'It does look like it's always been that way,' I tell her, the right hint of boredom at the edges of my voice. Though we are together looking up at the image of us reflected on her bedroom ceiling, the truth is every last pair of eyes in that image – hers, her reflection's, my reflection's and mine – each of us is really looking only at me. The need for reassurance is in every quavering word of what's left of her voice; every quiet, missable inch of her posture. I've won, and we both know it. Her world has reshaped itself with my world as the centre. It was that easy. Now all I have to decide is what to do with my winnings; to keep or to spend.

'So you like the mirrors?' she asks, turning her body to face us on the ceiling, trying to catch my reflection's eye where my real gaze has fluttered out of reach again. The leg beneath her apologetically long skirt, revealing only the curled tips of unpainted toenails, drifts so lightly over mine I barely feel the change in touch.

'Why shouldn't I?' My eyes drift briefly from my reflection to hers, before defaulting back again.

'No reason. It's just, well…' She adjusts the one open button of her disappointingly baggy, pseudo-Victorian gothic blouse. With people her own age it probably succeeds in its intention of projected maturity. To me, it speaks of how determined she is to have died before she's lived. 'Well, good.'

'Well then.' I tuck an escaped dull-blonde strand behind her ear, smile at the improvement. She flushes, self-conscious, unsure whether to be pleased or concerned at the latest subtle alteration I've seen wanting and made right in the time it takes her to wonder what it was about her that needed fixing.

'Good,' she says again, quieter still. She's almost beautiful, will be when she grows into that long, overly thoughtful face, those too-obedient, limp, pale waves of hair, less blonde than ghostly white against my carefully cultivated brown. Her hair is artlessly natural, where mine does the actual job of looking unaffected: chosen and perfected over time, selected to appear richer than it did a decade ago when the colour was real. *Anyone can be unaffected, baby*, I choose not to tell her. *The art of naturalism, that takes experience.* By the time she's no longer trying to be older she'll realise how easy she could have had it right now, how she could have played the game instead of handing over all her cards. She'll learn she was the one with the power, but that she *thought* too much and *cared* too cloyingly to play, to *use* them. And I, of course, am the last person with any incentive for telling her.

'Good.' I settle back against the pillows for another long stare into my own eyes. I didn't choose the mirrors, not in a way any court could convict. Didn't tell her to buy them, didn't directly sneak or summon the university's repairman from the official student halls to the unofficial, comparatively palatial student houses on the edge of town. Over here there's nothing but the university on one side and hills and rain on the other; whichever window you look out from tells you a better, bigger, somehow more real world is going on without you, somewhere you can just see the edge of. As far as I can tell this enormous house contains just this girl and her – also idiotically young – housemate. It is, technically, not the university staff's domain. But it's only manners to offer a name when someone needs a repairman. Why stand in the way of a man of business? Aside from telling her about him, and – in a different tone, man to man – him about her, all that I did was tell her how good mirrors would look up there, and how good we – I may have let slip an enticing use of "we"; not to be made a habit of – would look in them. Enough to send her scurrying off spending whatever money students have these days as grants trickle away to loans, fashioning my whimsy into material fact with all the industry she'd otherwise only be pouring into assignments. Why anyone uses anything as vulgar as graffiti when people are willing to repaint their worlds in your image is beyond me.

At any rate, I sealed the deal this end with a diatribe on how deliciously contradictory it was that this sign of immodesty, of literal self-regard, went against the spirit of the Victorian family house; how it would be pleasing me and displeasing the spirit of the house she'd escaped to do something so aesthetically inconsistent, so immodest.

I am not insensitive by nature: when it comes to getting what you want, there's a place for understanding how people think.

A moth is fluttering around the embedded bulbs in the mirrored ceiling, trying to find its way into or out of each one in frantic turn, before moving on to bash itself against the next. Much as she'll be doing when she's over me, which won't, in the end, be so very long after I'm over her. Real things will take over and this will all be an early memory, before the real business of life and love and power begin. Bless her.

'I used to be afraid of mirrors.' She presses closer beside me as our eyes return to the aerial view of ourselves. Every touch, every look is a question she is too shy to phrase. It wasn't like this at first. The speed of the turnaround from the person she was when her question stopped my lecture mid-stride is why I know it's not me she wants to please, but the idea of me; that there will be no need for real guilt or even real sorrow when it ends. 'Or that's what I thought I was afraid of. When I moved out, I realised it was just the ones at home. Not mirrors in general. Just the ones in that house…'

'Oh yes?' We're back to that house again. She never stops talking about that house, or how strange it is to have left it. She might as well not have gone, it's so very clear she's brought the damned place with her. Carried it in her every sensibility, nodding to it in every conversation, as my idiot mother would have to the crosses above each door in every room. Another disbeliever in life before death. 'Just those?'

'Oh yes. Just those. All the same…' She shifts herself another inch toward me. 'It's better when you're here.'

I shift an eloquent millimetre away, the creak of the bed echoing my unspoken response. She shouldn't let me see up her emotional sleeves like that. Show more leg, by all means, but not give away the full recipe of how to break her heart. Seem less needy, not more. Show less of your working, romance is not a mathematics paper. But she's readjusting, finding out who she is now she's not the good student, since the day the lecture became more interesting than its subject. So hopelessly, hilariously young. I'd almost forgotten how fresh freshers really are. Rather than have any of my confidence rub off on her, she's disintegrating, losing her grip on her own existence except in orbit of mine. Burning up, as the moth that's left the ceiling in favour of getting too near the candle on her desk is threatening to do, the flame flickering black at the edges, no doubt scenting my suit jacket with jasmine and wax where it hangs on the back of her chair. I'll probably move my jacket when I get up to swat that moth in a minute.

'...and there's something so ghostly about all one's memories being in one place, isn't there, and knowing the previous generation's memories are all there too? All over every corner, as if yours are just paper over theirs? I don't feel it half as much at university. No one stays long enough. People change too fast to feel like the walls are made of them...'

'Mmm.'

'People should be scared of houses, though, don't you think? Whether anything is still... there... walking through stories you'll never know anything about. It is strange, isn't it, when you think about it? That more people are dead than alive in any given space you sit or stand in, in any given room?'

'Hardly. There's equally unimaginable numbers still to come.' She was wearing a green pre-Raphaelite top in that first lecture; I think I spot its half-closed emerald eyes now through her insufficiently opaque blouse. I didn't recognise the face in the painting she wore – would bet real money she didn't either: an accident of fast fashion rather than an unearthed treasure of research – and was all set to remember the picture of the face on her chest more clearly than the breathing one above. Real faces never form separate personalities in my lectures that early in the term, far too many to justify the disc space. So many drop out anyway that I never give them real thought before Christmas, when the tutorials begin: auditions, really, of who has anything to say and who got this far by thinking they did. The latter with a sprinkling of the former will always get the furthest, and not just on the end of my cock: in art, later, as well as life now. She did make an impression, I seem to remember, with that question of hers, not that I remember what it was. But the impression, that I remember. Though even that was as much about Liane, about my wanting a change, as it was about the girl herself.

'...I mean, we pass through time in one direction and once a moment's gone it's no less or more real than all the others gone before it. They're all there, stacked on top of each other. Only our perception says they're not all still, you know, happening. Don't you think? Believing one's own perception is the definition of reality, surely that's the mad thing?'

'Mmm-hmm.' It's not even a race, between her and Liane. They'll both have lost, sooner or later. It's practically already happened. Being here now isn't really a betrayal of either of them; it really is all over with Liane in all but the saying so.

'Now that I've left, though, that house, I mean... I suppose I don't feel quite so...'

'Haunted?' I finish her sentence as I tune back into it with all the boredom and sense of her naïve predictability the best of actors could pack into that single word. She's spoilt it all, let it boil over too soon by showing me I could get everything I might (don't) want, for free. Liane – hardly an intellectual heavyweight – did at least work out that much very quickly. Liane who, if not precisely my girlfriend any longer in the mirrors-on-the-ceiling sense, is still the one to whom I am mated: the one with whom I share bills and a roof, the one who means my shiny new mobile phone, rich and solid as a gold brick (much like Liane herself, who purchased it as a gift not to me but to herself to keep closer tabs on me) is turned off. In that respect I understand the sense of being haunted. Except it's I who do the haunting; form the future ghosts I'm deciding on. Liane of all people would understand that mentality, the wish to have decided once and for all which way a thing is going to fall, being, as she always is, more overwhelmed by the options than enticed by the menu. Cut Liane and she would bleed administration. This girl, on the other hand, is an artist, albeit an embryonic one. One who (now that grants are being abolished) is willing and ready to buy her title. If she wants to know what's spooky, it's how fast everything is changing. We'll all have those electronic bricks making us available soon, keeping us honest or forcing us to be better liars.

She's gone quiet, or is trying to show me she has done so. I pretend not to have noticed, the best way to sprinkle what salt I still have ready to pour. 'Then what made you choose to move here, to a house that so clearly *mirrors*' – I pause so she can writhe in the cleverness of that stab – 'the one you're describing? I suppose you're not old enough for psychological patterns in relationships with men – there hasn't been the time – but what more fundamental relationship is there than that between yourself and your home? Why go for something old instead of something new?'

In the silence between us, she turns her back and moves towards the record player. She lifts the first album off the pile beside the machine, unsheathes something with lot of foliage and an unprepossessing young man in a cardigan. I vaguely recognise the figure: a young poet who didn't live long enough to be disappointed yet checked out early anyway, I seem to remember. Ungrateful little swine, with all that talent and all that time stretching ahead. The lyrics as they meander into the air turn out to be something about knowing someone, getting to see through the pictures they choose to put on their walls, the people who turn up to their parties. Except of course that it rhymes, and immaturely at that.

She's rattling the paper, trying to read in my face whether or not I want it changed or silenced. 'How on earth does someone as young as you remember someone like him?' I ask.

'Do I need to remember something to understand it?' she says quietly, into the sketchbook she's picked up. Surely she isn't going to draw me? Not that old chestnut? Get around an argument that way? 'You didn't invent the Seventies, you know.'

'Didn't I now.' So she's getting petulant enough to tease, is she? 'Why you'd have vinyl when CDs have obviously replaced it isn't worth asking. Vinyl is as dead as Betamax, not that you'll have a clue what that is.' She does have the odd cassette tape too, I've noticed, mostly with girlish loops of self-conscious emerald ink detailing bands and years in overly neat brackets as sanctimonious as the song titles. This whole room is a ghost in waiting. She'll grow out of all this. For most of her life this room will be nothing but a memory. For me, it will be even less. Perhaps I'll be the terrible episode that teaches her art doesn't stop on the page, that life is constructed just as carefully.

I might as well enjoy the role for now, after all I'm not sure yet how long I'll stay. It's a comfort to know that whatever I do here in passing matters so little. She'll realise that one day.

She pretends to have eyes only for the sketchbook, but it's tilted down far enough that I can notice I was right about what's under that self-conscious blouse: the same reproduction of painted eyes peer sleepily through, off her chest and over the observer's shoulder. The picture of a girl overshadowing the reality of one: an allusion to our meeting in more ways than she knows. When my eyes played that first time on that image, some obscure Byrne-Jones or other I'm sure, I briefly wondered in pure academic curiosity whether I'd run my hands over that face on those breasts. I could easily do so now, but the certainty makes it less worth the standing, when it's just as easy to sit.

She wants me to ask if she's upset. I shan't. Asking would give unnecessary ammunition. She wouldn't know what to do with it if she had it. Not as Liane would. No point my expending excess points or energy. Sets her a bad example. I channel the chance of catching up on whatever she was saying into a longer, pseudo-profound silence, while the moth flits from the ceiling to the candle on the desk, ignoring the open window and the mountains in the distance.

'What do you think?' She turns the sketchbook around; it shows my hair gelled up to a series of points in what, particularly under her inexperienced hand, makes a less than flattering scale. I didn't realise how far towards the centre my hairline had crept at the back, mirroring what I knew about the front; nor do I need any reminding from her that my eyes are slightly too narrow for the appearance of gravitas to triumph over perennial smugness. I don't look any closer at her pseudo-loving mockery than that. 'Come on, what do you think?'

'I think you're thinking enough for both of us. What could I possibly add?'

She goes quiet; quieter than before. This display is not for me, not this time; she's responding to the version of me she is trying to believe in, and starting to see it doesn't take. Yet still taking me too seriously, swallowing my opinions of her as objective truth. *You're making beginners' mistakes*, I don't tell her. *Caring too much. Behaving like the teenager you are instead of the adult my presence means you're all too impatient to be. Have some imagination, some ambition. Stop making this so fool easy*. Why can't she understand she's got the potential to be more interesting than this? That I wouldn't be here if it were otherwise? At least in not knowing she makes me feel like a big enough fish in the sad little glass bowl of a college that I may be passing glad to be who and where I am. That's what the select few are *for*. 'As a matter of fact,' I decide to take the opportunity her surliness offers, 'I was just thinking, probably an idea if I go before Matey gets home.'

'He's got a name,' her voice hardens just a little, into something that doesn't dare to be a snap. I've seen girls do this before, when one spots their platonic friend who would most rather be neither platonic nor friend, who will either destroy the friendship by not getting what he wants and overvaluing it as a result, or – by having got it already – not wanting it again. The more angrily they deny it the funnier it is when either the friendship shatters or they dump you for him. I wonder in which direction this one is creeping. It'll be amusing to find out, to hang around long enough to follow that long-drawn-out *I-told-you-so* to wherever it's going. It's sometimes fun to point the future out, watch them refuting with fury before asking with wide-eyed awe by the third year, in gaze if not in words as we're usually not speaking by then, how on earth I knew.

'Jack?' I ask, raising my eyebrows the way I did that first day with her far better question – probably nothing of importance, though she, if not it, was enough to throw me off my *pain au raisin*. 'Julian?'

'Jamie.'

'Ah yes. That's the chappie.'

'You know it's Jamie.' She hits me with a cushion. 'I've introduced you. Twice.'

'Yes, yes.' She doesn't know if I'm looking down on him as a student or up to him as a rival, but she is perfectly sensible in hitting me with the cushion because that's what she'd want to do in either situation. 'I knew it was *something* wet and arty.'

'Why don't you like him?'

'I don't dislike Matey. I don't have any feelings for Matey-boy one way or the other.' Simply that Jamie arrived first, and will stay longer, and whatever infatuation he is unquestionably harbouring for my disposable little blank canvas he is biding his time, if he's anything. Jamie is the reason all rooms but this one seem distressingly like a clean slate, like a destination and not an airport, which in the resulting vacuity of taste is not unreminiscent of Liane. 'You never met Liane.' I bring up her existence as revenge, to level the field of combat against her and Jamie. Whenever any room has the opposite of a history, like this one has in spite of its architectural advantage even before I suggested covering the ceiling with mirrors, I feel Liane's spirit at the door. Her expensively cheap candles and budget faux-sculptures; faux-nouveau frames and offensively cheerful soft furnishings, with their unintentionally hilariously meaningless Latin italics.

She stifles her reaction, face clouding and body stooping over her sketchbook as if stifling herself against a blow.

'It's been a term since Liane's near-resignation as departmental secretary – over the young lady she thought to be your predecessor, with much less basis in fact – and the new cohort of arrivals, of which you are but one fresher and she does not yet know which. *Yet*, mark you.' I let her contemplate the mathematics of her insignificance, before softening the blow with 'Liane left and returned following last term's dalliance. The departmental rumours went round – started by Liane, of course, an unfortunately eloquent receipt found in my trouser pocket upon doing the laundry. And for a while I went from catch-of-the-day to something less tasty and more pungent. She has a tirelessness when she perceives herself the innocent wronged. She will protect a perceived victim loudly and angrily, and will be equally loud and angry at the perceived cause. You, rather than I.'

'Does gossip worry you?' She only looks up long enough to check my outline and return to her sketchbook, as if the answer has no bearing on the map of my features.

'It certainly should worry *you*,' I tell her. '*You've* only just started. You should want your name to be your own, not a side-line of a story that will be doing the rounds long after your time and star have faded.' I'm never worried by gossip – my job is so safe that, when both the women in my life are distant memories to the university, I will still be a permanent fixture. Not one of my books – I might privately admit, in the darkest hour of a Sunday night – has made or will make humanity rethink a single thought, but they are enough to institutionally outlive the occasional genuine artist who slips through the university's courses, usually unspotted by the department. I, at least, stay. Who knows what this insubstantial ghost-in-waiting will do with her life, under the right direction? This girl might inspire me to be what I can, but Liane will administrate me into doing the best I – she – can with what we have, now. No, I reassure myself, the ratio of likelihoods is what I will always find it to be. Liane will win. She always does.

'You will stay tonight? Won't you?'

'I don't have any clothes here.' The trump card. It had seemed like one small, clear sign that could mean everything or nothing, depending on what transpired as most convenient. Nothing that would stand up in the court of personal recrimination, to provide evidence for my intentions or lack of them.

'You said it was over. It is over? With the administrator? Liane?'

'Of course it is, baby.' I use the practised tone, the one that is enough to convince even me of whatever is the most convenient truth. It is over, after all. In all but the saying so. I don't know why I'm even thinking about her. My phone is turned off. This is a cocoon from reality. Whatever comes out of it has yet to form and I will not be hurried. Not by either of them. Until then I shall phrase my thoughts as the compliment of an admirer, not the rehearsal of a puppet-master. There's no point in making her feel like she doesn't have some choice in all this, beyond the flipping of a mental coin.

'Good,' she says. That word again. As if saying it enough will make it true. 'Because I feel so safe with you.'

'Isn't that lovely.' She's lying. Telling me the version of me she wants me to believe in, of the reality she is begging me to convince her of. She says it quietly, though, making herself a victim to avoid an argument, to turn the tension from discussion into sex, to drown communication in self-delusion. Good girl. More instinct than she lets on.

She moves away, picks up the sketch pad. Opens it to a blank page. There's something in the gesture I don't like. Something decisive. 'Baby, put the damn thing down.' I stand her before me, at the edge of the bed, her free hand in both of mine.

She can only meet my eyes if she takes a false pose: life is only tolerable if it is disguised in art. Clever girl. She's not as short as she tries to be, probably nearly as tall as I am when she wears nice shoes and stands properly. She understands what her role is, has enough imagination to see things from my point of view, that she is art not life.

That voice too small, the body she tries to shrink, making herself less present in every way she can unless it comes with my express approval. I might even miss this when I leave.

'There now.' I press my palms to the join of head and neck, to make her stand straight, to make her feel I make her powerful, forcing her to take up more space. Of course she deflates again as soon as I let go. There's no belief when the cord is pulled, just what I'm directly powering, plugged to the mains, flickering more easily than the lights on the ceiling. There's a rattle of keys somewhere beyond the shut door. Matey-boy will be alone of course, will not be bringing other females back here to test his luck or her jealousy, not this early in a term. 'Is that Jack, Jimmy, what's his face?'

'Yes.' She smiles back at mine, as if it's a joke between us rather than one forced upon her.

'Sounds six-foot-three if he's an inch.' Perhaps she is simply not telling me that the friend is gay, or definitely out of her league in some tangible way to them that I can't pick up on in adulthood. I doubt it, though. A man's a man, for all that, and I'm not the first to know it. 'No generation since we stepped out of the ocean had any different view of tall, dark and handsome. They're top of the evolutionary tree. Maybe you should seal the deal, baby.' The masterstroke, right there. Nobody accepts a truth they haven't found for themselves. Working out she fancies him before she does should be enough to stop the whole potential thing in its tracks. I might not be around for long but feint heart never won fair student, however temporary the leasehold.

'What's the issue with height?' She looks curious now, as if I'm perched on a slide looking up the wrong end of a microscope, amused behind those wide, expressionless eyes.

'There is no issue. Don't be silly.' It's never bothered me being that bit shorter, my face that bit too boyish for manly seniority. But the point is if there's one thing we can safely bet on it's that Jamie's besotted with her. 'As it happens I'm barely four inches shorter than Matey-boy.' Why am I bothering to think about this? If it's going to happen I'll be long gone; certainly won't have waited around to watch.

'You knew, didn't you?' she says, her finger twitching towards the pad again. 'That this would begin. When I asked that question, in the lecture?'

'Knew I'd be here?' I ask, taking the pen from her hand and guiding the newly empty palm to my cock. 'Or knew you'd be *here*?'

'Not just that.' She knows I know which question, though she doesn't know I don't remember what it was she asked. Only the picture, the essential truth: the look of power, sex and challenge. Sadly, all the questions are used up; there's no power behind any of them now.

I have nothing to say on this she wants to hear, so I look for something to change the subject with. An easy, welcome target is the moth that had been flickering around between the imbedded bulbs of the mirrors on the ceiling and the candle on the desk, not seeing it's all the same small but lethal fire. 'Damn thing.' I prop myself up on the pillows, move a foot from carpet to bedspread, lift myself from the bed, arm extended, moving into swatting distance.

'No!' She pulls my hand away.

Her strength is next to nothing, but there's more vehemence behind it than I've ever seen, and that's the quality which makes me stop and look. I haven't been treated to the unexpected for a while.

'Please.' What's also unexpected: she doesn't look quite so absurdly young when I hold her gaze. Nor does she release the foot she's grabbed. She reaches for the knee.

The moth is now out of my range, somewhere behind me in the corner of the ceiling; she must see where it's gone before she lets go of my ankle and I land back down beside her on the bed. 'Whatever was all that about?' I ask.

She reaches in defence for her sketchbook on the desk, and the favoured emerald pen beside it. 'Just leave it. Please. It's as alive as we are.'

'"Alive as…"?' I snort the laugh this deserves. 'It really isn't. There's no chance in hell this dusty little lepidopteran has anything like our level of understanding. Baby, unless you're a lot less alive than you look, and God knows you try to be…'

She kisses me again, which is as easy to go along with as it would be to call out as the distraction tactic it is – there'll be plenty of time for that later, should I choose to stay that long – before her eyes return to the sketchbook and mine return to the mirror.

'A moth could never overthink like you,' I tell her. 'If that's what it is to be more alive.'

'No. Probably not.' I see the side of my face emerging from the emptiness of her page; I let her look at me and don't correct her on what she sees. I won't be correcting her line, her perspective; there will be no official credits for this assignment. But this does not feel like the time to let go. To give her any sense of a stalemate. Not yet.

I carry on as I left off. 'A moth could never sketch a man, observe his infinite reflections in the mirror. Distort them to its own wishes.'

Her eyes flutter to mine, just for a moment. 'I'm not doing that.'

'At any rate, it's not a life. And I feel very sorry for you if eighteen years is not enough to develop any inkling of what a life is and isn't.'

'But this is all it gets.' She looks at where the pathetic thing has landed, within easy reach now. It's walking around the outside of the bedside table's water glass, courting destruction like an idiot. The singer-songwriter has moved on to ask the listener to tell and show him all that they know and are. No wonder the young are so in love with death when their expectations of other people are that high. Rather than argue, I tease her about the record again. 'Why do you listen to this? Don't you have any idea about anything of your own age? Or are you just a little vampire for mine?'

She half shrugs, in a way that from anyone else would make me think I'd detected the kind of denial that exposed a deeper lie. But there aren't enough layers to her for lying. Then she smiles into the sketchbook and whatever she is haunted by does not have her interest anymore. She's a good enough artist that she isn't looking at me too hard, just the bold, true lines that will make her narrow the gap between the perfect thing in her head and the mass of intersections on the page. Looking at me as I am, taking from the world what the page needs, and no more. Good girl.

She gives me a flirty glare and takes the stylus off the record; selects a CD. There's no mistaking the choice, even for someone as far-from-modern as I choose to be. The arrogance and self-obsession of Britpop's current ruling scarecrows blasts through the room, the mirrors rattling. I burst out laughing but don't stop posing. Every song's the same as she draws. But there's a mellow reliability to the – shall we call it music? – the sound. I vaguely recognise the one about how today was going to be the day. But the next track begins with what is unquestionably stolen property.

'If the Beatles don't sue they're idiots.'

'*Imagine* wasn't a Beatles song,' she says, on autopilot, and then looks up with yet more apology. 'You're right though. And it's not their only steal.'

'Don't blame your decade for your own sense of being out of place. You'd have been just as lost if you'd turned up in mine.'

She doesn't answer, except in the spreading of lines into shadows, working as we all must from dark to light. Vaguer shapes of me move out from around the centre of her picture, so the artist herself in the mirror of the mirror of her own drawing is still just one small, vague element among my many reflections.

'I like to draw reflections,' she says. 'Rather than people. The stories we tell ourselves and hear back. When you draw, you can't state what's reflection of reflection of reflection and what's the real thing. Drawing a thing, it's already become a reflection. Just like all you ever see of yourself,' she nods to the ceiling without looking directly at it, 'is the mirror. They've proved that about memory too, haven't they? We don't see what was there, just the series of reflections. We only remember remembering, not the thing itself. So each time you think of an image you're photocopying a photocopy. Same with art. Other people's art becomes "our" songs. We want to disappear into someone else's image, moths around the flame. With the same results.'

'I can't say I've given it much thought.' I allow myself a glance at the hills beyond the windowpane. She changes the subject to my own lecture, what she understood of it, and I nod as much as is chivalrous in a man having his portrait drawn. I have only consented to be her model. If I'm her muse, that's her own lookout.

'I used to control my weight because it was something I *could* control,' she says out of a silence I wasn't listening to. 'Because of the mirrors. So I could control what I'd see in them. I thought that would work, for a while.'

'Entirely sensible. Nothing wrong with being seen to be beautiful. It's what you can offer the world. No problem in advertising it.' *You should try it sometime*, I'm tempted to add.

'At home there were things… presences… hanging around. I used to talk to them as a child but… after my parents died, I suppose I didn't want to be alone with… everything. I disappeared into clothes, into controlling the story people saw of me. Then as I got older I started writing the stories I used to tell myself. My language for what was going on in the house. Always other people's point of view. Those of the people who...'

Haunted you, yes, yes. 'Every little girl writes stories.'

As she leans and draws, the shape of her bust pushes against the baggy shirt. There is a woman in there, a real one made of flesh and blood, not manners and expectations. I am doing her a favour by being here, I really am. She says, into the sketchbook, 'I don't look into mirrors too long unless you're here.'

'Whyever not?'

'In case it can follow me through, into now, into the present. Whatever – whoever – I saw in there.' She looks up at the ceiling, and I see with an unfortunate rush of blood to the face how big a gesture those mirrors on the ceiling are. She wants to please me, and she wants to see how much danger she can put herself in, so the knight has to rescue the damsel even if I believe it's only from herself. I feel my toes twitching, my legs shaking to be stretched.

'You think too much,' I say. 'The only ghosts that exist are the ones we think into being. Pray into existence, in my family's case, for something to focus our misspent guilt on. Trust me, I'm an ex-Catholic.'

The moth flies past, breaking her gaze. Then she disappears towards the bathroom and it's just me and the moth, a line of brown on the purple curtain. She's through the bathroom door now, and in the growing dusk she won't see the difference when she returns: with nothing else to do, I absolutely may as well kill it as not.

There's no resistance as my palm comes down. Where first there was a small, brown clothes-moth, there is now my hand making contact with two kinds of brittle softness, then with something that isn't even a crunch, the first crumbles into the other and I stroke and brush the damage in, the remnants sliding off my hand, falling to the equally beige carpet. There's something reassuring in how a thing so fiddly and complex can be flattened into clarity, how simply a small problem can be solved.

The shower hisses into action two doors down, that door no doubt decisively locked, so I flick the new Nokia, futuristic and small and

Star Trek communicator-like (not that she would know what that was), and in the very second of freedom I give it, it screams to life, Liane's name a digital screech of capital letters across the screen. I turn it off again. It's that easy.

She comes back looking so underconfident in the negligee she only bought because of me – jade is a colour that's never done a thing for me; I only mentioned it positively to see what the reaction would be – meaning she'll only feel, so only be, sexy if I declare her so. I can create and recreate her as simply and easily as I destroyed the moth. How can she expect me to find her attractive when it's too easy? When I matter so much? All truth and no performance isn't just unattractive. It's unseemly. What I feel is as much pity, amusement, as it is anything approaching love. Looking at yourself reflected in the mirror is one thing. But making love to yourself? You can do that so much better alone.

She reads enough of my thoughts in my face to withdraw to the sketchbook.

'Surely you're not going back to that now?' I nod at my visible erection, what's left of my clothes sliding to the floor.

She smiles into the sketchbook, head tilted down a little more so I don't see it. 'I hadn't finished.'

'You've started though, I bet.' I slide one of the straps of the negligee off her shoulder, my other hand cupping the nearest buttock, sliding forward, down, in. She won't notice the absence of the moth I promised not to kill; she only noticed its existence when it was close enough to annoy me. Much like the flatmate, perhaps. Perception is reality. My reality, her perception. I've done nothing wrong, by killing the moth or by avoiding her unasked question, the one she thinks I've answered by staying here tonight. But that's just a picture. I haven't said any words I'd need to take back. What love there is can be enjoyed, for now. It's real enough for now, while I decide it is.

~

We must have left the curtains open; I wake surrounded by too much of the dawn over the horizon of her skin. One warm, bare shoulder has escaped the cover, hair spilling gently down to the groundsheet, an expanse of back, no longer pale in the warm gaze of the morning but gold as the sunrise over the hills beyond the window. I inhale her skin cream, the warmth she radiates under the single sheet. It's all so familiar, so thoroughly right, that my mind resists nothing. I take myself by surprise in that moment before truly waking, with an unfamiliar rush of pure affection. I realise, in the privacy of thoughts without audience, that I am letting myself belong here. With her back to me, her eyes shut, there's little danger in admitting just now with no visible reflection as witness that I am, right now, a very lucky man.

For a while I let the sun play as it will over our skin. But then a kind of fluttering through my body makes me aware that something is different from last night, something I can't place a finger on. Maybe it's the way the sun lands on my back, the verge of discomfort, untimely heat. Perhaps it's that I've been in one position longer than I'm used to, that the pressures of heat and light seem heavier than before.

To distract myself from uncertainty, I move from my head into the safety of my body. My fingers reach for her skin… but do not arrive in my field of vision. I reach out yet nothing changes.

Why can I not see my fingers?

I reach again. Nothing changes in front of me again. No hand, no arm is stretched before me, yet I feel unstable as if suddenly standing on one leg, although I am lying down. Aren't I? And how do I even know this is her shoulder I'm looking at when all I see is skin, rolling away into the distance, of a size I now realise is as vast as the hills I looked at through the window last night?

I try to touch her and her arm responds, comes towards me as it always does. But everything is different. Those white fingers, their long nails, no longer delicate but vast, no longer reaching to caress a lover but to scratch an itch.

Me.

The arm is coming through the air. It's bigger than anything I've ever seen. Before I know what I'm doing there is something instinctive that does it for me, that takes over my body and my choices and there is no more thinking; the desire is so strong it's action before it's thought and I am fluttering to the ceiling before fingernail hits skin in a streak of white. Before I know I've moved at all I'm suspended by nothing, powering up and up, climbing through nothing, nothing at all, fluttering higher, still higher through the air, towards the safety of the glass ceiling.

The ceiling?

I do not crash but I do land. I'm perched on the mirror, looking over at her. Except that over is down. From the mirror, I look down at her body on the bed we shared. It is the same, recognisable room. The record and CD players, the abandoned sketchbook, discarded clothes. And in the middle of everything, the girl. But she – everything – is different. Bigger, yet further away than I have ever seen these things.

Below me, all the way down there on the bed, the finger that had come towards me scratches hard at the shoulder I've left, leaving behind it a brief bright line like a vapour trail of pressure where the nail scraped. Then she is still again.

Fucking Clocks

[2015]

Either she's got a thing for hands, or the girl is fascinated by the way Veronica places the key in the door.

Veronica manoeuvres the key inside the lock, as slowly as she can so she can keep watching the girl. She's not precisely short, this one – no shorter than most women are to Veronica – but holds the world's eye in a way that makes her not so much tall as beyond height. She seems to Veronica as if she's constantly taking a picture, recording the details for later. A lawyer, perhaps, or a photographer. Her not-quite-olive skin and the buoyant, loose curls hanging behind her shoulders make her as far beyond geography as she is convincingly ageless, as modest and missable as Veronica is aesthetically loud. Yet Veronica has never seen anyone look so unapologetically themselves, unless she's looking at a cat. Or in a mirror.

Veronica takes the key out of the lock a millimetre or so, no further than seems plausible, jiggles it and slides it back in. The girl's eyes follow each movement. It is entirely possible to observe a thing without the observed thing changing, as long as you're wearing sunglasses, which is why sunglasses are Veronica's weapon of choice. Today is a convincing alibi, spring so impatient to be summer that Veronica can feel sweat tickling the back of her neck, collecting at her clavicle like an itch it would be too obvious to scratch. It's worth her skin's impatience with the sky; the prize is in front of her, or rather beside her, barely bothering to pretend not to watch the path of the sweat on her clavicle, waiting to be let in. Veronica stretches time as far as it will go; as if the lock is what's making her take all the time in the world. It's not the lock, of course. It's never the lock. It's the girl.

What Veronica really enjoys most about this moment is knowing, through precise imagining, what is going to happen. Like any other part of life, precise imagining is key to getting exactly what you want. She's going to start with the left bra strap: it screamed at her in the café during what began as a glazed look at the middle distance; bright and angry lilac demanding her attention beneath an unseasonable mesh vest, in a way its owner wouldn't begin to do in her own right. Veronica does love a lack of apology. Especially unapologetic underwear.

She's already forgotten the girl's name but that's no reflection on the girl. She's excited about this one, in all the usual ways and some of the older, simpler ones too. The ones she'd almost forgotten, before sex became straightforward, corporeal. When it was still magical and intense, strange and sacred. There is nothing magic in what Veronica does these days, except perhaps that it works like it. She's a straightforward person suggesting a straightforward arrangement. And straightforwardly available, if only ever to a certain point (she doesn't take Vincent's ring off). Short of exclusivity there is nothing Veronica doesn't offer, or doesn't want. And what Veronica wants first is to spend as long as possible on this extended drumroll of the front door. The girl has no way of knowing Veronica is the last person in the world to let a locked door control her.

The lock clinks, the door opens. Veronica is grateful as ever for the hallway mirrors, relishes the moment of checking in with the image of herself: the exact shade of purple hair, reddened by the sun; the exactly length of eyeliner wings, the exact shade of mauve lips. She is both as visible and as disguised as she wants to be; thoroughly and safely armoured in herself. She opens the door and steps back, pseudo-chivalrous, to watch the girl's figure in the moment of reaction as the well-positioned hall mirror captures and recaptures her expression as she walks in.

'You didn't say it was a family house,' is what the girl says, and for a moment Veronica is thrown before she enters the ring.

'That's an odd thing to say about an entrance hall composed almost entirely of clocks.' She closes the front door against the outside world they've left behind them with a satisfying clunk.

'And mirrors.' The girl leans back against as much wall is available, in the space where the coats end and the clocks begin.

'And mirrors.' The four or five Veronicas in the corner of the real one's eye share a tight-lipped smile. It's only fair to let the house have its moment. Veronica does not feel insecure about her own desirability but nor is she under any delusions about who wins in a battle of fascination between her and the house. She, after all, once stood where this girl stands now.

The girl looks around the entrance hall. She must be able to see the entrance to the downstairs painting studio, the faint smell of paint and turpentine just on the periphery of consciousness, beneath the eternal, mismatched ticking of the hallway. The kitchen is just visible from here, before the corridor slopes around to the bathroom and shower room, past the locked door of her mother-in-law's study. It's the first time Veronica can almost see the house as a stranger since falling in – and then (nine days out of ten) out – of love with it herself. She wipes a finger along the ledge of the grandfather clock's face which, it always amuses her to note, is where no one ever dusts. The only people tall enough to reach or notice – including her – are also the people who don't care enough. She's not precisely laughing at her mother-in-law in this but there is something amusing in how much certain people would care, how much happier they are not knowing, and how angry it would make them to know it.

Veronica grew up with cats, not just the increasingly doddery pair that live here now, at least one of whom is no doubt watching between the banisters of one floor or another like fascinated siblings (or disapproving parents, depending on what mood she's in when she looks at them). The teachings of cats have not been lost on her: Veronica steps back, body and mind, all confident politeness, not so much waiting as knowing the show will begin, the voyeuristic ownership of watching someone she hasn't touched in any significant way yet and knows she is going to. 'You like it, don't you,' is all she says.

The girl really smiles, and it's beautiful in the truest sense: there's humour in it, confidence. She's still looking at the grandfather clock that leans, as if masking extreme tiredness, beside the overpacked shoe rack and the light green wall peering out from under the cuckoo clock; at the vast black iron circular wall clock that's just a battery pack centred by a horizontal Stonehenge of mounted Roman numerals; at the train station one hanging at an angle from the ceiling; at the scattering on the opposite radiator, under the mirror, of porcelain and ceramic mantelpiece clocks; at the long thin olive green rounded diamond one with the yellow glass face and charcoal numbers. 'Yes. Among other things I like.'

Veronica decides to speed things along a bit. She allows the pads of her fingers to brush the back of the girl's neck as she takes her jacket and hangs it on the pile over the hooks. The girl takes a step away from her to kicking off her cork and leather platform sandals. There's a pixie quality to her that, had Veronica read it in a book, would have caused her to throw the book at the nearest wall, but this is not a case of someone turning herself into what she's read and waiting for the world's approval, not a reflection of a reflection of a wet dream. Veronica wishes, not for the first time, that Vincent wanted the kind of marriage where she would send him a text now, where he would share her happiness.

Veronica takes both the girl's hands and leads her the few steps up to the square of landing. She leans back for the cool of the wood to support her spine, the edge of floor above to press the back of her skull. She still can't remember the girl's bloody name. It was something that sounded unrealistic, something that didn't quite fit, so her mind had deleted it as misinformation. The girl's hand is cold in hers, the nails chipped at the edges, suggestive not of confident unselfconsciousness but the other kind, decisions going unmade just to get clothes on, get safely into the day and out of the backstage area of her head. Or maybe that was just Veronica's own, least favourite, memory of a time all this kept her safely sealed off from.

'It's a family house?' the girl says.

'How do you know?' Veronica hopes the answer is the girl wondering whether they were staying on the carpet or if a bedroom's on the cards.

'The coats.' She gestures over her shoulder but doesn't look back. 'A largeish family who aren't good at getting rid of things.'

'Or can't find their own things under each other's.' Veronica does not want to be impressed. She wants to be in her body not her mind. The opposite of stage fright.

'Are they your family?'

'They're expecting to be.' Definitely a lawyer, she was right the first time.

'So they're not relations?'

Veronica shrugs again. 'Everyone's related to someone.'

'Of yours?' The girl's expression does not change.

'Alright, full disclosure?' Veronica sits down on the stairs, chin cupped in her favourite of her hands. If it was hands this girl liked, she'd see a clue now. Veronica is very, very good with her fingers. 'It isn't the sexiest of truths but it's yours if you want it.'

The girl gives a barely visible nod, eyes steady and open and unapologetic as a tiger cub. Veronica, who has never been ID-ed in her life having looked (or walked) eighteen since she was eleven, wants to eat her.

'This is my mother-in-law's house. Well, technically my father-in-law's. It belonged to her parents – her father inherited it when her mother died early, or something like that – but they were all set to lose it after he couldn't keep up the payments. So he bought it from her. It's theirs now. But it knows its hers.'

She's never heard herself say that out loud. The girl doesn't react, as if what Veronica has said makes so much sense as to be not only sane but unremarkable. Perhaps it is.

'And their oldest son, who gave me this ring...'

The girl's lack of reaction to that is harder fought. 'Your fiancé,' she says. The tone is non-accusatory, except the consonants are too crisp.

'My fiancé, yes...' It's been so long since she met and picked up a card-carrying heterosexual like this one clearly is that she feels quite sentimental. And it really couldn't have come at a better time. Maybe the decision creeping into what's left of her heart really is asking to be made. Maybe this girl will be the break between her and the house, the life that would be enough for some other version of her. 'None of them are particularly pleased about it, don't worry, we're not disappointing expectations.' Veronica shifts up to the fourth step, the one that in the shoes she's kicking off gives her the perfect length to extend her legs and look her acquisition right in the eye. 'My fiancé knows this is what I do, what I want. What I believe. I don't think monogamy is ever honest. Or that asking for it is ever honest either.'

'And he...'

'And he, and I quote, "couldn't be bothered" with other people but understands I was being honest with him. That I was licencing him to do the same. Instead, he asked for one of his own rules. I named his the English Clause.'

'What's that?'

'That I could do exactly what I wanted, and so could he, so long as each of us make sure the other didn't ever find out.'

'Oh.' The girl looks like she feels a level of sympathy for Vincent that makes Veronica almost jealous.

'And I've chosen to take that at face-value.' But these stairs were her perfect rendezvous for a reason. Only the house's liminal spaces had enough room; its other, actual rooms were too full of books, boxes and litter trays, easels and accusations. And that wasn't all of it. Veronica only ever felt at home on the stairways, the landings. Those were the only places she ever quite felt like she wasn't lying about something. Where she was just a person passing on the way somewhere else. 'Also, living together in a place this big does not have the same connotations that "living together" would have in an exclusive relationship. Or a house that didn't have... demands.'

'We're not betraying anyone, is what you're saying.' She can tell the girl doesn't feel sorry for her, even if she feels sorry for Vincent, and it makes her want to fuck her even harder.

'Not through me. I haven't asked about you.'

The girl takes a step towards the staircase. Veronica knows women: the fuller the engagement in talking now, the fewer inhibitions when she finally gets what she wants. And God, all that hair. That's what she'd noticed as soon as she walked into the café. The girl lets it do its own thing, like she's got more significant things to think of. Lets it upstage her. Delicious. She'll know exactly what she wants and won't be too coy to demand it. Veronica doesn't have people making demands nearly often enough.

'Look, it's true what I've told you: it's only a betrayal if they find out. Their rules, not mine.'

'Not "he".'

'Sorry?'

'You keep saying "they".'

She stops, looks from one clock to the next, allows herself to hear the barely audible, peanut-butter-thick layer of ticking. 'I suppose I do.' She was fucking the house and everyone in it, and sometimes that was fucking them over and sometimes it was fucking with their minds and other ways it was fucking because that was the only way into their minds and what was she going to do to make the most of who she was now? 'The thing is,' Veronica says surprising herself with the thrill of someone else's truth in the silence of these empty currently non-accusatory halls, 'they cannot bear talking. The thing about the people in this family is they want nothing more from a conversation than a checkmate in three moves.'

Perhaps it's the moment of uncertainty, the sadness she felt float to the surface of her face that makes the girl brave – or horny – but she stands in front of Veronica on the stairs, almost eye to eye from down there, making Veronica's height seem a vulgar extravagance. 'Well, I'm half Australian. So all that English subtext isn't exactly my first language either.'

'Is that a fact?' She strokes the side of her leg. 'You seem to have picked up the small talk.'

'I don't speak to my Australian half.' The girl kneels on the step between Veronica's feet. She slides off Veronica's spike-heeled leather sandal and doesn't let go of the foot. With her other hand, she traces each metatarsal of Veronica's oxblood toenails and only puts the shoe down to take the other foot. 'Is it literally an hour? This coffee we're having?' the girl asks.

'Yes.'

Neither of them is pretending coffee meant coffee. That was why Veronica always used that line when she met someone in a coffee shop. A perfectly single entendre.

'How long now?'

'Fifty-two minutes, safely.' Veronica returns her attention to the lilac bra strap. She runs the pad of her finger along it, just missing the centre enough to whisper her presence on the girl's skin. 'My mother-in-law teaches in town. Her husband's on a book tour.'

'A writer?' Veronica's other boot hits the carpet.

'Illustrator. Artist.' Calling him her father-in-law would make it more of a betrayal of him. She can really only stomach betraying Effie. 'Royal Academy.'

'Right.' The girl kneels closer on the step above, between the knees and the split in Veronica's purple dress. Veronica shifts from her elbows onto the curve of her arse, leaning forward enough to press the length of her labia on the carpet through the material as she says, 'No further questions?'

'None.'

They aren't getting past the landing. She knows it as she feels the girl's tongue on the base of her thong, pulled lightly from her leg with a long, gentle bite. Before her dress goes over her head she's already realised her plan with the bra strap isn't going to work. The girl wants it to stay on, returns too far into her mind and out of her body as Veronica pulls at the strap. So Veronica lets go, gripping a slight, net cup and sliding her tongue over stitches and skin, finding the nipple below. The girl's body is soft against the expensive, discoloured carpet, and Veronica's palms flat to the girl's sides bring her down against the ridges of the stairs. When the girl does take her bra off seconds later it's because she knows she'd not being made to. There's probably about half a cup's difference; Veronica only notices it because she noticed the expectation of disgust, and Veronica has had enough lovers and owned enough cats know the answer is lack of attention, directing your interest elsewhere. When she kisses her again she lets her lead, doesn't touch anything except in reply, giving back exactly what she receives. But she is careful not to let her hands stay on the girl's breasts at the same time for too long, she will not be seen to compare. The best way to train a confident dom was always passivity. It was so easy to make people realise they could get what they want by knowing they wanted it.

'I knew you were going to be important,' the girl says, as her breathing slows to normal again.

Veronica doesn't normally have patience for shit like that, but 'Me too,' is what she hears herself admitting as she stares for longer than she ever has at the ceiling above the stairs. What surprises Veronica is not any of this, anything said or done on the staircase; it's how much she wants to talk now, as she leans back against the three steps from the small area of landing to the next floor. It's how the girl leans her astoundingly soft, pale back against the grass-green wall as if she belonged there.

Mirroring, Veronica leans her head against the banister, lets it take her weight, raises her eyes to the skylight, past the rails of the squared-edged spiral staircase. There's a cat looking back. She can't tell which of the two from here. They're almost identical shades of grey, that's the reason she gives herself, but perhaps the truth is she doesn't want to see a difference. She isn't staying that long.

They sit together on the top of the stairs in a nest of their abandoned clothes. Veronica's eyes move across her dress, lying on the girl's black skinny jeans, sleeveless V-neck and bra the girl's visibly forgotten she'd been so afraid to lose. Her eyes trail down the rest of the stairs to the front door. It seems like a riddle to solve, that strong, shut door. If they stayed there long enough, everyone who lived here would walk through. For a moment, in the silence between them, the two women on the stairs in a moment of perfect stillness, it seems no less likely that time would flow backwards as forwards, that everyone who had ever walked through this hall would do so again.

The girl smiles up at the cat but returns her attention to Veronica. Another mental brownie-point: no trying to show how good she was with animals, or avoid awkward silences or difficult conversations by pretending something being furry was a more interesting fact than it was. Cute wasn't real. It never was. Cats were people and should be treated with as much dignity and distance. More, if anything.

'I like how you made it clear we weren't betraying anyone,' she says.

Veronica shrugs. 'I know it's important.'

'Who betrayed you?'

Veronica opens her mouth to ask who said anyone did, then allows herself to think about the truth. 'She didn't betray me. She just grew out of me.' She hasn't thought about Meg for a long time. 'When we were babies she'd used me to stand up. Pulled herself up on me. And she started walking and I'd burst into tears. Just sat on the floor, staring at my feet as if I couldn't understand how I'd stopped being on them. They say the body remembers.' Veronica traces a hard fingernail along the girl's cheek, her clavicle. Swallowing the attention was delicious, like rich mousse. 'I still wear the platform boots that she discovered first. We lost contact. She had a baby. Or was about to. I say "lost", she asked me to read at her wedding. I don't think I'd ever felt so far away from anyone, or anything, as that church. Happy and clappy about everyone agreeing with them about their idea of God. Neither of us claims the end of our friendship but everything I felt changed when she told me the reason she hadn't asked me to be a bridesmaid was symmetry. She chose her sister and the two most popular girls in our class.'

'You weren't the cool one? You seem like you'd always have been the cool one.'

'I was never the cool one.'

'I can't imagine that.'

'That's how you see me?'

'Yes.' There was no embarrassment at all. Just truth, observation. A lawyer or a photographer, definitely.

'Well, it's lovely to meet me.' Veronica kisses her, eyes open. 'You make me wish I could paint.'

The girl looks at her, hard. 'Why?'

'I want to show you the version of you I saw.'

'In the café?'

'Everywhere.' Veronica remembers at her worst the torture of making the decisions of getting dressed, how nothing looked like her unless there was someone to sign off on who that was supposed to be. She wants this girl, this natural decision, the forest of hair beneath her fingers, when she breathes in the Aqua body spray of her neck, explores the heeled second and third ear piercing with her tongue, chews at the shoulder, subtle silver heart chain and skin alike, and brings her face around to hers to taste the cheap but perfectly coloured lipstick, she is mesmerised.

'Are you still sure we're not betraying anyone?' the girl says, when her breath returns and Veronica is staring at the ceiling again.

Veronica shrugs. 'Sex isn't betrayal. Falling in love, that's a rulebreaker.'

'You haven't answered the question.'

Veronica's throat and labia contract with fascination. She wants to be inside the girl in every way available. She looks at the skylight, over the forbidden floor that only her father-in-law ever walks on, beyond the glassy stare of what was now both unimpressed, dull-coloured cats. 'That's the sort of thing my mother-in-law says. And she should know, she gave up writing because she didn't like it anymore. She claims she lost interest and didn't enjoy it the way she enjoyed painting.' The cats go on staring from the edge of the stairs, two floors above.

'I mean of your...' she searches for the word. 'Emotional contraception.'

'Well, nothing's a hundred per cent reliable. But don't think I wouldn't have an abortion if I had to.'

'Right.' The sadness is back in the girl's voice, and Veronica isn't sure which of them she's feeling sorry for.

'Look, you... you don't know who you are yet. You don't go into a relationship thinking it's a cocoon. But be there long enough and you've taken the nutrients you can, and you fly.'

'Is that what you're in here? A cocoon?'

'I don't know.' Yes. She would fuck Meg out of her head and heart or die trying, if it took every other person in the world. And that sense of ground zero she experienced at the end of every orgasm was that of the phoenix she believed herself to be, she had killed off the previous version of herself, each successive version of her exploded in flames and something new and truer that had never been touched by Meg replaced it. But there was a freedom in this house hearing her history, witnessing who she truly was, even if those who lived in it weren't there to hear. Wasn't the whole point of being alive that people weren't exact, weren't fixed in time and identity? She feels an unfamiliar tightness that runs all the way from stomach to throat. 'I don't know what I think. All I remember is what you taste like. Come back here.'

She does.

Afterwards, another afterwards, with the clocks telling her this really has to be the last, staring up at the unimpressed face of one or other of the cats, Veronica says, 'How did you know it was a family house again?'

'I said it was the coats but it wasn't. It was you. The practised way you got my coat over the hundreds of others by tucking it like that. You're so used to not having to complain. To accepting what doesn't work.'

'Impressive.'

'Although I expect if you told him to, your fiancé would move the coats. But you don't want to tell him. You don't want the responsibility of what it means if he does. Or if he doesn't.'

Veronica turns her head to catch the girl's eyes in hers. 'Is it my life we're talking about here?'

The girl looks at her for a moment before she looks away. 'One of my earliest memories is a foot. Not of feet going through a door but literally a foot. I was walking past a car wreck, before I had any idea what that meant. I turned around as I crossed the road, I was holding hands with an adult, I think it was one of my parents, I knew I was safe. There was a shoe, too close to the ground, like whatever leg it had been attached to had sunk into the tarmac, like under the surface of a bath. It wasn't disgusting, which I suppose means I didn't believe it was real. But it was hypnotic. I couldn't look away. I probably became a photographer in that moment, whether I wanted to be one or not.'

'A photographer,' Veronica echoes. 'Not a lawyer.'

'Who said anything about a lawyer?'

Veronica looks at the girl, longer than she's ever looked at anyone except through sunglasses. 'I don't know if I've fallen in love you,' she says. 'Or if I'm just hypnotised by how much I'll end up hurting everyone if I have.'

The girl's colour doesn't exactly change, it's more that her entire face relaxes. 'I'd been going to that café every morning, trying to sketch. It just doesn't seem to be happening at the moment. But I knew something else would. Happen.'

'You really love drawing? Not photos?'

It was the wrong thing to say, or perhaps the right one: the girl's face freezes over again. 'I used to. I don't think I can do it anymore. Every time I see a blank page I feel my throat tightening like I'm running out of time. Like, literally running out of time. So really, in the end, I suppose I've stopped trying at all. I was glad of the distraction for real when it was you, but...'

'You mean unless you're inspired you don't do anything?'

'Maybe.'

'Waiting for inspiration is like waiting for perspiration. Nobody got fit by thinking about the gym.'

The girl smiles, enjoying the phrasing enough not to feel told off. They sit, silently, and the ticking in the air becomes audible in a way she'd swear it never was before.

'Fucking clocks,' Veronica says in the end.

'They're beautiful.'

'If you don't think where it's all going.'

'Perhaps.' And the girl who seemed too shy to have any agenda touches the contour of Veronica's cheekbone, runs a nail lightly down its length. 'I wish I had your drive. Your faith.'

Veronica swallows, the saliva that suddenly seems too dry and the face that word puts in her mind. *Faith.* She hears the voice that name conjures, so loud she'd swear the girl must hear it too. "Sarah got the wedding; I got the marriage. Which would you rather have?" It probably wasn't meant to sound like a challenge, it certainly wasn't meant to be received like a curse. But when Veronica looked back for the people who knowingly or unknowingly had formed her blueprints of what the fundamental centre of the world was and how it held itself and how she was built from it, she always thought of the moment Faith proposed a choice.

Whether her own guilt had pasted the words on their silence, she hears herself say, 'It would kill his mother.'

'I won't tell anyone. Ever. This never happened. And it was wonderful.'

'The world is small.' Veronica stares on at the clocks.

'I won't let them find out,' the girl repeats. 'Whatever we decide. We'll either meet each other slowly, or not at all. But I won't let it hurt them.'

'So there is something to decide?' There's hope in her voice that she can't dismiss as curiosity.

'There's always something to decide.'

'Look, while you could get a lot more than a coffee out of me, it's not fair on either of us.' Vincent had said the right thing: that he did not mind who her exes were, or what her future looked like. He said it because he'd say anything that would keep her closer, longer. And wasn't that the real agreement? That she didn't call his bluff? 'But my God, wouldn't it be fun.'

'Too much fun.' While the girl is re-wrapping her unseasonable skinny jeans along her pale, untanned, carefully hidden yet perfectly proportioned legs, there is a tension in Veronica's throat that only happens when an opportunity is going past without her, that has only ever happened when she's wanted to reach out and stop whatever was going past, catch it, stare it out. But she ignores that feeling because she has made her choice.

'You know what's scary?' she tells her instead, 'is how many stories that you don't have any say over form you in ways you've got no awareness of, and all those inadvertent programmers have all these inadvertent programmers of their own. And nobody's holding the bloody wheel. It doesn't feel it would be right to leave. But I'm not one of them. They don't trust me, in a way that isn't personal. It's an easy commute to his work, and with property prices being what they are it apparently doesn't make sense to share a flat. And I'm living with him, because if I weren't I would never come round and I wasn't ready to give up when I made that situation. He knows my needs. He has the same freedom. After a brief venture into what I hoped was empathy or experimentation, but was barely more than emotional tourism, he tells me he's lost interest. Beyond that, and a mumbled sentence along the lines that I could do what I wanted, there has been no real arrangement.'

'Or any discussion.'

'Or any discussion.' She doesn't flinch as she feels the girl wipe what she hopes is not a tear from her face and they sit looking at each other across the impassable void of all the other people's stories they'll never know. And it's almost worth the not knowing, Veronica decides, just to be here. 'What's that thing Bernard Shaw says about we're not meant to be happy so we might as well have a good time?' Whatever it was she doesn't believe it anymore.

The girl considers the half-quote a while, then says a very simple, 'Bullshit,' and retrieves her bra from where it lies beside the pot plant on the corner of the stairs.

~

Anyone who saw them, the tall, loud-looking woman and the short, quiet-looking one, walking down Nightingale Avenue to the corner of Richmond Hill, would have seen a perfectly friendly companiable silence. You didn't share silences like this with any old stranger. Damn everything, Veronica thinks. Damn George Bernard Shaw and damn all anonymous girls staring into blank sketchbook pages in cafés.

'I don't feel like this story is ending,' the girl says, when Nightingale

Avenue is just about to. They stop at the corner, staring down the hill towards the town.

'But it is. For now.' There are tears somewhere behind the girl's eyes, and Veronica knows she has the skill to make them show themselves if that was what she wants. But she still has the feeling the world is asking something better of her, and newer. 'You won't leave him,' the girl says.

'And you won't leave…?'

The girl doesn't offer the boyfriend's name. 'What if they aren't the story? What if they're just the distraction?'

'From what?'

'From our story?'

Veronica looks up the road, in the direction neither of them are going. The wind blowing straight into her face keeps her passive, gives her something external to defend against. Not everything needed to be measured in time. There were truths that were absolute, even if their only present was a matter of moments. It didn't matter how many clocks ticked on, the measurement or passing of time was absolutely nothing compared to the moments of connection. But what was paralysing was she knew one of those was happening right now. The world was paused on a pivot, and it expected her to do something about it. The girl whose name she couldn't remember knew her better in less than an afternoon than any of the people she had previously thought of as her home. 'You could be right,' she says. 'But you're not prepared to risk it, are you?'

'Are you?'

Veronica ignores the question, and hides behind answering her own. 'So this is how the story ends.'

Neither of them is asking for the other's number, and neither of them is leaving. Maybe Veronica is punishing herself, maybe saving the girl from the kind of complication she's starting to suspect, on this confusing and ridiculous day, she hadn't been enjoying as much as she tells herself and everyone else she invites into it. Veronica has an invitation on the tip of her tongue, that when both of them would, one day, be sketching in the same corner, would—

Veronica's eyes dart without her permission across the road, then look down aggressively at the pavement as she hisses, *'Don't. Look.'*

And even if it was ever so slightly too late that the girl obeyed, Veronica would later reassure herself that all the girl could have seen was half an idea of a late-middle-aged woman in a long, flowing ash-grey skirt and pseudo-Edwardian pale blouse, reading glasses on a chain perched on the end of her nose, a Kew Gardens tote bag dangling from one hand, a British Museum one from the other; that if girl and woman saw each other at all it would never have stuck in either's mind; that Effie would look away just like Veronica, only faster.

So it was Veronica that left first, never turning back to see if the girl was watching her follow her mother-in-law home. Veronica who would remember, each time she passed that stair she never again used for anything but walking, that she had sat with that girl in a space that defied every clock's ticking. Veronica who would always take longer over the stairs after that, and if anyone ever noticed at all, it would look like she was just being careful of her feet.

Toilet

[1970]

'How about now?' he says. The bowl echoes a whisper of the question back, sharpening his voice's singsong rise at the end of *now*.

She doesn't answer. It's not really her he's talking to. He's talking to the toilet.

'Perhaps a bit to the left?' He lifts the seat off, exposing two long, darkened silver bolts. He's holding the seat awkwardly in one hand as he stands, even more awkwardly, and gives a half-cough as his knees protest the change in state. Perhaps the loo seat only looks too heavy in his hand because it makes her so very aware of the wrinkles. They're always so much more of a surprise on her brother than on herself.

Or perhaps that's not what bothers her at all. Perhaps it's just that it's exactly the gesture with which their mother used to tell off her father. *You'll break your wrist*, she would announce, the proclamation echoing through these very rooms, Nightingale Lane's own Cassandra of health and safety in the home, fated to be disbelieved. Though also, happily, fated to be wrong.

'Ah, yes. Alright. Well, maybe further left.' Having contemplated the toilet at a distance, he leans the seat against the cupboard under the sink. He begins the orchestrated process of kneeling down again – screwdriver in hand, outwardly concealed and inwardly ignored pain behind his eyes – to adjust the bolt furthest from where she perches on the edge of the bath.

She's there for the pleasure of his company. It is not because she doesn't trust him. It's nothing to do with trust. Or age. It's nothing to do with either of those things at all.

We really can afford to get someone in to fix this, she's so far managed not to say. There is no way of saying it that won't sound exactly like their mother. She would rather everyone went on risking life and limb on a wobbly toilet seat than allow a sentence past her lips that so clearly belongs to her mother.

'A bit to the right, then.' He twists the bolt back the other way, begins fastening it down.

He'll tell the story about the goldfish in a minute. Any time a toilet is in the vicinity, physically or conversationally – any item of bathroom furniture, if she's honest – no member of the family could ever resist the goldfish story for more than a few minutes. She's even caught herself telling it in other homes, inspired by other toilets.

'I'm really not sure you should be sitting there,' he says instead, without looking up from the bowl.

'There's time before I get dinner on.' She speaks each word as cheerfully, as deliberately carelessly, as she can, dusting the lie as lightly as possible with the sugar-coating of irrelevant truth that bakes it to perfection. His hypocrisy would have infuriated her once: that he should be allowed to endanger his back and knees on the floor, at their age – and he the best part of a year older – while she, being a "girl", ought not even to be sitting on the edge of the bath watching him; that he, being a "boy", ought not to let her. The physicality of such injustice, the double standard of it, would once have been hot under her skin, swimming and burning in her thoughts and screaming to burst out from her body in the urgent relief of words and words and words. She'd never have expected to miss that need, the hard, hot press to let the words escape. Yet now it doesn't matter. It's amazing what doesn't matter now. Time, or the perception of it, is kinder in the end. If she could go back and tell herself that was what it would feel like there would be no point: she would never believe her. Or if she did, she'd just be angry. She'd pour it into more notebooks. Then lie awake at night wondering if it was worse to burn them, or to wonder who would read them.

'You know what this reminds me of?' he says like he's sharing a secret. 'It reminds me of the goldfish.'

'Yes,' she says, and the smile in her voice is real even if the surprise isn't. 'Barnes Summer Fête. Nineteen…?'

'Calico fantail,' he says into the toilet bowl. He doesn't confirm or correct the year, which means he doesn't remember either. 'Black and orange, barely any gold at all.'

'No goldfish is really gold.' She doesn't know why she says that. Another irrelevant truth. She just enjoys dropping them in these days, these limited days.

'No,' he says. 'No, I suppose not.'

'That wasn't the one from the fair anyway.'

'Wasn't it?'

She shakes her head, though she is too far over his shoulder to be seen when he only has eyes for the screwdriver. 'The one we won was pure gold. Orange, I mean.'

'Was it the same loo seat?'

'Was what?'

'The funeral. The goldfish's funeral, that is. Not Clara's.'

'Oh. Yes. Yes, I think it was.' They haven't mentioned the funeral – her daughter's, not the fish's – since they came back from it. Nor have they discussed how long either of them intends to give before making a decision about what will happen to this house when they leave it. Every day has been just enough like the last that she's almost let herself start to hope this continuous flow of *now* has become permanent, that no choices have to be made. She smooths a crease in her skirt. Perhaps she'll change before dinner tonight.

'You can still see the old paint just here.' He points to something she can't see, beside one of the metal circles that will fix the seat in place.

'Oh yes.'

'Two loo seats in three generations. Makes you think, it really does.'

'Yes.' The bathroom had been white when the goldfish died, the same colour as the fish's body had been when she saw it lying draped along the rainbow gravel. The other two goldfish, rapid and glittering with the fluidity of colour and movement of life, swam on in their abundant circles around the rocks and pond weed, while the one they'd brought home so proudly – a jewel in its watery bag, sparkling and vibrant, making them feel like the proud owners of living glitter – had been drained of the colour and movement the others still enjoyed. The other fish seemed to have quite forgotten that their fallen comrade had been any other way. But for her, seeing it lying at the bottom of the tank resulted in the opposite of forgetfulness. It translated into an avid, immediate and lifelong belief in ghosts, too instinctive to shake with any amount of growing up. It wasn't that she believed all that life and colour must have gone somewhere else; quite the opposite. It was as if that absence, that blank white, was somehow proof of ghosts in itself. The reason the goldfish changed colour when it died was that was what a ghost was: a white sheet that fell over everything that came before.

Clara's father was just the boy next door then, when the goldfish died. First her friend, later her "friend". Belonging to the house as much as they did, as if the house had selected him as much as she ever had, as much as her parents had. And later, much later, long after the second toilet seat, there had been Clara. And then Clara had Frankie. And now Clara was dead, and Frankie's face was so much like their parents'. Even now, in grief and maturity, it was heartbreaking to watch, Clara's face was so right in this house. She belonged to it. In it, that is. Belonged in it. 'Leo?'

'Lily?' He straightens up, as much as that's an option.

'I was just wondering if you remember...' She'd never been tempted to ask before, whether he recalled their fish turning white. It would be as terrible to know he did remember an experience so fundamental to her private understanding of the world, perhaps remembered it differently, as it would be to think that he wouldn't remember it at all; that the experience – whether it happened in the privacy of her own mind or in the external world – now existed only and entirely within her. All those years she'd been frightened to approach their toilet during the night – or any toilet, as it transpired when she left the house for three brief university years and found certain childhood superstitions moved home with one, even when, or perhaps because, one came home and married the boy next door – because night, logically, was when the ghosts would rise. Her father had impressed her with the fear, sure and certain as any hope, that some goldfish in the sewer did indeed go on living, and better there, where they might just swim back up into the light, than buried in the garden. Would the visible manifestation of the ghost she'd seen lying at the bottom of that tank – then stood and prayed for from her father's Bible while he respectfully slipped fish from net to toilet – emerge from the sewers to which it had been freed, or exiled? Would its spirit choose to return home? She was pretty sure hers would.

She was pretty sure Clara's would, too. If that were an option. Which of course it wasn't. Her daughter was not coming back.

'Remember what?' he asks, looking at her from the mirror where he's adjusting the loose bridge of his reading glasses.

'What?' She wonders when he moved. 'Oh, just what time the children are coming home.'

'We agreed seven, didn't you?' His voice doesn't register the change of subject, or that "the children" are adults, old enough to make plans over their Great Uncle Leo's head about what time Grandma Lily cooks dinner, about which he can be both irritated and relieved.

'Yes. Yes, we did.' She is determined Frankie will feel her family's presence, not just her mother's absence.

'Here we go…' He's back at the toilet, having edged the lid carefully, smoothly, on to its fastenings. 'There. Right. And off again once more for one more tighten…'

You don't need to be doing this, she still manages not to say. *We can afford to get someone in, we can afford…* She does not want to hear their mother in her voice – or her father in his, snapping back. Perhaps that's the real reason. Then again perhaps it isn't. Another thing that doesn't matter in the end. She just needs to keep the lid down.

The neighbours are having one of their hideous garden parties. She can hear the music starting up, beyond the fir trees that line the end of the garden. She knows the tune, for once. Simon and Garfunkel of all things. The one example of popular music she can't bring herself to dislike. Strange to think those neighbours, let alone her own children, children's partners and children's friends, weren't anywhere near born when she was first haunted by a belief in ghosts. Yet here she and the house remain, unchanging as ghosts-in-waiting.

'It wasn't that strange, was it?' He slowly, jerkily, reinserts the lid over the two exposed metal rods.

'What wasn't?'

'Being seventy. That's what they're singing, isn't it? That it's "terribly strange" to be that age. I thought seventy was alright. Had quite a jolly time of it overall. Didn't you?'

'I didn't know you could hear the music, that far away.'

He pushes the seat down, lid and all, lifts it, pushes again. He taps his ear, the right side, the one without the hearing aid in. 'You'd be surprised what I can pick up.'

'Perhaps I would.'

He stands, slowly, turns his body towards her while his eyes remain on the translucent glass of the bathroom window. 'I wanted to do this, Lily.'

'You always did. You've always loved Do-It-Yourself'

'As a last thing.' He rubs a finger and thumb down his nose, exactly as their father did, delaying bad news. 'You know we need to… the children and you and I, will need to… make decisions.'

She'd tried so hard to think tonight would be a normal dinner. Except that dinners together weren't normal anymore, and she couldn't pretend that they had been for a long time. She knew this was coming, the reason they were putting so many dinners off, of course she did. The sensible thing was not to sell the house, to make funds available for Frankie in the long run. It was was for Frankie and her father to continue living here, as they had done while Clara's illness was still barely visible. Yes, that was the sensible thing. But Frankie wasn't the reason. Her grandmother was. Her grandmother and her Great Uncle Leo. And no one was going to say so.

That sad young boy she'd been so sure Clara would tire of, not widow; he'd be here every day. Her poor widower son-in-law would no doubt be completely thoughtful and unpatronizing when she'd say "You know Grandma," – because she would always be Grandma in front of Frankie – "if you do think it's a good idea, that we can all be closer to each other… or even move in with you both? Officially?" Because wasn't that what Grandma always wanted? To be closer to everyone?

Yes, it was. It had been. But not like this. Not in a way that admitted everything this did. That Clara was dead. That she herself would be, before too long. That one day, little Frankie would too.

That's what they would decide tonight. Knowing, no doubt, before she made her kindly, dignified, well-chosen arguments that her answer would always be "If that's what the family wants" because that was always going to be her answer before any question was raised. She's not interested in any other answer.

She'd just thought, if she'd thought at all, they'd wait a little longer after the funeral. That they'd have time to adjust to living here without the person they were – technically – caring for, before the next generation moved in to care for them. Because however much fun that might be, she had hoped that there would be a little more *now* before the end.

'It has been six months after all,' he says into the toilet, opening and shutting the lid and peering at it as if he too expects one last goldfish to finally find its way, to swim back up, to validate all those years of quiet, gentle terror.

'Has it really?' Perhaps she knows that too, how long it has really been since the funeral, the way she knows the view from this window, the darkness of the fir trees, far too well to need to open it to see beyond the crystalised leaves to the real trees beyond. It just hadn't needed to matter. It hadn't needed to matter at all.

As she looks at her brother's face, failing to meet hers, it is impossible not to see the boy who'd offered her a freshly dug-up earthworm, or behind him and his outstretched muddy palm, the gap in the hedge and, through it, the neighbour who would become her father in law, whom she'd been so frightened of in the days when she believed in grown-ups, like giants and unicorns, before she realised that adults were just people, more afraid than angry, probably just doing their best to interpret the faces trying to interpret theirs.

It is nearly winter. She knows that. No point in taking it personally.

Having them here will make Christmas easier. That at least can be made right, for Frankie.

But winter is already here, a whiteness to the grey beyond the closed window, a translucency that still doesn't give any clues. From where she sits on the corner of the bath, she looks down at her brother. Did he used to be taller? They were the same height once. Nearly. She's pretty sure of that. But she feels taller now. The arthritis creeping up her toe, the careful way she has to think about never fully extending her knee, means one leg, the one nearest him and the toilet, keeps her tethered. She cannot be stretching, surely. Yet is she taller, now, for all that?

She stands, and moves closer to the frosted glass.

Poltergeist

[1973]

'And before you tell me I've gone bananas…' Frankie says, using her mother's lecturing voice. She really does sound exactly like Clara, more so with every day and every argument, and I'm pretty sure she catches me thinking as much before I turn away to face the window.

'Stop it,' I say, with no force of any kind behind it at all. I want to hear my wife's voice, whoever it chooses to speak through.

'…bear in mind it's exactly what she would have done in life.'

The pear tree outside our kitchen window is swaying. I never thought that tree would last. The garden centre was selling them at entirely the wrong time of year. It didn't even occur to the rest of us the sapling would make it. But Clara had, in all senses, bought it. She had admired its determination, insisted on our giving it its chance. And here it still is, nineteen years after it arrived and six months after Clara went.

'Mummy would call this "reading-in-the-garden weather",' I say, perhaps to prove I'm not avoiding talking about her mother. It's a little before midsummer now, and typically for midsummer the sky is offensively perfect, in ever more offensively perfect contrast with the conversation or fight or whatever the difference is these days that my daughter is about to demand I have and I am about to demand we avoid.

'I know she would,' Frankie says. The silence sets around us again. She's waiting to follow my lead, as she has every right to do. I am the adult. I am the one who should be helping her. I am meant to help her open difficult conversations, not to model for her how to shut them down.

'Darling.' I turn back to her, try to take both her hands. She almost lets me, before the pre-teen resistance kicks in. 'Your mother is not a…'

'Poltergeist, Daddy.' Frankie's eyes are blue like mine but with a steadiness and lack of apology that are pure Clara. 'I read about them. I didn't do a drawing because they're invisible. Words are all we get.'

'You mother is not a poltergeist. And if she were… if she were any kind of ghost…' I'm trying to laugh about it, to fill the silence; another way of not listening. Another way of making things as clear and simple as my fear needs them to be. 'Don't you think she'd have better ways to spend her earthly exile than putting our shopping away?'

Now it's Frankie who turns to the kitchen window, watches the pear tree sway.

'It's not that I don't want you to be right…' I'm laughing harder; no, worse, *trying* to laugh harder. 'It's simply that you're not! You can't be!'

'I don't know how you do it,' she says. It's a phrase we've both heard a lot recently, in varying forms, separately and together, from most of the people we know: my friends, her teachers, our counsellors. But Frankie's silhouette of perfect, quiet poise under that angular blanket of unfussy, straight brown hair remains my one answer, my only reason. The very image, not simply of her mother, but her mother's attitude. Though uniform grey replaced brown long ago, before fading and dropping to a lacy absence, nothing ever altered that outline of poised observation, of focus on the external. Clara focused on what was real. Not what it said about the observer. Just the observation. Clara's body was a mere vehicle; a tool for enquiry and not a distraction from it. For as long as her eyes could open, they focused on the external world. No prior assumption ever coloured a new fact, a new possibility; realigning her world view around a new idea, not blocking one because it didn't fit. Her back always turned, politely and firmly, against my well-meant avoidance. She was a true researcher. I am a coward.

'Frankie…'

'Daddy.' She doesn't turn from the window. I first saw Clara with her back to me, that very shape of certainty; I loved it, that certainty, at first sight. I still do, now that I can't see it except through our daughter.

But whatever Frankie plans to say, her shoulders sag – imperceptibly if you don't know how upright her usual poise – and she stoops to the lino where, true to family reputation, I have left the shopping bags all over the kitchen floor. Frankie opens the bottom cupboard, begins lifting things in. Box of teabags, bag of coffee, multi-pack of ready-salted Hula Hoops. She's very pointedly leaving the tins where they are on the floor. And I'm still trying to laugh the whole thing off. Both of which say this conversation is not over. I leave enough silence that eventually she has to pour truths into it, while I keep mine to myself, a technique I am ashamed to admit I always found worked with her mother.

'I don't know how you do it,' she says again. 'I don't know how you can spend your entire life with someone and still have so little idea – so little acceptance – of who they are. Even when they're exactly who you want them to be. And that person is there, and loves you, and… look. This.' She indicates the pile of tins. 'All the time. We both kept telling you someone was going to fall over it in the end…'

'But…' Yes, they had. Clara once snapped something about the indignity of eventually breaking her neck on chopped tomatoes or mushroom soup. 'But that's not what happened in the end, is it. The end had nothing to do soup cans, did it. It had nothing to do with anything.'

I'm smiling, making kind eye contact, but the slap under the words, the finality of them, still hits home. She rallies, trying to pretend not to have felt it, eyes flickering as she gropes for the words I pushed away. 'Picking up the shopping off the floor, your trademark pile of tins we both kept telling you you'd fall over and break your neck in the end if it wasn't one of us…'

'Which I didn't. No one ever fell over them—'

'BECAUSE SHE PICKED THEM UP!'

Frankie didn't even cry at the funeral; now she's almost crying because of tins on the kitchen floor. It's all control with her, I think it always has been. She wipes her face, determined as her mother would be for the substance and not the style to be what's heard. 'This is exactly what she'd do. Exactly what Mummy would do if she were… if she were *here*.'

'Frankie—'

'If she came back, if she wondered what to say or which of us to try and talk to or if we could sense her, if we wanted to, she'd do something useful first. Something practical. That was Mummy. Mummy *did* things. It's obvious, it's absolutely obvious she'd do that, and I don't see why after all this time you're choosing not to see her for who she is.'

'That's not what I'm doing at all,' I mumble, too indefinitely for her to bother disagreeing. I must ignore her present tense, for both our sakes. This is not the time for the past tense to hit her as well. 'But maybe I do see...' I wave a hand in what might be acceptance, might be dismissal. It probably looks more like I'm drowning in the middle of my own kitchen.

'What? Daddy? See what?' That hope. In her voice, her face.

'Why it's harder.'

Disappointment covers her face, translated into blankness. 'Why what's harder?'

'That who Mummy is to you, isn't who she was to me.'

The change of tense halfway through my sentence chills us both, clenches my teeth against the words that have already escaped, turns my face from my daughter as if they were spoken *by* her, not *to* her.

'Frankie, sweetheart...'

I want to apologise now that I've won, tell her I've never felt so alone as I do in the middle of the kitchen and its nearly tidy floor, with the knowledge that I have made my daughter feel as isolated as I do now, instead of doing my job of lessening that isolation. That I am making her believe out of – what? Spite? Denial? – that Clara is gone for me in a way she isn't for her. It isn't true. I just know that's what's supposed to be.

That hateful smile I felt on my own face is crawling over on to Francesca's; of laughter that sees the joke and doesn't feel it, that feels nothing greater than absence. 'I don't even know what I'd change if I could,' she says. 'Don't know if I'd follow you out of this...' she shrugs at our home, the world beyond it, 'stasis. Or if I'd pull you back in to wallow with me... Yes, actually. Yes. I would. I would pull you back in. In a second.' She snaps her fingers, smiles my own false smile in my own face. 'Not that it matters because there *is* nothing I can do.'

'What did you think you saw?' I ask, though I don't want to know.

'Nothing.' She's answering my wishes, not my question, her tone letting me know she knows it's useless to bring the truth into this. 'I'm sorry.'

I'm sorrier,' I say. As if it's her fault I don't believe her dead mother will suddenly pick our tinned tomatoes off the floor. 'We'll talk about this later. I have to go.'

'I know.'

'Charles and Heather are on their way over, I don't want you to miss going to—'

'I said I know.' It's not far from the longest day of the year, yet it still manages to be cold in here. It's definitely got colder since we started talking. For a moment I thought I could see her breath at the end of that sentence.

Frankie still has her back to me as I walk out of the kitchen. I don't get far. If

you let your feet trail as you climb the first few stairs, there's a place you can creep a silent step back. It was always very useful for leaving Francesca unsupervised for the first time at anything, and somehow over the years we neglected to tell her about our trick of watching when she couldn't see us. It's the perfect crime as long as no one turns the kitchen lights on. Although it's cold in there, it's always perfectly bright. I hover on that secret place on that staircase, that one step without a creak, and I watch as Frankie turns from the window.

The first thing she does is take in the empty kitchen. Her tears have dissipated with the source of her anger – me – and she returns to the measured, unemotional putting away of shopping, exactly as Clara would when that was what needed to be done.

Except that Francesca is deliberately leaving the tins out. The pear tree sways, somewhere beyond the window a blackbird begins an experimental trill. At first I think she's just forgotten about them, but then she stands still on the far side of the kitchen and looks at them for far too long. My daughter takes a couple of steps backwards, still looking at the pile of tins, until she's sitting on the stool in the corner where I used to polish shoes at the table. Clara always hated me doing that, asked why I didn't take them into the garden where, I would maintain, you couldn't concentrate because of all the damned birds. It's the same stool, the same white fold-down table, yet it's not. It's something and somewhere else now. What were associations have changed status, become memories. I'm not just looking through a door at the kitchen when I'm outside the room; it's the same when I'm inside it. I'm still looking back at where that place had been.

Frankie stands at the kitchen window. The sun beats on her drying face. I think she's expecting to cry again, is puzzled that isn't happening. I'd like to explain to her that I know why she cannot cry; her mother was the same. There was never an emotional reaction when there was still action to be taken, something concrete still to be done. Crying was for when there was nothing else to do. Maybe she's right. Maybe I have already let Clara go, already come out the other side of somewhere Francesca is still moving through. Because Frankie doesn't go through the world assuming it is as she always thought it was.

The kitchen is empty, I swear it is empty, except for Frankie and the pile of tins.

'Mummy,' my daughter says. There's a strangely muffled quality to her voice in the silence, as if something else is there for the sound to bounce off. But nothing happens. Nothing continues to happen. I'm just turning to creep the rest of the way up the stairs, when I hear Francesca's fists on the counter. 'Fuck!' she screams.

I open my mouth to betray myself with a reprimand for the language I thought she didn't know and—

Bang.

I leap in the air and towards my daughter in one instinctive burst. One of the tins is off the pile, rolling a semi-circle on the floor. Clara's raised eyebrows are clear in my head, the frown she chose rather than felt, the apologetic way she forced herself into shouting when she felt shouting was needed. I can't see these things in front of me and I never will again but somewhere in my mind, truer and clearer than anything before my eyes, I see them.

'Sorry Mummy,' Frankie says, alone in the kitchen, watching as the fallen tin rolls. I stand on my stair, and I wait, and watch Francesca standing and waiting. I didn't know I'd forgotten that facial expression, the one where our daughter knows she's done wrong and knows that Mummy will be angry and that the quickest way to the other side of the argument is to listen to the lecture and agree and nod at every word. I know perfectly well that nothing is going to happen. I know that it is pure coincidence the tin fell when it did. Or, at most, that some vibration from Francesca's fists on the counter somehow reached the pile of tins on the kitchen floor. And anyway, even if it were possible that she could be here, Clara wouldn't want to scare us – never wanted to scare us – that's why she explained the shape and process of her death so well in advance. So that, during and after the time came, we would always know the difference between sadness and fear. I know it all. Just as I know that the scariest possible thing the world could contain is not the fear of ghosts in an empty room but the certainty of that room's emptiness, of a world I have no right to be angry at for continuing to exist when she cannot be in it.

I know all this perfectly well, even as I watch the fallen tin of tomatoes tip up and rest on its corner.

The tin stands, solid and impossible, on its rounded edge. And then it clatters to the ground again. I watch the lack of fear in Frankie's face, the lack of anger and frustration that had been so present in trying to convince me of the possibility her mother was in the kitchen, frustration completely replaced by the open-minded, quiet interest that characterised Clara and herself with a new fact on the horizon.

The tin rolls in a perfectly natural way, until it runs out of momentum and is still.

'I'd… I'd like to be sure,' Frankie says. Her voice echoes a little in the empty kitchen. 'Can you show me again please, Mummy?'

The tin lifts back on to its edge. It lifts off the floor and sails the shortest of distances, the smallest of heights, onto the pile of tinned tomatoes, mushroom soup and baked bean tins it had fallen from. It's a perfectly normal gesture, one that would have been completely unremarkable had there been a hand to cause it, would have been one of many identical little acts of stacking after any supermarket shop.

Francesca must be thinking the same, because she opens the lower cupboard. Then she sits back down on my shoe-polishing stool and watches, with something approaching a real smile, as her mother, even more invisibly than in life, puts the shopping away for us.

I'm too selfish to give myself away, the questions too big to yell them like demands. Have we brought her back? Is my wife a prisoner in this house because I or Francesca refused to let her out? Have I made her a slave in her own home, a spectral presence to clear up the kitchen floor because I can't be bothered? If she is trapped by our inability to live without her, how do we set her free? And, if we can, do we have to?

'What do you want?' Frankie asks the silence.

The tin pauses in mid-air, as if awaiting clarification. Frankie's simpler, truer, kinder version of all my questions seems to have stopped it in its tracks where my volley of self-indulgent terror would have got nowhere.

'I mean,' Frankie says, 'I'm happy to… see you. But I don't want you to think you have to do this. We'll catch you up, won't we? It's just for the time being, isn't it? I mean, isn't everything? You don't have to wait for us. We'll be… alright. We'll get on with…' She shrugs, smiles, pushes her hair and the threat of her tears from her face. 'With… for… the time being. You don't have to worry. I promise. I love you.'

For a moment, nothing continues to happen. The chopped tomatoes tin remains stationery in the air. Then it continues its journey to the cupboard. The next tin rises off the floor and arcs in the direction of the first. It floats there, as if unsure.

'Alright,' Frankie says. 'One last time. But then you have to let us do it.'

The last tin of chopped tomatoes sails gently onto the messy pile inside the cupboard that has been my lip-service to enforced tidiness. Then the cupboard door shuts, on its own. By the time Frankie's mother has put the shopping away one last time, I still don't know if I believe she's there, or if she knows I'm watching, but I know it's not about what I believe. It's about what I do. Clara wouldn't give away our hiding place whether she sees me in it or not. I pad quietly on the spot, before walking, audibly, back down the rest of the stairs. Frankie is picking up the empty supermarket carrier bags, stuffing them in the plastic half-moon container by the door. I lift the last few with her, until the kitchen floor is clear.

The Moth, Part Two

[1993]

It took what felt like three days for her to truly worry. At first she just cried, not with any apparent fear for me; nothing worse than my having gone without saying goodbye.

To that version of events, the absconded lover in other circumstances I'd have had every intention of being – have been on more than one occasion – her housemate responded with brotherly consolation, endless cups of tea and solid hours of not telling her she was repeating herself, at a rate and timescale that would have made me scream. Now he stands in her doorway, looking at the gap left by the pile of clothes on what was my side of the bed – nearest the door, as befitted the situation – while I look down on the tops of their heads, the bed, the gap where the last evidence of me was. Even from the ceiling, there's no missing the expressions on their faces.

'Mate,' he says.

'I know.' The sight of his friend cross-legged half on and half under the duvet in her tartan pyjamas, her usually limp hair messily wild and last night's make-up ringing her eyes, holds the same apparent focus and respect he'd given our departmental meeting (that's where I'd seen him before: the student rep. I knew there was a good reason I'd taken against him). All of which means I can at least comfort myself that no man could be even half-tempted by such an image as the one she presents today. He doesn't look directly at the gap on the floor from which the police took my clothes. She rarely looks anywhere else.

'I know,' she says again, still gripping the t-shirt to her pale, mascara-slashed face. The police are long gone; all that remains is my anonymous brown suit jacket over the back of her desk chair. I'd never seen how shiny the material was until now, how… inedible, is the word that comes to mind. A strange thought.

'He's everywhere,' she tells him. Liane bought that t-shirt she's gripping to her face. I find I like seeing her holding it, purifying it of the past somehow. Then I remember I'm not there. I'm becoming part of that past. I'm playing voyeur to a future I suppose I always expected to cause, never to be part of. 'He's the first thing I see when I come in, when I go out.' I flew at her only once, that first day only; throwing myself at her, yelling at the top of my lungs who I was. But she was thinking too deeply of me, crying too strongly into the t-shirt she'd taken from that pile that I registered as just another tear on her cheek. I stayed only long enough to feel how easily she could crush me without a thought, without awareness of her strength, her power, before fluttering back to the ceiling. She pulls one leg up, leans her chin on her knee. 'This isn't… he wouldn't… I know you don't like him. But…'

'I'm not disposed to like him,' Jamie begins.

'I know you're not disposed to like him, Jamie. He wasn't disposed to like you either.'

Jamie visibly brightens, either at the information or her use of past tense.

'Isn't,' she corrects herself. 'Oh God.'

Jamie nods, interlocks his fingers, tightening them, and stares at where the blood is draining from the knuckles. 'But…'

'But, to leave without his clothes…'

'I admit that's not the commitment-phobe I took him for. A streaker is not a commitment-phobe.'

She almost laughs, then the joke wears off and reality closes over her again. 'They've covered his lecture. He hasn't turned up for work. That's not like him. His job is everything, it's all that's real to him.'

Although she says "job" and not "career", it's the accuracy rather than the inaccuracy that stings. A plethora of friends have been over every night since I, as they see it, disappeared. The girls interrogate the emotions and leave no space for the facts. They'll make terrible painters, all interpretation and no observation. No sense of scale. Hugging and crying and repeating; no clear outlines to a conversation so you can't tell what the picture is supposed to be. But their faces looked nothing like each other, which made me doubt myself as I ran through the groups I'd taught, blurs of ages and not individuals. I have colleagues, fellow intellectual heavyweights, brothers in arms. But when the armour is put down, few of what these students would recognise as friends.

She stares over the t-shirt Liane chose into the middle-distance of the closed curtains. 'The smell's almost gone. It was the one thing I had of him. Every time I touch it, breathe into it, I'm replacing what was him. All that's left is me, my version of him.'

'Sounds like role-reversal to me,' Jamie quietly tells his trainers.

'That's not fair.' But it is, and her face shows she knows it. And though he sees this as surely as I do, humbly staring at the blood leaving his knuckles, still he apologises for what they both know is the truth.

But I am right here, I want to laugh at the stupidity of it, that I am witnessing the effect of the end I have chosen. But my lungs don't have the capacity. Moths, it seems, cannot laugh. The lives of moths don't provide the reason, the necessity, or therefore the equipment. I want to scream from the mirrors on her ceiling, yet I might as well be as far away as she imagines me, because I can tell her nothing. I was right when I told her this isn't living. Not as humans are lucky enough to call living. Moths cannot laugh, any more than human beings can smell how the taste of cashmere differs from cotton, which I'm starting to learn as I flutter absentmindedly away from these giants and towards the wardrobe at the far wall.

'Why aren't you?' she asks. 'Disposed to like him? Really.'

He gestures to the desk-chair and at her nod he takes it, leaning as far away from my jacket as feasible. 'Do you? Really? Like him, I mean?'

'Jamie...'

'I mean, you love him; that's nobody's fault...' He tries to stop himself, but I see the flash of it, the moment he catches a taste for telling the truth. 'He's not in the room when he's in the room. We're all extras in a play he's already written. Every look, every snide comment screams "I told you so".'

'He's not like that.'

Jamie doesn't answer. The telephone rings in their living room and he responds at the speed of relief. Then we are alone. She's still cross-legged, still gripping Liane's choice of t-shirt as if it was ever a part of me. She doesn't change, perceived or unperceived by Jamie. That was just for me. She is herself, with him. And I never met her.

I immediately try flying at her, screaming who I am into a world so much bigger than I am that it simply cannot hear even if it chose to. She barely notices me hit her face before she bats me away, gently, slowly enough that I'm in no danger; I just grip the back of her hand before the too-gentle-for-swatting arm extends and I right myself in mid-air, returning to the curtain and landing almost exactly where she still hasn't noticed I swatted that first moth.

It doesn't matter how hungry I get. I shall not eat her clothes.

I wasn't truly hungry those first few days. Not before they removed the pile that would have been mine by right, before I adjusted to what hunger feels like in this body, let alone how sating it would work. The day after that I still didn't understand that's what I was – hungry – that this was hunger was for something so small and missable. Not until I found myself called to her old mahogany wardrobe, its cacophony of textures singing to my scent receptors from the dark, delicious cavern. Part of that was the smell of her but part was something more, something that spoke directly to my body's screaming, yet still I stopped myself before the first bite. These new desires do not feel new; they feel old, heavy laws written in the material of this new body. The keyhole of her wardrobe was like coming home in a way I never let my previous body feel about her bed.

They've been sitting silently, the two of them, propped up by her pillows, for what feels like hours when that doorbell rings. There's a steady dull drizzle over the hills but it hasn't quite reached the houses. Something in the length and strength of the ring means I know, somehow, when Jamie leaps up and says, 'You want me to come with you?' exactly who will be standing there.

'No.' She looks in the mirror for what feels like the first time since I disappeared. 'We don't want to look like we're ganging up on her.' I follow her to the door, down the short hallway, keeping my movements apparently random, circling as far out of reach as possible. She barely pauses before she opened the door. 'Hi,' she says.

There is no humour in Liane's face, but then there rarely is, unless she's the one telling the joke. Her eyes, set back under the expensive, tasteless self-conscious blonde streaks of the mud-brown bob; cheeks sagging the way they always do when not lit up by external stimulation; laughter, anger, indignation. 'Hi.' She throws the word back, the first thrust of swordplay at this girl, half her age and never knowingly her enemy.

'Would you like to come in?'

Something in Liane's face stir at this, recognises however reluctantly a fellow traveller sharing in her pain. 'No, thanks. Look, I… this isn't easy.'

'I know.'

Her narrowed, dim blue eyes follow the corridor beyond, taking in me, if she only knew it, as part of the architecture. 'So this is where he was, then.'

'Yes.' To her credit and my pride, she's deciding not to notice the attempted insult. Liane's tone goes entirely, effortlessly, over her head, just as I do, crawling from the top of one doorpost to the other. 'I've honestly no idea what happened. Liane, he said nothing. I didn't even know he had… that you were…'

'I'm sure you didn't. You sound exactly his type.' She tries to laugh. 'That wasn't fair. Look, it's not… none of this is about you.'

'I know.' She picks up the cardboard box that's been sitting by the door. 'This is it, everything. The police returned it all after the tests were done. It's just the clothes he was wearing. He never left any here, for what that's worth.'

'I see,' she says. And then, with some of the guard dropped, 'Thank you, I suppose.' In the nod, given and returned, there's a part of both that recognises an ally beneath where I created an enemy.

When she's gone, we – woman and moth – go back down the corridor to the comparative familiarity and safety of bed and mirrors. Except that when she sits beside Jamie on the bed, she leans her head against him. He puts his arm around her in a way that suddenly makes me feel more jealous than his height and silly name ever did. I have returned to my favourite patch of ceiling, but cannot settle, so flutter to the accusation of empty coat hangers, the half of the wardrobe she must have thought my clothes would occupy. If they had, I'd have eaten today.

If I do succumb, when I do take a bite of one dress, and then another because another is always what follows a first bite, what I love will be gone. Even though I hadn't noticed myself listening at the time, I know what each of these identical hanging dresses means. That's my alibi now, my reason to tell myself I cannot eat. The holes I took such pleasure picking were nothing to those I am eventually going to bite. Not taking a bite of a single dress. In the middle of the night, hungry and alone with all the food I could ever need and the woman I love in one room. The truth seeps over me just as the fluff or dust that seemed the natural deposit of my wings has started to leave itself over the dress I skirt the hem of, the scarf I perch on, hung on the back of the door.

I flutter around the faces of one and then the other and back again, unnoticed where once I was the largest thing in the room. They both see me and think nothing of me, except that Jamie is closer to the window, so it's Jamie who stands, politely turns the handle and angles it to let in the minimum possible drizzle while giving me the option of escape. He returns to sit beside her in the most companiable silence I've ever seen. Neither of them looks at me again to see whether or not I bother to fly away.

I don't remember the last time it wasn't raining. The insistent tick and patter on the window has become my understanding of silence. The embedded lightbulbs are off and there's just the one jasmine candle burning on the desk. Jamie sits on the edge of the bed, and I see her look away from this in the way I did from what I, too, meant to encourage. I haven't been mentioned for weeks, or perhaps it's days; any difference is long behind me.

'I always wondered,' he says. There's a wisdom, a thoughtfulness to his face no nineteen-year-old has any right to. 'Why art?'

'What do you mean?' My disappearance used to be her excuse to need him, his excuse to hover in case needed. But even as I become little but my own hunger, barely able to fly from curtain to wall, I can tell when she is talking of me. Her voice patterns change, tighten, drop away to something choppier, unsupported. To what I thought was her voice. Because it was her voice when I was here – when I was human. The looser, lower, streamlined gushing river of her real voice is a freer sound, the sound of their world gently closing over the gap I've left.

'Art, not English. Coming back as a mature student, given everything…'

Mature student?

'What do you mean, everything?' she says.

He looks at his feet, the way he used to in the doorway. 'I've never asked you about the book.'

There's a silence I don't understand. 'I didn't know you knew,' she says.

What book?

'Hell, you were on every bus stop, every newspaper. "The female…" who? "Tomorrow's…" what was it?'

'Does it matter?'

'They were tipping your second novel to be the Nobel Prize-winner.'

'It wasn't the Nobel. They tipped me for something.'

'Several somethings.'

You were what?

'Yes,' she sighs, 'I wrote that. And then I dyed my hair and waited until the fuss blew over and started the college course I was meant to take. And no one even realised I was a mature student.' The LPs aren't ostentation but birth-right. She is not trying to look older. She is dressing and thinking her age and looking young. The CDs creeping past the floppy discs and cassette tapes, the mobile phones learnt along the way, just as mine were. 'People talk about an ageless face. What they really are talking about is their own expectations. But, I don't know… it was reassuring to be around so much certainty. It doesn't need to matter how wrong he is about most of it. It's so different to how those of us who see more in the world feel most of the time.' *I hear you, I see you*, I try again to scream, frozen to the ceiling, but she exists on such a grander level she has no way of hearing.

'Well, I had something of a gap year too,' Jamie says. 'It included a divorce. She was older than she looked too.'

They look at each other as if for the first time, smiling in a way I never smiled with Liane. It's not the smile of shared habits and histories but of mysteries, futures, curiosity. And trust. 'Which of us is older, Jamie?'

He smiles. 'I suppose only administration knows. So if I don't tell you…'

'Liane might?'

It's not that Jamie was closer in age, that was just my pet reason to discount and distrust him. I didn't believe she was serious about me. I respected Liane little enough, was little enough inspired by her, to know forever was an option. That's the truth about myself I didn't perceive until I was looking down from this ceiling, able to see it all from too far away to do anything about it. He has been there for a history I have no concept of, he was winning before the game was mine to play. Set and match, young artist. It's all so obvious from up here.

'And what's your real first-name again?'

He cringes, like his response or her question is half-joke, and she picks up her sketchbook and hands it to him. He scribbles something and shows it to her.

'Gerald? What's so bad about having that as a name?'

'Nothing, except it's my father's. To me, anyway.'

'Then it always will be. Unless…'

'Unless.' He nods, the tips of his hair touched by a breeze blowing through the window from the hills, ruffling my wings and barely acknowledged by them. I can't help missing the hair I thought too coarse, that I covered in too much gel for the breeze to make a difference. 'I didn't have my name at school. There were three of us with that first name.'

'You don't even want to say it, do you?'

He shrugs. 'Perhaps I'll claim it one day. Anyway, two of us with my name also had first names as surnames. So for the convenience of others I was Jamie.'

'Why not James? It's a perfectly sensible surname.'

'Two of those in the class as well. James the First and James the Second. It was that kind of a place. I didn't want to be James the Third. Why do you hate your name?'

'Takes up too much space. "Francesca".' She mock-shivers, and it's confident, unapologetic. I'm treated to a glimpse of someone real and unselfconscious I never met. Never took the trouble to listen for. 'Too many letters and you can't hear half of them.'

'No, I mean why don't you shorten it to something that doesn't take so long.'

'My parents did. I was Frankie at home. I left it behind when I came here, met you, met… him.' It's the first time I've been mentioned, I realise, in days, and apparently I don't have a name at all. Her voice doesn't lose its projection, her sentences don't tail away again. 'I didn't even fancy him at first.' Her voice isn't even all that halting anymore. 'I just remember looking up and thinking, carelessly, "if he were attractive, would I fancy him?" And then of course I deserved everything I got, didn't I?'

'Why?'

'Because I fell in love. Because how dare I be so snobbish about what counts as attractive? He knows and thinks so much about everything that matters to me. It answered something in me too, to be taken down a peg, to fight for worthiness. I suppose it's why I walk less tall, why I don't argue when people think I'm still so young.'

She is. They are. They have as near to forever as anyone gets. I call her name again from the ceiling. It might as well be from outer space.

'I feel…' She looks up at him, then back at the duvet, the curtain, the duvet again. 'I feel most like myself with what you call me.'

He looks at her directly now, echoes her light smile. 'I'll do it if you do. Change my name back. Take it back. Metamorphose into whatever we are.'

'Or are going to be.' She holds out an open hand. 'Hello, Gerald.'

'Hello Effie,' he replies, shaking her hand.

I want to fly away but there is nowhere of any relevance to go. Anywhere at all is merely further away from her. And perhaps I fall asleep at some point because all there seems to be is darkness.

Methodically, efficiently, my mind as far out of my tiny, breakable, irrelevant body as I can keep it, I take my first bite of the collar of her black wool dress. The series of chomps seems to echo around the wardrobe. But what is loud to me will not register to the human voices beyond my side of the half-shut wooden doors.

The wool dress was the logical choice, the most substantial meal and, there's no difficulty admitting now there's no one able to hear, the easiest to bury myself in. That and the past. The first time I saw the dress. What notes I'd prepared I left at home in the middle of another fight with Liane. Library café pain-au-raisin cupped in a brown paper bag I grabbed as I threw down a fifty, skipping the queue, calling out to the face I hadn't taken in to keep the change. I arrived not exactly breathless, in the same way I'd not exactly been breathless in the argument with Liane that morning.

It had been about my tone of voice, apparently. The proof of how little respect I had. I never asked a question, she informed me. Even when I spoke the words of a question my tone made it rhetorical; told the world, this tone of voice did, that she had nothing to add. I would still have been in time if I hadn't taken the path of most resistance, the crueller, funnier path of sitting on the edge of her thousand-pound sofa and saying – asking – and what if that were true, Liane? If I admitted you were using me to make yourself feel cultured and intelligent as much as I am using you for money and access to the levels of culture you wouldn't otherwise find, let alone understand? Have you read a single one of my books you've lined up on your shelf, Liane? A single book at all, mine or anyone's, in the time since I've moved into your cathedral of inherited, expendable wealth? Or have you outsourced education as well as culture? Am I those departments of you now? Literature and politics and wit and intelligence? Do you see how little history there is in this room, Liane? How the books are height-and-colour-coded rather than shelved by author, subject, significance beyond the colour of their spines? I would so much rather be cruel than be you, Liane.

I was still riding high on my eloquence when I realised too late in the walk to campus I was doing what I never do: going without breakfast. I can forsake love, I can even go without sex if there's nothing new or safe on the immediate horizon, but to caffeine and breakfast I am a slave.

It was easy at first, the way comedy is under pressure. It didn't matter whether the students knew I hadn't prepared, only whether the stand-up act was strong enough that they didn't care about the difference. I was lecturing, I found, on colour and perspective, asking whether my enjoying this exquisite pain-au-raisin was as much about my expectations of it, the colour and consistency of the visible spread of fruit beneath the surface of the dough, as it was about the last aspect of the pastry: the taste. Aesthetic was distraction from content, rather than a summation of it; if you took away colour, you took perspective too. How Esher at one end and Klee at the other agreed we brought ourselves to what we saw, interpreted not the world but ourselves. I don't know if I meant a word, yet out it came, glorious because it needed to be, and perhaps I was fooling no one but I was entertaining everyone, and wasn't beauty truth in the end and…

…and I still cannot remember the question she interrupted with. Just the moment my soliloquy became a monologue. The crumbling of my fourth wall. The realisation the audience *was* there, listening, looking back at me through worlds of their own, histories, observations just as much beyond me as I knew mine to be beyond them.

'That,' I do remember saying, taking the last bite of that now thoroughly tax-deductible pain-au-raisin, 'is a profound question.'

'And what's the *answer*, Professor?' she asked. I wondered, not with any great passion but more with detached academic interest, whether the day would come when I would slide my hand over the breasts that underlined that two-dimensional Byrne-Jonesian face of her emerald sleeveless top, or if this moment's fork in the road of potential and kinetic, of fantasy and reality, was the happier place to leave things. I could almost feel Liane glaring over my shoulder at the little pre-Raphaelite, threatening to drag us all into a new, unpredictable era. My intrinsic lack of respect for Liane was winning out from under my material gain. Had this child promised me the safety, the sedentary reassurance of Liane's offer, there would have been no contest. But even as it stood, I was bored enough, interested enough, to risk changing everything, even myself.

I am not this body, biting into her wool dress.

I am the potential in her eyes as she asks that question, which I don't have to close my eyes to see more clearly than the inside of this wardrobe, the chomp and tear of the wool in my mouth. I am the man she started to smile at in spite of herself, all those pairs of eyes upon us both, invisible to us then as I am invisible to her and Jamie now, though the wardrobe door is open and she could see me if she only knew how to look. I am not this body. I am the moment we locked eyes where she'd aimed for horns. I am the moment that, even if there was no blinding light, unless it was that I was looking for the impetus for escape from Liane and her comfortable, monied overconfidence that I was hers forever, I was intelligent enough to admit that I had spotted what my bravest self was looking for.

But that would have been one transformation too far.

I still don't remember her question. Just the way it lacked apology for itself, or deference to me.

This was the dress she arrived in on our first official date, how it framed a face I stared at so much I was amazed I had forgotten it, had thought the art she wore could possibly upstage those real eyes. A scarlet trilby and suede grey shoulder bag, platform boots straight out of a time I'd thought – no, not thought, assumed, the opposite of thought – she had no right to remember. She was going to treat me as her inspiration and I was going to treat her as a pleasant dream, nothing more substantial, nothing with any of its own strength, its own obligations.

Perhaps there is a way she can end this. One where she doesn't even notice what she's doing when she pushes the book shut, then the pages will be falling, lightly at first, then with the combined strength that not a single one of them possesses but together will give me no time to think anything, no time and nothing to think at all. Perhaps it will be a reflex action, some less than accidental afterthought, a hand on the curtain or a shoulder to the wardrobe door.

They'll never kill me by choice. The only way this will end is if I choose it to. There are so many options I've imagined: trying to drink from her tea mug of water and falling inside the china, my last conscious moments being of floating in a surface on which I'm light enough for it to first appear hard like chilled jelly, until in my lack of hurry to escape it I feel myself sinking, no further than a millimetre below the surface but it would be enough; a shallow death. Or, instead, I could choose to land for the last time on the open sketchbook beside the cup on her bedside table, and would I feel anything at all as she lifted the hardback and the pages around the spine flattened and shut, taking me with them until I am preserved, exactly as I am, biologically accurate and perfect and flat as a pressed flower?

I don't need to leave the wardrobe to know why the words have stopped. The whisper of their kisses is just about audible, louder to something as small as I am.

'We'll need a lodger who isn't scared of mirrors,' she says into his shoulder. Today is the day they've chosen to move the most important parts of her room into his. Soon our mirrored ceiling will look down on someone else's reality. 'They seemed like such a good idea at first but who wants to be staring into your own eyes the whole time?'

'People can get used to anything,' Jamie replies. I creep nearer the bright angled shape of the keyhole, dare myself to venture in, to see them rather than imagine them truly together.

'It's too soon, I know,' Jamie says. But they're both smiling. I don't exist for them. There is no one else in their world.

'What is?' But she knows. She understands now, all of it, everything, the science of the art of living. She's bringing stagecraft into the truth. Theatrically waiting, trusting him to give her cue.

'Well, just that when… if… as I was thinking of changing my name, would you care to join me?'

'You mean…'

'My surname,' he says. 'Perhaps we might share it?'

Neither of them has moved. Yet everything is changing. The air is clear yet it swims with terror. I cannot see a way beyond my own perception, the prison of it. I'm locked inside my own reality, voiceless and immaterial.

'Are you asking me what I think you're asking me?'

'Not yet. I will, though. One day. It's a thought, isn't it?'

And there's a smile in his voice, a hope and a joy and a maturity that makes me see an entirely different person in him as well as in her. 'It is.'

She tickles the edge of Jamie's light brown hair with an intimacy we never reached. I was on a pedestal, she a groundling. She would not have dared, had too much respect for me for anything approaching the thoughtless truth of that affection, and they're looking at each other the way they did when I first saw what it was for two human beings to truly see each other, only now they're both fully clothed and instead of being happy for her, instead of patiently and sadly and bittersweetly watching her life move on, instead of all of that now I am flying at them, I'm in her face and in her hair and she's too distracted by what is important, too focused for obstacles, and I'm flying at them, and as her hand comes down I know she's who she always was, because she doesn't crush me when she has the chance.

She stays awake longest, looking up at the living moth it would never occur to her or Jamie to swat as I would have, at far more of a stretch than it would be for him. It would never occur to them to enjoy destroying, to enjoy power in that way. They are true artists, creators, taking the option to study to become what I could have been. Her glasses are on the bedside table so if she does seem like she's looking at me as she smiles into the darkness, it's only because I happen to be there. She doesn't know me, doesn't think of me, none of this is for me. Yet I feel privileged to watch it begin. I creep to the edge of her dress's shoulder, fly to the curtain, hang, stood to attention, behind him so I am looking directly at her face, over his shoulder.

I still don't remember her question.

It was the first and last time she told me what she really thought, rather than asked me, after I'd tamed her. And I don't remember the question.

Jamie says her name, their new version of it, over and over again. As their eyes lock I see a truly perfect mirror image, every angle of their bodies reflects in the mirrors on mirrors and it's nothing like her drawing, nothing like the two of us lying beside each other on her bed staring up at the flat, lazy ceiling. Their true reflections are in each other's eyes, as their realities blend and merge and mirror. They are becoming a new story. I see it in the rhythm of their bodies and their smiles that are not for any audience in the world, reflected and re-reflecting forever in each other's eyes.

She tried to tell me. She really tried to save me from a hall of mirrors, of realising in the middle of it how alone I was. But now I'm outside the story and the major characters are looking at each other – not away, as I always did – with such visible love.

I fly at his face a couple of times but he pushes me away until I land on the open sketchbook beside her on the bedside table. With the last of my strength, I crawl towards the spine of the pages. Would I feel it more if the pages shut from above, or for death to come from both sides? The question is academic: there was a drop of water from the glass beside the book and by the time I know this, I can feel it spreading, sealing my wing to the page like pixels on a screen shut off one small light at a time.

There's the sound of a spark and a change in the patterns on the ceiling as she lights the candle on the desk, almost invisible from here on the other side of the bed. The air is full of jasmine. Then the hand is coming and the pages are thundering to a roar that is greater than any sea and the pages are coming from both sides, pushing and pressing and compacting and compressing layer by layer as what little there ever was of me is crunching and flattening into dust.

Ladybird

[2022]

One minute he was fine. He hadn't wanted a viewing of the body, he'd been absolutely clear on that, and he was pretty sure his mother would have been as well. But he had been fine. Everything had been exactly as it needed to be. They'd been solicitous, the undertakers, when it came to handling the speed, conversation, fees, how quick the approach to the room itself, whether or not he wanted to be alone with the thing that was still there where his mother had been. They had let him stand there, looking at the thing that was there where she wasn't, the shrunkenness of the familiar features, as if he was looking at her from far away. And as he stood, paused in the workings-out of the visual puzzle, outstaring those permanently shut eyes, they stood too, he realised after – they must have stood without seeming to be waiting for an answer, without seeming to be waiting at all. And after a while, when he remembered they were there, he said thank you, he would go now. And he'd been neither less nor more sad, no less nor more anything, than he already was. Nothing was different. Nothing at all. Perhaps, if anything, what he had seen was evidence that she was dead and wasn't here anymore, but he hadn't needed evidence. He'd understood already. And then he'd driven home, put down his keys on the umbrella stand, spoken to Adam in the kitchen, their father half-reading yesterday's paper and coughing every time he turned a page, then while the kettle boiled he'd walked up past the bedrooms to the balcony outside his father's office, and up the fire escape stairs to the upper balcony. And if he hadn't stopped to lift the ancient crisp packet he'd swear hadn't been on sale since he left school, he wouldn't have seen the ladybird. And a moment later he wouldn't have been on the stone ground of the ash and leaf strewn balcony, a twenty-nine-year-old mess of tears and snot, palms clasped and flattened over his face so no one would hear him screaming for his mother.

What had been the ladybird was attached to the corner of the windowsill, held in mid-air by a tiny roped-off theatre-curtain of grey cobweb. There were many webs on that balcony. No kind of surprise, given how long ago the space had fallen out of regular use, if it had ever been regularly used at all. The colour, Vincent noticed, was the first thing to go, before the body itself. Not at the funeral parlour, obviously, but when nature was left in charge. The structure remained, but the absence of anything inside was what came across. Vincent sat on one of the ancient, unloved chairs, the one attempt at denial of the dead space it had been for so many years. The ladybird, like the balcony, was long on its way to being something else. Not precisely nothing, but all the same, just being here he understood where ghost stories came from. And somehow he knew – perhaps it was a self-fulfilling prophecy but still he knew – that he would always picture ladybirds when asked about his mother's death.

He couldn't call to mind the face on the table anymore. Which, if he was honest, was an enormous relief. The reverse had been his main concern: that what he saw in that innocuously pink, softly-lit room would replace everything he'd ever seen before, all of their lives together. All his life. All of it. He'd feared that thing would replace her in the only place she was now – the pictures in his head. That was really all that was left to fear. But maybe his memory had rejected the picture because of all that false colour. Vincent had software that could have done a better job than the undertakers. His mother would never have called herself a goth, obviously; the idea of a person expressing themselves through their physical body instead of their art, external to themselves, was always distasteful to her. But the black and white that comprised so much of her wardrobe and the number of times he'd heard her say she wasn't a goth seemed qualification. That was the one way of telling who was on the goth spectrum and who wasn't; people who said they weren't, but their friend was a proper one, had always been the real thing.

His new girlfriend's sister wore bright red velvet crucifixes, dyed her hair peroxide blonde and liked to tell people she was a goth. Vincent didn't find that annoying because there was no permanence to his relationship with Amber. There was only so long any of this would matter.

But it hadn't ended yet, and the possibility hadn't occurred to him how often he'd have to hear her say that. This all felt like a new series, continuing due to public demand, but whose characters would never quite be as real as the originals. It didn't feel real yet, anyway. Maybe it would. But, for now, none of this did.

At least the funeral meant he'd be seeing Veronica.

How many ways was he betraying his mother, thinking that? How short a route it was from anything, even from the false colour of empty skin, to Veronica. His mother had never liked Veronica, but then she'd never liked anyone with power or intelligence, anyone who did the things that, if Vincent was honest, he knew she'd wanted more than he did…

He didn't want to finish that thought.

People with power. Intelligence. They were as bad as people who didn't know they had it, with whom his mother had no patience at all. She liked art better than life. It stayed in its frame. It didn't argue with you about your interpretation. If he was honest, he sympathised. People were too malleable, too complicated, too much possibility in too many combinations. He still wasn't quite sure how he'd ended up with Amber, and through her the *I'm-a-goth* woman auditioning to be his sister-in-law. If only Kerry-Alice was there instead or, failing that, as well. That would have been good.

The proportions of the ladybird were all absolutely correct. The ladybird was utterly recognisable as what it was – what it had been – but it was also just as clearly empty of whatever it essentially was. It reminded him of his mother whenever she passed a hapless canvas in a shop or gallery or on a son's easel muttering "photographic realism", like she was swearing under her breath. Never with the students. He'd had to pass through the studio their downstairs living room had become to get to the kitchen, and he'd never once heard her muttering when she was her official self. The mutter was just for them. It was accompanied by that noise that somehow involved yet avoided her nose, to express not even disapproval or distain, but anything that tried too hard to be something else. Was death why photographic realism was such an insult? He'd never know now. He could google an answer, but he couldn't ask his mother, and his mother was his true dictionary, his translation, his encyclopaedia.

But now that sound was gone. His mother's disapproval was gone. He could still hear it in his mind, but no one else could hear it.

It was dusk. He only noticed when he realised he was shivering. Dusk had crept up on him, the balcony, the ladybird, over the trees that stretched their shadows the length of the garden all those floors below. And only he felt it.

There had been plants out here for a while, in the days when his father's colleagues smoked his father's cigars, drank his father's brandy and stubbed out the smoke in the flowerpots. Vincent still couldn't look at a mint plant without picturing cigar stubs. You weren't meant to do that with cigars anyway. When they turned up at work he took great pleasure in extinguishing them properly, much more than he did in the smoking.

The cigars, and everything that went with them, were why his mother withdrew from the territory, he remembers now. The friends who only came for the atmosphere, to feel part of the art world because the man of the moment listened to their opinions. Had she actually said that, or had he felt it at the time? Whose anger was this, that the fame had been his father's yet the ground they walked was always his mother's? Did she think they were using his father, living through him too much, or her not enough?

Whenever Vincent tried to remember the colleagues' faces, he saw them only like a spread deck of cards, barely separate, repeated and mixed versions of the same established aesthetic pattern, the same sneer, the same way of talking down to women and children that embarrassed, angered and shamed him all at once. In theory it was the smoking and talking outlet, but as fewer and fewer meetings were needed (or wanted) over the years, as his father made it more and more obvious to everyone, including himself, that the kind of happiness you got from work you loved in a space you loved with family you were perfectly comfortable in companiable silence with, the more of an extravagant interruption the outside world became. The friends that did visit came for dinner and drinks downstairs, the ones his parents wanted to talk to instead of smoke with, who gradually stopped separating the genders and Vincent watched his father realise he'd been providing so much for. Friends that weren't really friends, obliging him to be the artist they needed him to be, their romanticised vision of where their own lives could have gone.

But here it still was, the place she never went so the one place that hadn't changed in his eyes for her not being there, the best place he could think of to go and think about the unthinkable: that she was gone. Still kneeling on the ground, fingers and chin on the stone of the balcony wall, he found himself counting the now-obvious, now clearly important things he had never thought to ask her. Which order had she studied at which college, which university? Hadn't she nearly married someone other than their father? What other lives had she given up to be his mother? Was he supposed to be a girl, or was that just Adam? Why had Kerry-Alice disappeared, the same day the cat died? Was it something he could have done anything about, if he were better at listening? If he'd married someone she liked better than Veronica? Would she have never found Kerry-Alice and never lost her? Could he have done something to make everything as easy as he wanted it to be, as it so easily could?

The silence after Kerry-Alice was nothing to this one, though at the time it was the loudest silence he'd ever heard. His mother filled each room she walked into with a buzz of defence against whatever it was she hadn't told them had happened. Now she was gone (he'd keep trying "gone" in his mind, until it clicked. Dead was easy. But not here? Not ever coming back? Not there to glare through his wedding if Veronica – if anyone – ever decided he'd have a real one?), the silence the rest of them shared was less pressurised. Their empty conversations – full of information, whether a window needed putty or a bill was too high –were always pushed by his mother as if they were supposed to be talking about something else the whole time, as if they couldn't simply exist as they were. As if there was never quite enough time and if they didn't hurry they'd never reach wherever they were supposed to be going.

And then she'd go and wind all the clocks. Every Sunday, his mother would wind the clocks.

Who would wind the clocks now?

Would he have to do it? How did you wind a clock? Were they all the same? Or did each one have its own mechanism, its own ritual he would have to learn? And why all those clocks? He'd never thought to question the clocks. Why was the hallway packed with them? They predated him; were as natural as Grandma's pear tree outside the kitchen window, the rhubarb climbing the back wall, the strawberry plants forever dying and being enticed back with new ones, the blackberry bush that seemed to take pleasure in lashing out at people, the thyme bushes they never cooked with or maintained but nothing from snow to drought had ever managed to kill. The pair of gardening gloves his mother had bought to replace his father's moth-ravaged ones that were more hole than glove but that his father refused to wear because he was "keeping them for best", infuriating her. But Vincent telling her it didn't matter infuriated her more.

It was so much easier his way, for all that didn't matter to float past, yet his mother had never seen it like that and what it did to her made him see it all the clearer. Maybe that, and not Veronica and not silence about whatever had happened with Kerry-Alice, was the real betrayal. Was that what he'd done wrong?

It was getting colder. He should get up, go in. But the ground was so wonderfully solid, so reassuringly cold. The trees were so beautifully calm. If he rolled over, perhaps he'd see the stars. They were probably there, by now. He'd probably roll over, in a minute.

When his father had come out of the bedroom where they found her, when she hadn't got up at the usual time, two days after Boxing Day, and asked if he wanted to go in, he'd said no. It didn't change anything, he'd thought, seeing or not seeing her, in there. Adam had seen, stood at the doorway, hadn't gone in, hadn't touched. She never used to like being caught sleeping. Lying down, closing her eyes, that was for offstage. She didn't want them to see that. It had never been said, but Adam must have known it too. He'd watched Adam in the doorway, and what he saw Adam seeing haunted him so much more than looking would. That was why, when the undertakers asked if they wanted a viewing, he'd wanted to go. Just to know and stop imagining. And because the males of the family didn't overthink each other's decisions, not unless she told them to, it had been accepted without a lot of embarrassing discussion. He'd been almost glad she wasn't there. They would have had to discuss it then. She was the one who needed words, even if she said she preferred painting.

This was the one place there wasn't a memory of her everywhere he looked. He had once locked Adam out here by mistake when they were playing Hide and Seek, but even then, even when he worked out where the crying and shouting were coming from and his father had searched the house for the key to the door and he'd sat on the other side of the glass with his palm against Adam's palm until his little brother was freed, he'd never stepped out there. Why else he'd be attracted to the balcony he didn't know – alright, he did. It was the only part of the house he had no memory of his mother being in. She could never just sit down and relax, and that's all there ever was to do up here. No plants, just a bare table, two unwashed chairs and an ancient mosaic ashtray. The balcony on this level was over the edge of the world. Maybe he felt closest to her as well as furthest from her here.

He tried standing up. Rolling, at least. Sliding, from shoulder and leg. He thought about not turning around, not taking his leave of the ladybird before he went back down.

He turned to the window, to the cobwebs.

The ladybird was still there, faded by dusk and its own unpleasant processes to black and not so much white as greyish yellow. It was more of a ladybird than his mother had been his mother on that table. He didn't need to be able to see it properly to know what was there. Or maybe he just thought that because he wasn't so close to the ladybird. That was why the corpse was fine. It wasn't his mother, he didn't think of it as his mother. He thought of it as the corpse. He'd gone to see a viewing of the corpse, of the thing left where his mother had been. He wasn't in denial. He was in absolute acceptance. She wasn't there. That wasn't her. It was not life, it wasn't even really having a go at photographic realism. It wasn't frightening, it had been her face but the eyes were closed, sleeping, severe, what she'd never wanted them to see. It made him remember an article from before lockdown about something they were calling "resting bitch face". And he'd wanted to laugh when he thought that, but he looked instead at the face she'd occasionally muttered was too skeletal, the way her forehead had too many lines, how very unadventurously straight her white-blonde hair had always been whether she curled it or not. It knew who it was, she'd said.

"What was it like," Adam had said to him in place of hello, as he'd dropped his keys on the coat-stand shelf and headed, as they all did on walking through the front door, in a straight line down the hall to the kettle.

"It wasn't like anything," he'd said. "It wasn't her. She'd gone."

And Adam had accepted that, and asked how much water there was in the kettle, and he said there was enough, and they'd stood and watched the kettle for a bit and remembered just in time that he would only need three mugs and there was no need to shout downstairs to the painting room, only upstairs to their father's office. And when he'd remembered what Adam had said he briefly put his head round the study door, accepted Kerry-Alice's condolences, came within a millimetre of asking her... something... but it was a question he couldn't form. Anyway, it probably didn't matter.

Vincent walked down the hall, and sat on the stairs on the landing. If anyone had noticed how long he'd been gone, or how much cold he'd brought in with him, they didn't comment. From where he sat on the stairs, those first few Veronica used to take so much trouble over, he noticed through the living room door the book he'd been reading that morning open on the arm of the sofa, that he'd left it like that when there hadn't been a bookmark from a corner of newspaper, and yet it hadn't been closed and tidied somewhere it would take him weeks or months to find and retrieve, and then he really knew that she was dead.

His father's sound-effects of standing up from the armchair drifted out from the concealed half of the living room. He saw him, and came down to join him, on the stair. Neither of them commented on quite how much this was something one simply did not do. As they watched the empty hallway full of clocks, Vincent realised for the first time in his life he could hear them ticking.

'One doesn't notice them ticking usually,' his father said, at exactly the same moment.

'No.'

'Defence mechanism, I imagine. You were born with it like this.'

'Yes.'

'I hated them at first.'

'You did?'

'Noisy things.' His father passed the notebook he was holding from one hand to the other. 'Not a single clock in our student flat. Then she brought me back here, to all this. New ones every year.'

'What's that you've got?'

His father gave him a sidelong look, and showed him what he was holding. 'This is an old sketchbook of hers. A bit racy, drawings of another man in it.'

Against his better judgement, though not feeling as much repulsion as he expected, Vincent looked at the drawing of the man, reflected in directions all across the page, above as well as around, as if by a ceiling of mirrors. 'Do you know who he was?'

'Actually yes.' Vincent's father's voice tightened around the words. He shut the sketchbook and placed it back down on the carpet of the stairs. 'Is the kettle on?'

While the kettle boiled again and his father's back was turned, Vincent lifted the sketchbook. A dead moth pressed between two of the pages fell to the stair by his feet, reminding him he really should throw away that disgusting moth-paper on the shelf in the office. He hoped Kerry-Alice hadn't noticed it. He'd never seen a single alive moth in his mother's office in all their time in the house yet there always seemed to be a full moth-paper on the shelf. He wondered how often she changed it, and then wondered why on earth he was wondering, as if it mattered.

She'd chosen this. The ladybird hadn't gone looking for the web, but his mother had. And she'd told them, rubbed it in their faces above all how sane she'd been when she made the choice. As if choosing to die was better than spending more time with them, as much time as the creeping thing inside her would have allowed. As if death was something to be efficient and timely about. As if death cared.

Thank God it was pills. His mother knew about art. She knew the image of her swinging was worse than the image of falling asleep. And she'd known, presumably, it would be his father who found her. She'd just stopped taking one thing she was supposed to take and then taken a lot of it when she wasn't supposed to. It had been her choice. It had been that easy, that straightforward.

Meanwhile, Vincent's little brother, the one he was supposed to protect, had phoned the sister they'd always wanted, the daughter his mother had always expected to eventually produce, and had exiled when she couldn't have her to herself. He didn't know what had happened, but he'd known it would, and that it didn't need to. The diagnosis came late because Effie ignored evidence that wasn't within her control. She hadn't wanted to die. She just didn't like losing control. Kerry-Alice or cancer, it didn't matter.

He never knew what to say to Kerry-Alice. He always felt on the verge of telling her about Veronica's experience with his mother, warning her what happened when you offered information about who you were like a gift, that all you got back was competition. And then Kerry-Alice was gone, as totally absent from their lives as she had been suddenly present when she appeared in them, and his mother switched from praising her at every opportunity to never speaking of her at all.

That was what had sent him upstairs today. The things he would say to Kerry-Alice if he said anything to her at all were just too big to fit the kind of conversations that sat in the air of this house, that the house allowed. He'd never managed the balancing act. He'd never been rude, but he'd never been interesting either. And that was fine when it was just him and Adam, they ignored each other and took each other for absolute granted and that was a perfectly reasonable and acceptable form of love. But Kerry-Alice had been auditioned as a sister. And Vincent had held back the information about his mother that would have secured her the job. And maybe she's have been able to…

No. That was too long a story. And anyway, it was all too late to matter now.

'Adam and Kerry-Alice have gone off for a drink, I believe,' his father said, taking the open pages from him and closing the sketchbook.

'Right.' The clocks ticked in the silence. 'She looks well.'

'She does.'

He stared at the remains of the moth on the stair carpet. He wondered how long it had been between the pages of the sketchbook, what chemicals meant the pages did a greater job of photographic realism than the undertakers. They sat and listened to the quiet ticking, the one that for so long Vincent couldn't hear it at all.

'I hate them, Dad,' he said. 'Not them. Not Kerry-Alice and Adam. The clocks.'

His father looked into the distance, where the stained glass in the front door cast scarlet and emerald tracks over the stairs, not quite far up enough to reach their feet. 'The grandfather clock can stay. I'm partial to a grandfather clock.'

'We could talk to the auction house, for the rest.'

His father ruffled his three-day moustache, slid it down his beard. 'What's that charity shop at the bottom of the road called?'

'Should we talk to Adam first?'

'Only to ask him which one he wants.'

'He'll pick the cuckoo clock.'

'Yes. Yes he will.' They both smiled, without looking at each other. 'But ask him anyway.'

His father made the sound effect that showed he was thinking of standing up, and then did. 'I'll call. You get started.'

Vincent stood, moved towards the landline on the table to the left of the door, turned back to the square of landing. Over his shoulder, he said, 'Thanks Dad.' He didn't know quite what for, but it didn't matter.

'Not at all.' The slippers continued over the carpet.

The Rabbit-Hole

[2016]

She was perched on the very edge of that perfectly comfortable chair they always had just beyond the doorway, where the art gallery stopped and the clubrooms began. If the chair disappeared from under her, I'd often recall thinking in those seconds before I quite remembered which of my students she was, the girl would simply leap up and be perfectly safe. She might not even register anything was different, so little belief did she have in any solidity beneath her. I liked her – or my idea of her – straight away.

'Mrs James!' The duty manager's overplayed, over-bright smile brought me back to her over-protesting "welcome" desk. It had been an *information* desk in the perfectly good years before the sign, and before her. 'Wednesday already!'

'Already indeed.' I bent my knees to place my tote bags on the fake-marble floor, spine unbending, eye contact constant without being actively rude. She would have the length of time it took me to sign my name in the book, no longer, and I meant for her to know it.

'I regret there has been a hold-up with the charcoal delivery. We can only provide the two rather than the three kinds per easel today...'

'Right.' Beyond the club door, the girl looked away, but only to the floor and back again. It was her hair I remembered. Thicker, wavier than she let it be, brushed into a messy, anonymous ponytail. As if there were more important things to think about than her. Even to her.

'However, the easels are all set up and ready to go.'

'How lovely.' One had to suffer this weekly recitation of irrelevant victories and invisible problems that, as her customer (patron, even, through Gerald) she should prefer me to know nothing about. The attention the woman drew to her stage-managing, it was as if she'd missed the whole point of stage-management: invisibility. Good administration is the structure beneath the façade. If this woman's business were placed on my easel, it would be a fury of over-pressed lines. How could she run a gallery and not understand that the façade of effortlessness is what any viewer applauds?

'And how is Mr James?'

There it was. The reminder none of this ceremony was for me. All of it was Gerald. 'Quite well, thank you.'

Puce lipstick parted to reveal expensively natural-looking teeth. I remember when only Americans had teeth like that. My eyes brushed past the edges of the woman's face – Suzette? Lynette? Some other kind of Ette? – and returned to the next doorway. The girl on the edge of the chair met my eyes, but dropped hers before the slight smile arrived there.

'And the biscuits, tea and coffee will be right on time…'

'Thank you.' They wouldn't, and we both knew it. I picked up the bags I put down to sign in, turned towards the corridors that give the Rabbit-Hole Gallery a right to its name. My burrow. It had been mine before she arrived and would be mine after.

None of which stopped her continuing the conversation I'd so demonstrably left. 'If I could also request that full newspaper coverage be maintained over the Danish side-tables…'

'Yes, yes of course.' I never argued with this but kept my usual mental arguments to myself, such as why they let art groups use the room if they were so reluctant for the clientele to be inconvenienced by the process, the creation of art – but right now it was easy to move past the usual rehearsed silences. I already knew something far more interesting was waiting on the other side of this conversation.

'Three o'clock as usual? The teas and coffees?' Her voice echoed and bounced on the mirrors in the slight hallway between public and private worlds.

'As usual,' I called back. On both sides and above me, my reflections marched in union, away.

The girl stood as I approached, my perfectly sensible boots surprisingly loud, decisive as stilettos on the echoing tiles. A whispered sensation fluttered through me of memory in reverse, as if I could almost see what I sensed she did: the artist and teacher walking into this glorified shop that to her feels like the gallery it thinks it is. Or perhaps this emotional equivalent of incidental music came to me later. There was no building crescendo, no drum roll then. No sense at all that one era was ending and another, quite another, the best and the worst of everything, was about to begin.

'Do you have a minute, Effie?' she asked.

'Of course, Kerry-Alice.' The name came back to me from last week's register, perfect in its unlikeliness. 'Let's see if there's anyone through here.' I marched ahead of her to the end of the club room, a small area out of the way. The gentlemen's club the building had once been allowed for copious withdrawing corners for conversations one would have expected them to think female: minimum visibility, maximum cover of sound of other people's conversations, the buzz of life a strong enough wall between the conspirators and everyone else.

There was a kind of reverse nostalgia for the conversation I thought I was going to have. I had always been above these girlish confessions, their apparent sadness and significance no more than glorified gossip. A bust-up with a lover, no doubt. Something that would call for the one piece of advice I remember from my own mother along the lines of time healing all possible wounds and there being plenty more fish at the fairground. 'So, how can I help?'

She looked up at me, from the traces of lilac nail polish chipped from her chewed fingernails, and down at them again as she said, 'My boyfriend's father dropped dead in front of us last night.'

'Oh.' It was an inappropriate response, but it was out before I had an appropriate one. 'What happened?' I managed, mentally picking up the pages of script my mind had scattered. The "plenty more".

'He arrived about seven, I asked if he'd stay for dinner the way I always do. And he said no, the way he always does.' I hadn't thought the girl wore make-up, but there must at least have been mascara as it became visible in the discolouration of her tears. I never had that technique, my efforts with make-up never appeared natural on my own face. 'Did. I always asked, just to make sure, because it's about measuring time. If you know when he's leaving then you know the maximum time the argument can last. They always argue, that's what's so sad. Danny's his only son. His only family as far as I know.'

'Right.'

'Danny always says it was like this before me. That it's not directed at me. But it is. It's about Danny's decisions. He disapproves of every decision Danny's ever made.'

'And that's what you are is it? A decision?' I can hear the one thing my education really gave me – eloquent disapproval – in my voice. Sons never wanted your advice. Perhaps girls would have been the same – and girl I saw her as; she looked very little older than the boys.

'I can't even remember what he said he'd come over to talk about. It always ends the same, Danny getting more and more silent, his father shouting more and more. You wouldn't think there was more silent you can go, but there is.'

I nodded. This was a much more interesting story than anything I expected. At home they had never come to me with anything that mattered as much as a corpse.

'He'd come round on a pretext, a phone bill he thought was wrong, an object he thought Danny should want back. He's lonely. I get it. Since Danny moved in, that's the furthest they've lived apart. It's only a few stops on the mainline. But this time he was shouting about something to do with the house…'

She was half-way through the small packet of tissues she'd taken from her bag and I instinctively reached into mine and gave her another.

She nodded thanks. 'It's why Danny never argues. With me, with anyone. He's never seen disagreement without violence. It's not a compliment that he doesn't yell at me too. He never really saw me as a person, because of the age gap. I'm not worth arguing with. I'm just more evidence of how wrong Danny is. I mean for God's sake, nine years? If we'd met in a bar that would be nothing.'

I didn't ask where they did meet: she'd presented the information as her statement for the defence which eloquently screamed of a crime. If I interrupted with advice it would have been that this wouldn't end well. But the disappearance of one man from my life, probably before she was born, certainly before she was sentient, did not foretell the disappearance of another. That kind of advice reeked of the wish for control of one's own life in retrospect, and the stupidity to believe the feeling could be reached through someone else's. Besides, there had been no corpse yet, and I knew enough about composition not to be distracted by background detail.

'He was just getting angrier and angrier. About nothing. And the angrier he got, the quieter Danny got, and I used to try and jump in and help but that isn't what he wants, it never is. He doesn't want things to get better.' Her face clouded. 'Didn't. At the time, I thought that's why his colour was changing. But then I realised it couldn't be that. That that wasn't the colour people go when they're angry. And I hadn't heard him shouting like that before and I didn't realise at the time, but I think I already knew I wasn't being polite by not stopping him, he was getting all the words out as if there wouldn't be room for them, wouldn't be time, they had to come out now. And I just decided, then, I just thought it was time he dealt with it himself. And I looked away because something flew past the window. I only looked away for a minute. But in the time I looked away the words just stopped.'

'Go on.'

'He was still standing. But there was nothing inside him. I knew. I think I already knew, before he fell, before he hit the carpet. It wasn't a process. It was a moment. And I hadn't been looking when he died. Died shouting at his son.' She was crying more now. 'I'm not sorry I'm not sad. I'm sad I'm not sorry.'

'That's still grief,' I told her. 'That's definitely grief.' I took out another tissue

packet.

'You have a lot of tissues,' she said.

'I'm an art teacher,' I replied. 'Go on.'

And she told me what it looked like for a man to die just as you realise how much you hate him. She described the way that, even though he was in his late sixties, he used the Brylcreem he would have been using at twenty; that his face always looked permanently tanned so she didn't understand why he'd ask her what it was like to be "half-caste", as if anyone ever says that anymore, yet he was more orange than she was any colour at all. She told me how he wore shirts that were too small for him, as if he was trying to dress as the person he used to be, denying whoever he'd had the chance to grow into. A chance her parents never got. And when she mentioned her parents she stopped and asked if she'd been shouting, even though all she did as she got angrier was whisper. How as he fell on his back, he'd kept the same head gesture, the one he'd always had, chin tilted up, away from the person he was shouting at. Which was always his son.

I placed my remaining few tissue packs unobtrusively on the small round table between our armchairs.

'His face hadn't changed. He was focused on the ceiling instead of on his son and the expression was the same and it was always going to be and I thought, typical. That's absolutely typical of him. I wasn't scared, I don't think. We just stood there for a moment and then Danny's done first aid so he was checking airways and everything and saying 'John? John can you hear me?' and I asked him why after and he shrugged and said if you knew the victim's name you should always use it. I didn't say anything, I didn't say why aren't you calling him Dad? And I'm calling the ambulance and giving our address and offering to help with CPR but Danny's twice my size and he's trained and I suppose because he used to be my teacher there's a part of me that sees an adult and doesn't argue if...' She looks at me, quickly, and looks back at her fingers. 'Anyway, I just went to the door to make sure the ambulance knew which house it was. And they dealt with everything from there. And oh God, Effie, I'm so ready to paint.' And she starts laughing and crying more at the same time. 'I'm so glad it's Wednesday. I've only been here three weeks but... I should have done this such a long time ago.'

I didn't laugh, didn't smile, didn't let her see how amusing it always is when people half your age tell you how late they are to the party.

'It's more real than everything else. Even other people's death. Is that terrible?'

'I doubt it's terrible.' It was easy to be the person she needed, to give her the excuse note she needed to present herself with. In her eyes, I felt more like a person in my own right than I ever had, the artist who taught the class in the back of the club, not the wife of the Royal Academy member who kept the gallery alive.

She wiped her eyes. 'He's... it's... he was the same shape but something is completely different. Like colour and movement are the same thing. You don't realise when you're looking at something alive but you realise when you see something dead. Empty. Like all that was left was the outline of shadows you started with. Sorry,' she said, and I could hear the offered end. 'God, what must this sound like. I wasn't there to draw him.'

Sometimes, very occasionally, I've let myself realise how much I lacked a daughter. Not in front of the boys, not in front of Gerald. But this was one of those times. 'It doesn't sound like anything but what it is, Kerry-Alice,' I said.

She smiled.

'What is it?'

'So many people get my name wrong. I like that you remembered.' For no reason at all I remembered my previous life as a writer, and with it the kind of instructor who told you past tense was "better" than present. Trying to normalise your writing, rather than make it more itself. I had no wish to name her something more normal. But perhaps in truth that was because I'd already decided what I wanted her to be.

'I do get that, you know, it isn't about me.' She had misinterpreted my silence as disapproval. 'I didn't like him, he was horrible to Danny, but he was still… a person.'

I shook my head. 'Being a person is absolutely no excuse.'

'Sorry?'

'Painting is a perfectly acceptable response to anything,' I continued. 'It's the contribution you have to give the world. It won't bring him back but neither will not painting.'

She shook her head now, as if to dislodge what she saw there. 'It's so clear in my mind.'

'Then bring it out.' I ferreted in my handbag again, but not for tissues this time. 'We still have fifteen minutes. Use every one of them.' I handed her the tiny sketchpad that stays in my bag at all times. Familiar voices passed us, through the bar to the club's staircase. I did not remember the last time I'd not been first to my room, any room, as teacher or as student. 'Honestly, Kerry-Alice, the one thing worse than waiting for inspiration to do all the work for you is not catching the sketches when it does.'

She nodded, and the fascinated obedience I saw in her eyes was the best present I'd ever received, that I was licencing her to be herself, that she had wanted this so much without knowing it was possible. I too had told this comparative stranger, this comparative child, my truest thought, on two Wednesdays' acquaintance. But I thought of none of that while I watched as she drew. There was no future in those fifteen minutes, just a contagious, continuous flow of now that transcended, stretched the time.

She had talent, I'd recognised that as I watched her with no particularly greater interest than in any new member of the Wednesday afternoon set. What characterised those that could do this regularly in the middle of the day was that they had the time and money to procrastinate for years on whether they had the willpower, the self-esteem, to truly invest in their own voice. She was something else. She was not one for whom an art class on a weekday afternoon was a birth-right instead of something that had to be thought about, saved up for, committed to through a step of taking command of your own life. She achieved it, chose it. She had not found me because she was bored, but because she was in the gallery and, it would turn out, had moved her work schedule around to accommodate investing in this. And I watched as the world around her – the bar, the sounds of the gallery, me – disappeared around her and she poured herself into turning every white space she could reach into the picture in her mind, the truth of what was there when everything else was scraped away.

I did not know the man emerging in the pictures, but I believed in him. I could see the indication of the hairline, the expression that had been left on his face when whatever was truly him fell out of it. I also noticed with how much familiarity and simultaneous lack of enjoyment she'd sketched the younger man holding the telephone. She was too concerned with detail, which reflected in her storytelling. I'd heard everyone else's motivation except her own. The girl in the background of her sketch – herself – seemed to interest her the least. The people in the foreground were so much more real for her than she was. She didn't seem to need a face at all.

But watching the process of someone exiting themselves, not through death or procreation but through pouring themselves into something outside themselves, making the internal reality eloquent, I understood what it was I was doing, or had been trying to do, for all of my life. I grieved as I watched her, for my younger self, as I never had. I had once known how to pour myself into the work outside my body. It was nothing to do with how I felt about the boys. I was meant to be a painter, that was what I was for. Being a mother, even a distant, unattached one, took so much time. I painted at night now, when had that begun? Watching her sketch with all of herself in my club, where I never came except for the work of others, the sun blaring through what were essentially my windows, contrasted with the dark and dirty secret painting had become in my own life. A part of me found Kerry-Alice more familiar, already, than my own sons. Or found myself more familiar in her orbit.

In that moment, I decided what happened to me must not be what happens to this girl, forgetting herself in the time and space my silence gave her. I was proud, jealous, hypnotised by the ritual of silence, space and time I created, the circle of attention my presence and her belief formed around us. She was far more eloquent than I ever was in her details, even if they were overwhelming, even if she had no time for her own face. If she could maintain this forgetfulness, she would be a proper artist, the kind Gerald was. The kind of focus that was not on others and their thoughts but on the one call that, once you truly listened, deafened you to everything else. I'd never heard such a call, but now I heard the call of a protégée.

'What I can't get over,' Kerry-Alice said out of nowhere, breaking the silence I'd forgotten wasn't eternal, 'is the way one moment he had been as sarcastic as I'd ever known a human being able to be and the next... nothing. The corners of my mouth started turning up, as if the universe had told me a massive joke, as if the joke was in poor taste but in my very muscles I knew it was funny. People aren't meant to feel like that.'

'Are you sure people are *meant* to feel like anything?'

She looked up for a second, but the work pulled her back. Good girl. 'I felt like I was betraying Danny, by being happy for him. It feels like a lifetime ago, when I was really angry with him, it was probably only a year ago, maybe two, I don't know... He was going clubbing with... someone, and I wasn't invited. When I was out on my own and I realised how many possibilities I shut down by being with him, I just needed to find out who I was without him. So I went out and I did meet someone I could have... I was tempted. Hugely. I didn't know which of them I would be using if I did. That's what put me off doing anything I couldn't take back.'

I wondered in passing if the person she was tempted by was a woman, and surprised myself with the itch of curiosity that was almost jealousy. Not of Kerry-Alice, but of the options ahead of her. I don't know what I was hungry for, or how she promised the sating of it.

Perhaps she was the choices I didn't make, that perhaps had been mine only for the asking, the sketches beneath the picture I'd painted over them.

'Do you know about Gerald?' I asked.

She nodded in what at the time seemed the way people did when they knew they were supposed to have heard of someone. I would convince myself later Gerald had all been part of her plan, but if I was right about that there was no way the plan had started to develop here. She did not see Gerald when she looked at me. She saw me.

'Gerald and I, really I, have decided to look for an assistant. We might be moving the classes out of the gallery, there's a perfectly good studio at home, looking out on the garden. Perhaps someone to set all this up on all that social media nonsense.' It was all so obvious a plan. It was irrelevant that it only existed inside my head. It was the truth that should be.

I watched her eyes brightening, and the contrast with the drain of colour she'd described could not be clearer, like we both felt her moving out of the world she'd found herself trapped in and into the one where she was meant to be. She looked like someone whose life had begun as she nodded, and stared into her lap, where her watch had been pushed to allow her more space to draw. 'Oh God, it's almost time. I'm so sorry.'

It was never more than five minutes since I looked at my watch. Not ever. To realise I hadn't checked it was to realise time went on without me. And that was when I should have known.

I thought, as my shoes echoed ahead of her, sliding her portfolio along the marbled floor, that that folder was probably heavier than she was, yet she climbed those rich, unassuming carpeted stairs with so much respect for them, for me, for it, and so little expectation of any for herself.

～

'To make anything feel real, we start from the shadows,' is what I remember telling them – or rather her, with them around us. 'What's counter-intuitive about that? It's light – in life, rather than art – we consider real. So what I'm asking you to do is the opposite of what a brain tells itself about the world. Light is where we take information from. But shadows tells you so much more, if you have the courage or patience.'

I found myself glad the model was not Veronica that week, but a friend of hers from the same agency where Vincent found Veronica for me, and then for himself. I selected a lying down position, knowing that Kerry-Alice could work with the image already residing in her head. She looked at me once as if to confirm what I'd done and I gave the smallest of smiles, the smallest of nods: *go for it.* In the brightest I'd ever seen this room to be, I'd given her strength and permission to find her way into the darkness. There were no tears up here, no fear of what was waiting in the corners. There didn't need to be. She was looking directly into them. I suppose proximity to death would make any afternoon feel as eternal as this one did, that there was infinite time ahead and infinite potential to do and be all one wished.

'Our shadows define our shapes, tell the truth about the object, place, person. Our imaginations are drawn by the things we don't see, hence the brain interprets from dark to light. If you're lacking inspiration, what you're actually lacking is curiosity. The courage to look at the things your mind has waiting. To follow in faith, instead of hold back in judgement. Your unique responses to the world, your questions about it. There are no bad ideas, no inappropriate subjects.' I look at Kerry-Alice only a little more than I do at the others. I can only really see her eyes, as her easel is at the back and I am not, in truth, as tall as I walk.

'There is no inspiration, only listening and engagement. Light is just so much misdirection. Don't try to look away from the dark. Start with the dark. There's no such thing as black. Get dark adapted and start painting.'

'But if the light is what draws our attention,' the loudest of the Slone clones asked, the ones who had not saved up to take a mid-week afternoon off work, the ones for whom this was a perfectly normal day and who, with all the money in the world, still did no work in between because they didn't have "enough time", 'why don't we start with that?'

'Try it,' I said coolly.

A few near-identical Sloany heads look at First Slone. I don't have to watch their easels to know they're following my advice and not hers.

'The path to being unique,' I continue, deliberately looking nowhere near her, 'is knowing what the rules are so you can break them with intention at positive change, rather than pointless rebellion. From dark to light, whatever rule you decide to break,' I still don't look at First Sloane, but smile over the easel at Kerry-Alice at the back. 'Look around your own houses – homes – to practice, if you have a habit of overdrawing. Get too much down on a sketch and the only thing it does is keep you too strongly tied to preconceptions when you reach the canvas. Try not to let your canvas feel like a disappointment to the sketch that conceived it. No one likes an overprotective parent.' There were titters around the room, from those who understood and from those who wanted to pretend they did. 'Sitting around waiting for inspiration is like…'

'Waiting around for perspiration?' said Kerry-Alice. We smiled at each other across the easels.

$\sim$

'That was brilliant,' she said as we walk down the stairs, before I had a chance to say the same. Her portfolio moved like it was a thousand times lighter. I'd swear she was an inch taller than three hours ago when the class began.

'Thank you.' Kerry-Alice had stayed and offered to help the staff put the easels away, which for the first time in my time here inspired me to do the same thing. I don't think I'd ever laughed in there before. The frustrations remained, but having someone to share them with was already almost as much fun as if there had been no frustrations at all.

We were in the hallway for longer than I'd ever spent in my own club by choice. I never came here with Gerald, brought the boys or Veronica, or any of their other girlfriends, yet in one afternoon with Kerry-Alice I heard myself saying I would arrange an end-of-term drink for the group. She offered to help.

'Kerry-Alice,' I said. 'I mentioned we've been looking at the possibility of hiring an assistant for a while.' We hadn't been, but if I told Gerald I'd decided we should he'd agree quickly enough, and then forget the timing of the conversation, that it was as good as being true. 'How would you feel about that?'

'I would love that.' She still looked like she felt like all her dreams had come true, and I let myself enjoy that. 'But are you sure? Do you want to think about it? Get references? A contract?'

'Don't be silly.' It was a sensible question. I barely knew her. But she respected me, she wanted to learn, to help, and I wanted to feel like the person I saw her believing was standing before her. Those were the most comfortable shoes I ever stood in. I wanted to go on walking in them, feel more of how she made me feel, and I was prepared to pay. 'Come round to the house next week. We can have coffee and talk about a regular day.' I hand her my card. 'Send an email and we'll arrange a time.'

She looked more grateful than I have ever felt for anything in my life and, looking back, I was even jealous of that. But this was my new start, not hers. Everything and everyone else – Vincent and Veronica, Gerald and our non-retirement, the books I knew I'd never write and still half-believed I'd never wanted to – were extraneous detail. I had created in someone the sense of possibility to be who they could.

'Bye, Etienne!' Kerry-Alice waved to the duty manager, in a way it has never occurred to me to bother with in twenty-five years. I had, I realised thorough our contrasting colours, the manners of a teenager coming home from school and dumping their bag in the middle of the floor. The reason I gave myself – for that and what followed – is I've never been good with those who wish too hard to please, to satisfy. Too many bad memories, of myself. But here she is, looking at me and seeing an artist, her teacher, and not just Mrs Gerald James RA. It felt like such a victory to be one of the founders of the Rabbit-Hole, the bright new world we were taking back from the dusty moths, the leerers and bottom-grippers. But now we are the moths, and she is one of the bright young things. 'I must sound so naïve, But for the opportunity to be... I don't know. Useful. Useful is really all I've ever wanted.'

'I'm sure we all feel like that.' Or did. I hoped I concealed just how much wiser she is about herself and others than she realises; it wouldn't be long before she saw what a fake I was in comparison to this view of me I imagined she had. 'Thank you, Kerry-Alice.'

I paused to move out of the doorway for the path around the corner, around the corner of the cobbled side street onto Richmond Green and towards the bus stops for what my sons call a pointlessly long journey that takes me through so very much of my town and almost directly to my door.

'I'll give this everything I've got, Effie.' That's what I remember her saying. The breath of fresh air was exactly what the house needed, the perfect time and reason to be moving the work home.

It took the bus it took less than a minute to arrive, as if the town itself was giving me its blessing. As I climbed the stairs, and shopping centre fell away to river and hill, every corner was the edge of a different picture, a different version of potential stories: the flower shop on the corner, with lavender and honeysuckle plants outside that, even though they changed every week, always looked exactly like they'd grown there forever and knew they belonged; two teenagers each with a labrador on a lead mirroring each other's body language, one with purple lips and cobalt dreadlocks, the other with freckles and red hair, the dogs not making eye contact; a black kitten dozing in a lighting shop window's gold and white display; two women, obviously sisters, in the same colour scheme in identical front doors, arguing; a ginger cat on a graveyard wall, pretending to sleep while watching a red setter leap in the air to catch a bright purple frisbee. It was not possible to feel anything but exalted to exist within this exquisite jigsaw of lives, ever separate and ever connected.

As we turned from the river up towards Nightingale Lane, my religiously silent mobile phone shivered in my blouse pocket. I put down the bags as the bus took the corner, the words veering and wobbling and beautiful: Kerry-Alice's text message, thanking me again. If I were to believe I had to thank anything for making the sun come out on a cold day, it was that too-long sentence and the even longer series of incomprehensible emojis. I had, and there was no point in trying not to admit it, always wanted a daughter. But I was being offered a friend. I had colleagues, I had family, I was acknowledged. But when Kerry-Alice looked at me, I felt liked. As I stepped off that double decker at the corner of the road, I realised in the moment of its happening, as one almost never does, how truly happy I felt.

I would grow to hate Kerry-Alice, and most of my life, within a calendar year.

Roof

[2004]

The two women sit on the same sofa, a few inches and entire respective worlds stretching out between them. I try to swallow and it feels like there are hands inside my throat, pushing back.

'He's worried about the pepper plants,' I say with the false cheeriness I only ever hear my voice fall into in this exact situation. The sound seems to come from further away, crackly, dark, like it's arriving on the wrong frequency. 'Apparently we planted them too close together. It's nothing major. A little light repotting. I'm sure he won't be long.'

Faith smiles at me, a fairly recognisable attempt at her real smile, the one that almost never leaves her face, except for when she and Sarah are here at the same time. But as soon as the smile has been attempted her eyes return, magnetised, to the tray I've placed on the coffee table between the three of us, like some kind of limp ritual to resurrect conversation that isn't working and was never going to.

Even the teapot is an accusation. I see it in the way Faith looks at the tray as if it might slap her, never at the same time that Sarah looks at it exactly the same way, but with exactly the same practised lack of expression. They're looking at the same twenty-year-old burgundy porcelain but seeing totally different stories, different accusations. Faith sees evidence the woman beside her is more real here, a story that happened first. Right beside her, Sarah sees only the subsequent: how everything but the teapot has happened since; that the teapot is chipped, outdated, maintained out of loyalty or politeness. There's no direction either of them can look without seeing the other, and nothing I can do about it. The harder I try the more obvious that is, to them as well as me.

'That's a lovely hat, Sarah,' Faith says, and means it. She even manages eye contact for a moment before she blushes under all the extra foundation she doesn't need and looks at the teapot again.

My adopted mother looks back at my stepmother, from under her black trilby and metallic blue eyeliner. She recrosses her vegan faux leathered legs, obviously searching the enemy's face for sarcasm. Then, even more obviously, she tries to find something nice to say about Faith's layers of neutral make-up and pink dress. 'Thank you,' she says when she's visibly failed.

I should have let Faith do the tea, that's obvious now. That would have been kinder. I should have thought to let Faith stake her claim as living here now that she is, indeed, living here, as much as Sarah ever lived here first. But all I saw as I planned the day was my own story, advertising the dutiful daughter I too am trying to prove to myself that I am, as if that was ever going to halt the silent war of who gets to be more my mother in the other's eyes.

'So, Ronni sweetheart.' Sarah sits back on the sofa she chose when I, and probably Faith, were still at school, not long before Abraxas, barely more than a kitten, was prolifically sick on it, making her re-cover it in the current ochre, to which Faith eventually and respectfully matched the rest of the living room. 'Twenty-two tomorrow.'

'Twenty-two tomorrow,' I agree cheerfully, though when Faith had said the same exact thing in the same exact tone over breakfast all I did was roll my eyes. I'm in audience-mode with my own mothers, my ever-too-low voice trapped in self-conscious cheerfulness, which I can't seem to drop, though I'm sure it isn't fooling either of them. *You both have your own lives*, I want to scream. *You are both real. You have nothing to prove, to me or to each other or to him. There is no competition because you've both already won. You have happy lives. All you have to do is get on with living them, instead of looking for someone to award you marks, or someone else to beat so you can deduct them from yourselves. There's no point to any of this. It doesn't exist unless you make it exist.* But saying anything at all would acknowledge the problem, which would only make it more present, more real, contradicting my own point. So that's why I don't – except it's not. I don't do it because it's *not done*. So all I can do is sit in the armchair with my back to the garden so I can't be tempted to glare constant psychic messages at my father's apparently innocent back.

'Will you have a party?' Sarah asks. 'Work friends, and so on?'

'Tonight,' I reply, and realise too late my eyes have wandered to the little Nokia on the arm of the chair. I don't look up to catch the knowing sparkle in their eyes. They both want to ask me about it all, the new "friend", the new job, the new diagnosis. But more than that, they both want to be the one who asks the right probing question so I bring it all up myself and they get to win the "mother" competition in front of each other.

'What colour was the sofa before Abraxas was sick on it?' I ask instead. My voice is so bright it makes me want to go and lie down in a dark room. 'Do you remember? I must have been what, seven?'

'Six and a half,' says Sarah. She doesn't follow up with how she knows, how exactly she remembers, because it's to do with the time of my adoption, and that would be an own-goal in front of Faith, who's lived with me now longer than Sarah ever did. I can almost hear the silence lasting exactly as long as it takes all three of us to do the maths in our heads at the same time.

'Yeah, that makes sense,' I continue, as if there's nothing in the room or in the words. 'It was that really prolific liquid sick cats almost never do...' Abraxas was a kitten, though a giant panther to me then, bought so I could have someone littler than myself to look out for, someone more puzzled, someone more a different species in the house than I already felt. Abraxas became a surly teenager before I did, of course, because that's what cats become and stay. Since coming back from university, I've seen how much he's aged and I haven't. I'm fighting so hard not to slip into surly teenage mode because I feel it, pushing at the surface of the life I'm determined to make real. It's the easiest version of myself to be, the most reliable. This is part of it, the need to shut up and the need to fast-forward the silence into something, anything, else.

'Anyway,' I say, 'Gray'll be in soon. All we did was pour a bunch of seeds from cooking into the flowerpots so how he thinks we can have made a wrong choice I don't know...'

'Oh, Gray's always been like that,' Sarah says to Faith, as if she's introducing someone Faith's never met, though Gray has been Faith's husband longer than he was Sarah's. 'The more options available, the more unhappy he'll be with the one he's picked.' The tone sounds like a genuine attempt at friendliness; a shame she's making it sound like Faith won't have made her own observations in eleven years. She can never let go enough, never stop trying to win the conversation instead of have it. 'Always wanting to go back and check out the ones he hasn't.'

'Yes, Vee said that used to a problem. Outside the garden.' Faith looks at me with an easy smile, making it a favour she's covering for Sarah's embarrassment at going too far, making me implicit, a decisive finale of friendly fire.

'Vee?' says Sarah.

'Ronni,' says Faith. 'As was.' Her smile is sadly convincing now. She doesn't want me to change my name, though she respects it. You genuinely wouldn't know how scared she was of Sarah, that a previous reality was under the ice waiting for her to fall into it, unless you knew how successful an actor she'd been before her ankle gave in.

'Yes. Well.' Sarah fidgets with the tassels on her faux-leather trousers. 'It's been over a decade hasn't it, so perhaps it's not a problem anymore.'

Somewhere outside the line of fire, I hear the sprinkler and turn to the French windows, swallowing a whimper that just makes it into a sigh. I eyebrow the back of my father's head, too far away to feel, see or hear me, deliberately standing as far away as it's possible to be at the very back of the garden, staring at a yellow geranium.

'Though in my experience, there's always a next time. Patterns are patterns, aren't they? Soon as you least expect it…'

'Excuse me a moment, I must just…' My stepmother's voice is faint. Behind me, I hear the knock and slide of Faith's high-heeled slight-limp head out the door and up the stairs towards the upstairs loo. Which she only bothers doing if she's going to cry and doesn't want us to know. I must never mention this even if I want to, because if there's one thing family life has taught me I can't afford, it's to give up any amount of the tactical advantage of information.

'I was sorry to hear the African violet died.' Sarah pounces as soon as Faith is out of the room. But with only one of them here instead of two I feel my body let itself be angry; she honestly thinks she's making conversation but I recognise the accusation, and the length of the silence tells me even she does too as soon as it's out. Her mother bought the plant when we moved in here. I don't even know if I thought of her as Grandma then, or just as Sarah's mum. Aside from the day of the adoption and Abraxas being sick, I'm pretty sure it's my first clear memory. Of course I'm angry the plant died, but I'm angrier that she takes it as a worthy sacrifice, that the plant gave its life so she'd have something heavy to throw against the enemy.

'Yeah,' I say.

'How's it all been, Ronn... Vee?' Sarah's looking at me too hard, desperate to show she understands what I'm feeling.

'Good,' I say.

'Good?'

I pick up my phone, perched politely on the arm of the chair, and look at the text that's waiting for a reply. I'll get through this conversation, then reward myself with the future. I don't want to mix them, need the doors to stay locked between them, even in my thoughts. 'Yeah, really good. If you're talking about the diagnosis?'

I don't need to look up to see her squirm, knowing she's lost and won: we're talking about it, but because she wants to, not because I've confided in her. 'It's good, like when you've got enough pieces of the jigsaw that you're seeing the picture underneath instead of all the distracting little lines. Or, like, you know that magic eye poster I used to have? The eagle with the fish in its claws I used to have on my bedroom wall, remember?'

'Of course I remember.'

'Well good like that. Like somebody's seen me, seen what's really there.'

She's trying to understand, and the sensation of string tightening around my heart and throat makes me realise how much I want her to. 'And you realise you were starting to think that's what life would always be like, all the little lines, but then at last the picture underneath makes so much sense.'

'So you're...happy?'

'Yes. I think I actually am.' You'd think a diagnosis was the problem itself, not its solution. As if labels are bad things. As if knowing what's in seed packets stop a gardener expressing themselves. 'Is that such a surprise?'

'No. No, not at all. And you have a job now, Dad said... I mean, Gray said...'

'Dad's fine, Sarah. You can call him that.' I do too, in my head, where it doesn't need to be policy decision. 'You always did. I don't mind.' They always called each other Mum and Dad, though I always called them Sarah and Graham. I don't want to tell Sarah about Meg. Not yet. That's another door still locked, still just for me until I'm comfortable in there myself. Or because I'm still superstitious enough that if I let too much of myself through while it's still forming I'm sure the new shoots will freeze, or disappear back into the soil they sprung from. That's why I know when Faith feels the same thing. Except I sprung from this place, at least was chosen first, and I don't want what she longs for, to grow naturally and happily in. I don't want my identity to just be a part of theirs.

I hadn't noticed myself flick the phone off silent, but my spine ripples with frosty joy at the notification of her name. Another text.

'Sorry, Sarah.'

She says something polite. I check the text. It could be anything. Then the tune I'd never know but for Meg erupts.

Can't talk now, miss u tho

Sorry wrong button, talk later :)

The spinal chill of joy spreads to my face, too sharp to hide the smile.

'Who's that, Ronni?'

'Friend. Old... new friend.' I'll reply on the roof later. The roof will still be there, whatever happens below it. That's been a comfort as long as I can remember. The roof hasn't changed with eras, even what graffiti I applied over the years has faded with the rain. I didn't go out there a single time when I came home on university holidays. But now this is home again, though not forever, I am safe there, whole. I am exactly who I am.

The one thing my adopted mother and stepmother really had in common was the conviction that one day I was going to fall through the roof, where I like to sit outside my bedroom window, and crash to my grizzly death the kitchen below. Faith in particular was convinced to this day that I was going to die a horrible, noisy death of slate and plaster before finally stabbing myself with the kitchen knife harmlessly drying on the draining board. She always brings it up during the washing-up argument. My father leaves the knives with their points up; they argue about the washing up and drying when what they're really arguing about is my safety, her position an adult in my eyes, his eyes and, via us, her own.

'Is he not back?' Faith says when she re-enters the room. Her make-up is as perfect – by which I mean careful – as when she left, but her eyeshadow is dark fuchsia now, when this morning it was bright salmon. Faith's got Meg's magic power, that she can cry and her face will look completely normal five minutes after she stops. I don't have that. I look like a puffer fish and continue to look like a puffer fish for hours after. It's one of the reasons I've got so good at avoiding it. But the first time it happened in front of Meg, the day of the education psychologist report before our finals, that was the day of the puffer fish. I lay on the ancient eiderdown of the bed in Meg's room in the house she shared with two other literature students, a barely literate, dirty-nailed gardener, and told her how it felt to be told by a piece of paper I needed help to read that I could be entirely myself, that I *was* entirely myself, that it wasn't my fault that I learnt in a different way to other people, was brilliant at things others didn't understand and paid it back in the categories they found easiest: writing, reading, stories. I was fine when I was present in a garden, present in the world, and she took the hand that lay beside her and told me being present was enough. She said that's what the strange song that was playing was about, the dragonfly and the lamb were two sides of the same person. It wasn't a love song to someone else, but of standing on the windowsill between two versions of yourself, and the only way was through, that being true to yourself was growing, leaving a previous version of yourself behind. It was like attending my own funeral. Or birth. I said I didn't know which.

'Always both,' Meg had said.

Meg's ring tone trickles into the silence again, the strange old song she taught me.

'What was that?' Faith asks as she comes back.

'Wings?' I say. 'A friend likes them.'

'That takes me back,' says Sarah, and starts telling us about how a friend of hers was one of the ballroom dancers on the film version of an album the guy who wrote the song released a few years after. I'll ask Meg about him, when we're alone. Finally.

Faith interrupts a couple of times with stories of getting up at five am to take her under-eighteen friend to meet another band on a TV show I've barely heard of, and the sound of friendly fire continues as I text Meg what's happening and get a reply, *That one wasn't even Wings. He was solo by then.* Nothing any of the three of them are saying makes any sense to me at all, and that makes it easier to just enjoy listening.

Meg didn't seem to have any of this, relatives at war. I remember her telling me about Wings, in her bedroom covered with well-chosen pictures of people I wouldn't even think to listen to, about how that song is about leaving behind the part of yourself that isn't serving you. Not because Sarah didn't understand, but because Gray never missed a chance to remind her how great Faith had been about it, which just served to remind her what hadn't worked.

'And you've told them?' Sarah asks suddenly. 'At the new job?'

'I'm a florist, Sarah.' I don't look up from the phone. But the living room returns around me, pushing its way towards the part of my mind I want to keep separate and safe. 'Dyspraxia's about co-ordination. It means I need to be careful with scissors and diaries, and that if you throw a ball at me you'll see it go past my head before I lift my hand to catch it. It's not like telling them I'm severely allergic to pollen or colour-blind.'

'We just...' Faith says.

Sarah joins in. 'We just don't want to see you get hurt.'

They nod identical nods, exchange identical glances. They're on the same side now and I don't like it any more than I liked barely keeping the peace.

'I'm not climbing Everest,' I say. 'I'm not jumping out of a plane. I'm just doing what I want. For the first time.' And, also for the first time, what I want wants me too. Exactly as I am.

'All the same.' The fear in both their eyes is so real that I know, when I look back on this, it's going to convince me the future is frightening too.

~

Dad climbs through the window behind me, onto the roof. I'm back from the pub and I'm no more sure I should have climbed out here than he is. Faith's gone to bed and Sarah's gone home, later than any of them had planned. They'd played their roles of getting on almost convincingly once they could unite against a common enemy: my future.

'I'd forgotten how clear the graves are from the roof,' he says conversationally.

I nod. It's too misty to see much; if I didn't already know what I was looking at I wouldn't see, which means he can't see them either, which means he's just trying to think of something to say. I tell him so.

'Don't you think you're overthinking, Ronn... Vee?' he says.

'Why does no one ever say that when someone comes up with something they actually like?' I snap back.

He's looking at Innes's grave on the far left, the laminated brown scribble of my earliest attempt at drawing a cat still recognisable against the dark green of the dusky garden, then the tortoise-shell-and-white scribbles of Nowell and Stanshall.

Beside me, shifting his bum between tiles to get as comfortable as the slate allows, he gives me one of his ever-present earphones. It's Moby, one of his favourites. I never got this one. It's absolutely no comfort that we're all made of stars and I don't know why it should be, but that we're here at all is comfort and awe beyond words. It is enough.

'So, twenty-two,' he says as he sits on the roof beside me, and for the first time today I let myself roll my eyes, until they fall on Abraxas, staring up at the roof of the shed, willing it to get shorter, closer in reach.

Dad follows my eyes to the black fur and green glare. 'He used to do that jump easily, didn't he? In one spring.'

'He did.'

'How's the flower-arranging going?'

'It's going well,' I say. 'And I grow things. I don't just arrange them.'

The mist is starting to clear. The moon will soon be rising.

'They only want what's best for you, you know. Both of them.'

'And you.'

'I know.' We watch Abraxas get bored of staring and walk back towards the house. 'And, at some level, maybe even each other.'

'You left me alone with them.'

'They want time with you. I thought it would be better without an audience.'

He's not going to understand. There's no point trying to explain what he refuses to hear. There's no way I can word it that he'd let himself understand, so I just say 'Yeah' again, because I always get away with it, because they're all too stressed and tired to change the rules now.

'They just don't want to see you get hurt, Veronica.'

I look at him to see if he's joking, copying the words they wait until he's gone to say. But of course he isn't. 'Of course they don't want me to get hurt. Nobody wants anybody to get hurt. But Faith's ankle injury isn't what stopped her acting. It was not going for parts at all. Giving up stopped her acting.'

'Well, yes, obviously, but…'

'But it doesn't work like that. I'm not going to unhurt myself by not… not *trying* to be whoever I am. If people can't deal with me because they're embarrassed or they don't understand, that's not going to be less embarrassing or understandable because I give up. You can't go through life making choices based on not getting hurt. I'm going to be as me as I possibly can, for as long as I possibly can. I don't care who my birth parents are. I don't care if they gave me up because they had to, or because they wanted to. I don't care what anyone – from the ed psych to you – thinks that says about me as a person. I don't care if you think I'm suppressing more complicated feelings. I don't care if I am. I am going to be myself and I don't need to define that by anyone, visible or invisible, in my life or out of it. If I get what I want or if I don't it is not going to be for someone else's sake. I am going to be as me as I could possibly be and if that isn't what the three of you want for me then you're not the parents you want to prove to each other you are.'

'They both just want to feel they're…'

'I know! And how do you think that makes me feel? That both my mothers think they're not my real mother?'

I didn't know I thought it until the silence after. The words echo in my brain, jiggle into place, and fit, as true and real and had been there all the time as the magic eye poster, the picture in the jigsaw.

'Maybe you should talk to them,' he says. 'Maybe if you give them a little piece of you, you'll get the same back.'

'This from the man repotting pepper plants for two hours.'

'It was never two hours.' He's right, though. Of course he's right. Below, at the kitchen door, is the faint, business-like plink of the cat-flap. 'We should go back down.'

'Meg's going to be here during the day tomorrow. Faith's working, so if I ask her to stay it'll just be the three of us.'

'Right,' he says. He hides the excitement like a pro. Faith's been teaching him. Or he's learning from her, whether he knows it or not. 'Right. Meg. As in…?'

'As in Megan.'

'Right. Okay.' In the silence between the words and the silence after, the inaudible cogs whirring in my father's head, I know he's decided to be okay with this whether he understands any of it or not.

'Thanks, Dad.'

'For what?'

The moon is rising over the line of firs at the bottom of the garden. The plants growing at the flowerbed at the back are standing at perfect angles; whatever he did out here for two hours he did it well. The yuccas at the back I usually ignore and the new pepper plants spreading their shoots like wings, flying up and out like solid water, as if each one is a slow-motion waterfall. How long would I have to sit here to realise I'd been watching something growing, moving all the time, even when it was perfectly still?

Behind us, at the window, there's a small, insistent miaow.

'Coming Abraxas,' we say at the same time as the moon rises over the yuccas.

Cauliflower

[2017]

She's always so bloody on-time. What point is the little bitch trying to prove?

I'm conscious of my speed, the view of my work-slippers on the carpet, one beige step in front of the next, as if I've never watched myself race to answer the door before. What in hell do I think will happen if I walk instead of run upstairs from the kitchen to the hall? They all have mobile phones these days, don't they? Especially her generation. The one time I didn't hear the doorbell she called the house, and Gerald's voice three floors above shifted from his age-old, dour recitation of our telephone number to an ecstatic and thunderous "Kerry-Alice!" as if he were exalting the blessed virgin. My name certainly hasn't sounded like that in his voice since before Adam was born.

Her hair is unmistakable through the frosted glass, thick and busy and visible in a way that puts me in mind of how much taller she manages to be, though she'd be lucky to scrape five-foot-four. It's not so long ago she used to tame it, flatten it, beat it into submission. My thinning, greying bob is a bad joke beside her dark forest of piled curls. At her age, curls like that were brushed out of us. The place for beauty was within the frame of a canvas.

'Morning, Effie. I—'

I only see her face for as long as it takes to open the door, then turn towards the stairs again. With any luck she'll think it rude to follow. She'll turn right before the stairs and into my study as she does every week, drape her coat over the spare chair opposite the window as usual and start checking if the paintbrushes need washing, setting up the easels, placing the three kinds of charcoal on the ledge of each one, in pedantic symmetry. I only realise I've frozen at the bottom of the stairs when she's right behind, and right above, me. 'Effie? What's wrong? What's happened?'

'The vet is coming,' I say. My eyes can't seem to leave the carpet. There are pieces of purple tinsel walked into the threads. It's closer to next Christmas than to the one gone. I never took the cards off the shelves in the office. I should do that. But then, it was done, wasn't it? And suddenly there they were in that plastic pocket in my correspondence tray and what business are my Christmas cards of hers? Hadn't she hounded and harassed enough information out of my friends and family at the Christmas party I should never have invited her to, should never have blurred the lines between assistance and friendship, watching those bitten nails grow into elegant talons twitching towards the future of my business?

A beat of silence, a moment of how my house used to sound. Just the ticking of the hallway, the clocks just out of time to give a single, solid, supportive murmur over the worst of the silence. Then she says, 'It's Cauliflower, isn't it?'

It's not as if it's so clever of her to have worked it out. Cauliflower has been "on the way out" since before Kerry-Alice. The first thing I told her was how my loping, indestructible smaller grey tabby of the pair didn't make friends easily. Seconds before the indifferent bastard leapt straight on her lap. 'Gerald can't be disturbed,' I say. 'He's in a meeting.'

'Do you not want me to check if he wants to come down? It's only two floors up, Effie. I'm sure he'd want to be with you when...'

'Oh yes, what are you sure of? About my husband? What else are you an expert on about my marriage? My life?' It was out, that cork from the wine, in a minute's exquisite release. I taste it in the silence that follows, louder still. 'Gerald can't be disturbed,' I snap with the firmness of twenty-five years of art instruction. I've tasted it now, the truth in my mouth, the clarity of it still burning on my tongue.

Were she closer I could step away, respond to inappropriate, disrespectful proximity. I manage it anyway. One step, enough to let her pass. She takes the hint. For someone who didn't know silk-coated from cartridge paper, she's strangely aware of the blending of colour in life as in art: foundations and eyeshadows, expressing and enhancing her features, making her look like herself but more so. She's never offered to share any of that with me. Hungry as she is for what I could teach her it never occurs to her to offer me any of herself in return. I can do what she does on canvas, but make-up was always like poster-paint in my hands.

The top of her head disappears as she kneels where Cauliflower, invisible to me from this angle to the edge of the counter, lies in a half-sleep. She disappears entirely from my sight as she kneels further towards the basket. 'Oh, Cauliflower.' I can't see either of them, but his gentle purring-come-gasping is louder than it was before. This morning it was only coming in fits and starts. Now it's so confident it feels like that's what silence sounds like.

I speak over it. 'He was sitting on the sofa beside me, over breakfast. He leapt off. His breathing...' I don't need to finish. My memories are mine, will not be hers like everything else seems to want to be, forcing me to watch all of my life warming towards her as thoughtlessly as I did myself. The soft familiar grey of Cauliflower, vibrating, straining just to breathe, then collapsing forward as if to get his breath back after nothing more than breathing. He has become a glove puppet of a cat, sometimes finding the spirit of movement had sneaked back inside him and for a few moments everything seems familiar and normal, until he would collapse forward again, straining and squeaking each insufficient breath. I always promised myself I wouldn't be selfish and sentimental, that too soon would be kinder than too late. Yet late came so much sooner than I expected. 'I've called the vet. She's on her way. She's bringing a trainee of some kind. She said that... that that's why there would be two of them, but she would be the one to do the procedure...'

Kerry-Alice comes into view around the side of the counter as she slides to lean back, still kneeling. The mauve curve of her slacks meets my lino, my words falling like water off her plumage. Her curls falling forward so I can't see her face as she talks to him. 'I'm sorry, old friend.'

Old friend? She's worked for me less than two years. This assured little interloper who from the very first seemed to think she was part of the house. When I met Kerry-Alice, she was so afraid of giving some offence, of being caught out as unworthy. She listened so carefully, so overly aware of the world around her, her sense of perpetual apology for being in it. Then she convinced everyone else in my life she was an integral part of it. I see the way Adam looks at her; Vincent too, on one of the rare trips my vacuous Napoleon of a daughter-in-law allows him downstairs without her. They're so *interested*. They *shine* around her, brighter in her light. Veronica has something of that too. Maybe that's why I never see them together. Veronica always has a reason to be absent when Kerry-Alice is here. It's the only thing that stops me feeling they are upstaging me together, in an agreement. It all worked as well on me as it did on them, before I spotted how damned convenient it all is. Every thoughtful little gesture to help me, knowing what I want before I do, I know perfectly well is for herself, that it would be ludicrous for her to think she needs me for anything. She must know she's a better artist, a more instinctive one, taking a pleasure in a blank canvas I never knew. A blank page is always laughing at me; it entices her. I see it in every class, yet she is the student, the assistant. Praise God I never got around to contracts, that she trusted me too much to ask.

The doorbell rings and I don't move, so it's Kerry-Alice who lets the vet in, introducing herself as my assistant, not my friend. At least she has that much tact. Being beside me in this moment as my friend would have been a step too far – so why am I disappointed? Whose side do I think I'm on?

'Mrs James, hello.' The vet is not much older than Kerry-Alice is. She has a measured voice and equally measured smile that leaves a respectful distance, lets us both believe I'm taking in what's going to happen (though I could not explain a single thing I'm hearing), how long it will take (that too leaves my mind as directly as it came), what Cauliflower will and won't feel. I only look away from the carpet as the trainee approaches the basket, bending down with her hands on her knees and a bright "Hello!" that knocks me off balance. It seems inappropriate, unseemly, to address him the way you might greet to any cat you met at a friend's house, or on the pavement on the way to the shops. A cat, in short, whom you were not about to be paid to murder.

'It's absolutely fine if you'd prefer to stay where you are, Mrs James.' She looks at me as if it's perfectly normal to glue oneself to the kitchen doorway. 'Or we can bring his basket onto the sofa, onto your lap?'

'He wouldn't want that,' I say.

'But you…'

'He wouldn't want that!' I'm staring at the carpet and no one is taking the hint, not at all. Why can they not understand I do not wish to be here, I want to disappear into the circumstances, the background. Kerry-Alice, God damn her, can make herself truly useful for once and work out what I mean.

I don't really hear the silence. The fibres of the carpet I'm staring at again shake from side to side as I give my only response. I don't want him moved for my sake. Cauliflower is perfectly happy where he is, with them, with her. With Kerry-Alice. Everyone is. Do they think I don't see that? Do they feel so sorry for me it's supposed to be a secret? Better to stare into the carpet that was in this house before Kerry-Alice was, before I was.

There's movement around the basket. The trainee's head comes up far enough for me to see, beside Kerry-Alice's face. The extraordinary pain it registers, but she never looks away, never flinches, takes all of the pain into herself as if she is the friend who gets to know him better than anyone else does.

The vet has her back to me, and is bending too close for me to be able to read her expression. And while I haven't moved, Kerry-Alice is saying over and over again that she'll keep on stroking him the way he likes, talking to him through the sound of a shaver that rips the silence like a threat. That must be where they prepare where the needle will go in, and because I can't look I don't know which of his beautiful grey legs they are shaving, and because I can't look I only hear the click and peel of the needle being prepared, the slide of it being filled, and Kerry-Alice with tears in her voice saying how Cauliflower likes his ears rubbed, the left one more than the right one – *how dare she know that? Did I know that?* – and telling him everybody loves him, that she loves him, that Effie and Gerald love him, that Adam and Vincent and Veronica love him, even though I know perfectly well she's never met Veronica because Veronica is never bloody here on Kerry-Alice Days, and yet she recites us like one of those ridiculous yoga mantras.

And then, even though I don't truly know what's happening, it's happened, and the tears shoot from Kerry-Alice's cheeks so that I know what I cannot see and I know the one thing I still have power over is that I refuse to feel as powerless as this ever again. That this crisis will not be without opportunity, that this feeling ends today.

All that in less than a second before the vet says, 'There, that's all done for him.'

'For him?' I ask. 'Hardly *for him?*'

And I can't remember what happens after that except for the sounds of Kerry-Alice smoothing it all over as I run for the stairs.

∾

Our garden is big enough that it's really just about digging the hole. His body stays under his favourite blanket, the boys' old picnic rug, the outline of his shape a tartan mound in the corner of my eye as I dig. I dig the hole alone; he and I are the only ones together for that. She cannot take this from me. She will not take anything from me anymore.

∾

Long after Kerry-Alice has left, barely an hour earlier than she would have left anyway, I hear Vincent's key in the door. He sees my face and immediately calls upstairs for Gerald. There's none of the *what*ing I would get if I called Gerald; the men of this family respond to each other because they only ever contact each other with specific reason, never on a whim.

I did get almost as far as removing the blanket. Just far enough to look into his eyes, yellow and filmy, that weren't gazing back into mine. His body not his own either, but frozen already, stiff from not needing to move anymore. I didn't say anything to him; there's no point in the face of such proof that he simply is not here anymore. I look into those eyes that, in the minute they froze, were looking into Kerry-Alice's, and I find myself jealous of a dead cat. Who was she? What did she want? What was it about her that made me warm to her so quickly, then turn back to fire and flame so that I had to get her away from me before she burned my life down?

Their faces, drained and still, thoughts of past and future dismissed and existing in this moment only, give me a comfortable sense of power I realise I'd lacked all day, since seeing Cauliflower in that state this morning. 'I'd said I wouldn't wait too long,' I remind them. 'And the truth is we *have* waited anyway, far too long. But it's done because that's what was right for him and that's the only thing that matters.'

I look directly at Vincent as I say that, and Vincent shrugs, which from anyone else is the equivalent of stomping out of the room. His father, on the other hand, is less convinced and I feel inexplicably like I'm being hauled up before the headmaster. At our ages, the gap between is a matter of so few years it's laughable. Yet I feel exactly as I did standing in this kitchen with my parents.

'I don't understand why you didn't tell me,' Gerald says, *sotto voce* as Veronica, who I hadn't even registered arriving, slips out for her business-call-and-cigarette, while Vincent and Adam talk loudly over the dishes. 'I was two floors above you, Eff.'

'There was nothing you could have done.' I cut, hard, through the last of the Emmenthal, trying not to remember I was with Kerry-Alice when I bought it. That and the chocolate mousse we're having for dessert. On one of our final admin days, a blazing summer afternoon. Kerry-Alice followed me from department store to delicatessen and back while I insisted on finding exactly the right ones.

But all I see even as I ask myself these questions is what I couldn't look at. I know the room so well, every angle of it. I can see where the basket was, and the space where Kerry-Alice's knees met the edge, can see the shaver as they took the fur they needed gone so they could see where to inject him. And he wouldn't have argued, he was always the politest of the cats. If Cauliflower didn't particularly like something but sensed that one of the children did, he'd let it happen. Let the soft pad of his paw balance on the pad of a small thumb, his claws curling and uncurling as he purred and only remove it after a polite elapse of time so as not to offend the child in question. The vet was much the same age as the children are now; would have seemed to Cauliflower like just another child to be patient with, to please. And then the injection would have gone in, and his eyes would have glazed over into what I saw in the garden, still yellow-green as they ever were but further away, the animation gone out of him, paused mid-action, mid-purr, and that was all there was.

And I saw none of this. So now I must see all of it, again and again, in glorious technicolour, speeding up and slowing down as time moves on outside me and does not move on inside me. And I know that if I feel this today I will feel it for all days. I betrayed him. I let that bitch's kindness become a necessity. Never again. At least that one thing I can be sure of. I was decisive there at least.

Gerald takes my hand, looks into my eyes with the spirit of unembarrassed enquiry I fell in love with. 'I could have been there. Is being there not doing something?'

I don't have time to answer. Veronica returns, reeking of Marlboro Lights and brandishing her iPhone like a Stanley knife, placing it too hard on the table as Vincent and Adam return with the coffee pot and mousse plates.

'How was the rest of the day?' Gerald asks. 'It was a Kerry-Alice Day today, wasn't it?'

I feel the boys look up like the name is a dog whistle. Even Veronica listens with something approaching neutrality: as far from dislike as her settings go.

'I never quite know what day it is up in the studio,' he goes on. 'But it feels like it was time for a Kerry-Alice Day?'

'She was here,' I say. The last mouthful of cheese is strangely complicated to swallow. 'She's gone now.'

'Well I should hope so at this time! Lovely girl like her, gorgeous evening like this.'

'She arranged for the bill to be posted, and made the calls that today's class was postponed.' I have pasted the chocolate to the side of the bowl, a technique for pretending to eat I'd forgotten I was once so good at. 'Very rude of her to tell rather than ask me she was doing so, as it happens.'

'Sounds like it was the right call to me,' says Adam, in that infuriating way of his father's that makes every person he disagrees with feel like they've received a compliment. 'I mean, we've had Cauliflower since… I was what, eleven?'

'Young enough to decide that Cauliflower and Artichoke were excellent names for cats,' Vincent nominally tells Veronica, but really just enjoys the dig at his little brother. 'He was so proud he could fucking spell them.'

'Language,' Gerald observes into his chocolate mousse.

'It's the example not the issue,' I snap.

'Spelling?' Adam asks.

'Kerry-Alice,' I state as calmly as I can. 'It simply wasn't working.' I take the coffee I hadn't noticed Vincent pour and try to swallow. It's hard work, like the cheese was. Much hotter – or is it colder? – than usual.

'Okay. Oh, by the way Dad, can I borrow the car at, like, nine?'

Gerald nods and Adam has forgotten the Kerry-Alice conversation, Vincent has his coffee and Veronica has her phone, but Gerald in his silence has not forgotten.

'Kerry-Alice won't be returning,' I snap when the silence is too loud.

'What?' my sons and husband chorus as Veronica says, 'Really? Why?'

I know that I'd decided how to answer this, and I try to remember my answer. They'd never understand the truth, so I'm trying not to think of that but to remember what I believe they will understand.

'But you two seemed to get on so well,' Gerald says. He reaches for my hand again but it does not – cannot – move from where I've set it in my lap. 'I honestly thought you'd never been so happy.'

And that's when, in the only language anyone truly understands, I throw down my cutlery and burst into tears.

~

'She's fired you, hasn't she.'

'Yes,' I say. Somehow I knew the unknown number would be her. The evening is unseasonably cold; I've walked the town centre more than I ever did when I had a right to be in it, when I was a student at the gallery that became a shoe shop, after it failed within a year of Effie pulling out and moving the classes to the house. I walked around it rather than going home, trying to find where I was standing when I was exactly who I wanted to be, or was walking towards becoming it. When I thought Effie saved me, when I swore I'd do everything I could to make her happy, for the business to be everything I knew it could.

Everything I've done, everything I tried to do, every suggestion she didn't want to hear meant keeping my promise, making the business everything it could be, being all about that and not about myself. Not reading a single sign that it wasn't what she wanted. I don't say a word of this to Veronica. I just cry into the silence.

I haven't heard Veronica's voice in all the time I've known Effie. But I remember every cold, precise syllable. The absolute clarity of it, like perfect crystal. This voice has existed like a ghost over everything, under everything, a simultaneously pure and dirty secret. I never knew her name, not until I came alone to the same house she'd brought me to only a year before I found Effie's classes, before a conversation about someone else's death started a new version of my life, exactly where Veronica once offered to do the same. As I walked towards it that first time, I prayed it would be a different door number, and prayed it wouldn't. And then the door opened, and I saw all the clocks and I knew. The house had called me back a second time.

We had avoided each other, in wordless mirroring agreement, all this time. Until now, as she says 'What the fuck happened, Kerry-Alice?' and I press her voice as close to my ear as the phone will go, letting the silence wrap itself around my name.

She says it like they all do, like it makes sense as a concept. Like I make sense as a concept.

'She says I'm a terrible influence on Adam, that I'm muscling in on every aspect of her life, That her friends like me more than they like her; that the cat does; that her sons do.'

'In that order?'

'In exactly that order.' And we're both laughing. Laughing at the things we make important, the people we misrepresent as gods. 'It's good to hear your voice, Veronica.'

'I couldn't be there. I couldn't see you.'

'I know. Vincent's nice. I can see how... I can imagine he makes you...'

'Where are you?'

'Nearly home.'

'Home still means Danny?' When I don't answer, she adds, 'So nothing's changed.'

'Nothing at all.'

'Take care of yourself, Kerry-Alice.'

'And you. Veronica.' The name tastes sweet and rich, forbidden and wholesome in my mouth, a gâteau of a word. I've never said her name, not to her, not to anyone, except in my head. We hadn't known each other's names, then.

Neither of us hangs up for five, ten, fifteen seconds. I'm counting to calm myself, but I realise as I reach twenty that neither of us is hanging up.

'Where are you?' she says again.

My eyes flick, unbidden, to the café I'd been sketching in when I had first discovered Effie's flyer, and where Veronica had first discovered me. 'Where do you expect me to be?'

Moth Paper

[2022]

They're exactly as I left them. If I try, I can still see what I first thought I saw, the picture I thought I was looking at. Distant birds, frozen in flight. A water colour, perhaps, of a greyscale skyscape. But under it the suggestion of unnaturally straight lines, a whispered noughts-and-crosses board across what I took to be the sky. The cross-hatched lilac-on-white of the grid, too straight, too clear and accurate to be anyone's picture of nature. I feel the creep and hit of the realisation again that this wasn't art but life – or, rather, death – not artist's perception but immediate reality; millimetres from where my hand rested, and rests again now, on Effie's bookshelf.

The moths had mostly hit the paper mid-flight. I wondered then, and wonder now again, if they would have had the strength to struggle. How they haven't decayed where they landed.

'And if you want something to remember her by, I mean, go for it.' Adam's soft, pleasant voice jolts me back to where, or rather when, I am. Everything is acutely, aggressively familiar, as if the time since I last walked out of here were a commercial break in an ongoing programme; as if I never really left.

I thank him, and say something about how well the room has always suited itself. That it always knew exactly who it was.

'It does, doesn't it?' Adam looks pleased at the idea. His gaze moves around the room in a quick, simple line, as if he's trying to see his mother's study for the first time: the bookshelves that cover the walls and even the space above the door, circling our – no, not ours, not anymore – two desks like three-dimensional wallpaper, their dusty books unadded to in all the time I was there, and I'm pretty sure in any of the years since. Adam's eyes are more like Effie's than I remembered, or maybe noticed, except there's none of her urgency behind his, no sense of being pulled in a million angry directions. He sees what's there. And that's enough for him.

No wonder he was such a disappointment.

Adam moves from the study doorway to what I can't stop thinking of as my chair, facing the ever-jammed sash window I never once saw open, the curtains I never thought to ask to close however bright the sun. He begins filing Effie's collection of paint brushes from the top drawer into piles. 'I totally still think of you as a day of the week,' he says.

'You do?'

'Yeah. I still think, "Oh, it's a Kerry-Alice Day".'

'Every week?'

'Totally. We all do. Well…' *Not quite all*, he doesn't finish. I can see in his face that he never said it in front of Effie. 'How long's it been?'

'Five years,' I say.

'Five? No way.'

I nod. 'Just over.'

'Well, maybe anything with Covid in the middle only counts as one.'

'Maybe,' I say. He doesn't seem like a man whose mother's just died, and I realise in thinking so that I've started thinking of Adam as a man. He's grown into his father's good-natured patience and, also like his father, carries himself like he's floating not walking through life: taking in the view, not competing in a race. I never noticed any of this when I only had eyes for Effie and her approval, gratefully and arrogantly determined as I was that the world (or, failing that, triple her existing number of students) should know what an excellent teacher and painter she was. Every week I arrived with more and more plans, suggestions, social media and marketing advice, when the last thing she wanted was anything more than what I gave her in our first conversation. But I was too busy trying to show her who I saw her as, who she was to me.

Adam was so young when I was fired, second gap year and university behind him and a blank canvas ahead of him. I wonder what's happened in between. I don't ask now, even though he's obviously staying to keep me company, while delicately averting his eyes to let me wander, cry, do whatever I need to. Effie never liked me talking to her sons. I have no real idea who this man is. We were scenery to each other. I could reach across that now, but instead I'm at the windowsill, looking at the collection of vases, gemstones and sand in jars, all of which look back at me, blank and unapologetic as the dead moths. This is already the most I've ever said to Effie's youngest son. He was out of bounds, for reasons I didn't understand.

But reasons were irrelevant. I hadn't cared that my home and relationship were imploding, that I had no other prospects and my whole sense of creativity and individuality were now channelled into being her assistant. I didn't care, because there were two days of clarity to every week and I lived for them. Painting at the club, assisting with the students, and the administration at her home on Thursday. Adam's Kerry-Alice Days. That's what they felt like to me, too: the days I was absolutely myself, the days I truly felt I was Kerry-Alice.

It was so wonderful to feel absolute love, excitement for the future and gratitude to match, and with it the freedom from sexual attraction. I'd never had a mentor I didn't want to fuck; life with Danny had confused so many things. Effie was the opposite of sex. I knelt before the altar of her, her refusal to link artistic expression and personal aesthetics, her broadcasting of asexuality, yet still I reverted to type, offering too much love in return for too little and feeling gratitude for that. What a waste gratitude without self-esteem was.

'Five years,' Adam says again. He taps at what was my computer. It's smaller than Effie's, beside it on the taller desk. Still, there's more desk space at what was mine. 'No way.' It's a friendly contradiction, a cheerfully glib, rich white alpha male's answer and I've always found it a guilty comfort to be around such certainty. She had that too. But there's none of the force Effie would have used in her son's eyes. Still, every time I meet them I remember that scowl, the one behind her passive face, the look of a bird of prey (a thought I pushed away a thousand times as I saw her not meet the eyes of waiters and barely acknowledge gallery staff), with nothing personal in the fact that she would eventually pounce.

I wonder if she told Adam what had happened, what her version would sound like. Did she tell him the actual accusations? No, actually, I don't wonder at all. Of course she didn't, she wouldn't have done.

'Listen, I think that's Vincent now. I'll put the kettle on. Would you...?'

'No. Thanks, Adam.'

He leaves the door ajar and I hear the light, confident tread of converse on stair carpet to the kitchen down the hall.

I am alone.

Or so anyone else would think.

I slide around between desk and bookcase, and return to the moth shelf. *Hello, old friends.* The outlines of the corpses haven't changed, the shapes they left while their life blood – if life can be beige – seeped out. A faint, stained halo leaks and fades around each tiny set of remains. I never mentioned the moth-paper, but from week to week would look and think whatever happens today, here is a thing that will not have changed when what I'm going though today is all over.

I had no idea how right I was.

A small breeze blows through the uncloseable opening at the top of the sash window, and instinctively I turn to the empty doorway. I realise I am behaving, even as I stand perfectly still, as if a woman I know perfectly well is dead is watching my every step, following my every thought. And I know this is not even *because* Effie is dead. It felt exactly the same when she was alive.

Adam is on the floor below now; I hear his gentle pattering around what I still think of as Effie's studio. I wonder what it's become now. There was always a kettle and a biscuit tin, so no clues there. Another living room, perhaps. Unless Gerald moves his studio downstairs. I bet he won't. Gerald's position at the top of the house was as symbolic as the days of creation. There would be nothing more ghostly than nothing being above them, vaguely and benevolently looking down. Much easier to know there was nothing below. I decide not to ask what's changed. I don't belong in this future. I'm here on Adam's charity, just as I was here on Effie's. Anything else was my mistake. I thought the house called to me, wanted me to be part of it. To help it become itself. Effie made it clear how wrong I was.

The person I thought was Effie has been dead a long time. If she ever existed. The real Effie was nothing to me. That's what she told me. She was Adam's mother, and Vincent's. She made it clear that love, and as a result grief, was an inappropriate imposition. If she were looking down on me now, she wouldn't see a friend saying goodbye, but an enemy crowing that I had outlived her. I shouldn't be here. I should have made some kind of excuse and followed her unspoken wishes. The way she expected everyone to. But loyalty to Effie would have been rudeness to Adam, a refusal to acknowledge kindness.

My eyes return to the moth-paper, the way they did when only Kerry-Alice Days made any sense, were islands I swam to and from each week. When all I could say to myself was, no matter what would happen in the days between, next week I would see this again and everything that mattered – Effie, and the world created around her – would be the same. The books would still be dusty. The moths would still be dead. I would have made it back.

I'd managed to conceal the shudder the first time I realised what I was looking at, or thought I had.

Effie didn't notice me jump, if I did. She had eyes only for her work, and the things that affected it. I didn't ask myself at the time why she seemed so much less jumpy outside the house, how Wednesdays were an era of perfect calm and yet when we met here, invited and suggested by her, she was following my gaze as if I could steal something – or someone – by looking. All that happened was Effie tapped her hard, unpolished nails on the end of the shelf, smiled that business-like smile that was in itself a command and not an offer, and I obediently went to what was about to become my chair, sat carefully in the middle of the darkly shining velvet cushion.

The chair looked straight into the sun. I would come to blame that, and myself, for not being sure if I'd read her wrong. I could barely see her face. But even her voice was inscrutable, a different tone to her certainty, or at least to the way I heard it in the classes at the Rabbit-Hole. It was as if I was talking to someone I'd never met before.

If I'd just explained the sun was in my eyes I would not now wonder whether she thought that people were – that I was – scowling at her. But I only had eyes for her, blinded as they were by the light behind. Maybe if I'd said it was uncomfortable in the direct light she wouldn't have misread my face and everything would have been different. What I said, that first time, was "This is wonderful. The studio downstairs. I don't think I've ever been happier than in my school art room.'

'Do the classes remind you of that?' Effie asked. 'You're clearly a strong enough painter that some of the advice will feel constrictive.'

'It's the freedom,' I said. Her body language suggested I'd contradicted her but I kept going, desperate to show her what it was I loved so much about the world she'd created. 'Three hours on a Tuesday afternoon there's only me. Absolutely me. Freedom to get things wrong.' She didn't ask what I was thinking about, and I could feel she was uncomfortable with me being uncomfortable. 'That's how you make discoveries.'

'I see.' She always said that when she didn't see. Or when she disagreed. Or when she chose to disagree in spite of not seeing.

'And this your first term here? At the house? Downstairs?' If I'd only kept the admiration out of my voice. If I'd only seen a reason to.

'My first for a while. When Willow and I began the classes, before the club was suggested, our children were so much younger, so not working from home was the goal. The quiet. I do value quiet.'

'Me too.' I wondered who Willow was and decided I wasn't supposed to ask. But the way she dropped hints about betrayal, and the things she would accuse me of, made me wonder if I was simply the new Willow, a self-fulfilling prophecy in a role I didn't understand. 'I think I have a bit too much of it at the moment.'

'You can never have too much quiet.' A tone that demanded not to be contradicted, opinion that demanded to be fact. Anything but intimacy. Anything but a way in, to the person behind the words. Unless it was her doing the talking. Her life was to be endlessly interesting to me. If I brought up mine, tried to offer her information as a gift of intimacy in return for hers, she looked at me as if I'd been impertinent and changed the subject. She'd fill every conversation with information about herself and damn with distance any offering in return. And I didn't notice any of it. Just tried to work out how to please her. If Effie's ghost wasn't glaring at me now, this study should be laughing at me.

But before all that I sat opposite her, light streaming into my eyes as she asked, 'Which days did you say suited you?'

'If Thursdays are best for you they're not a problem for me.'

'Arrive at about ten-thirty, we'll have coffee and talk about the day ahead. The first thing will always be setting up the easels for the morning session; normally I ask Vincent or Adam to help with this but Adam works during the day and Vincent is rather busy at the moment.'

And it was only then I remembered I had something to feel guilty for. But the house was already Effie's to me. The way my life had gone when I didn't take Veronica from this place was to bring me back to it, to be of genuine help. For a moment Veronica's face was in front of me, but then the present was superimposed.

'Make sure every easel has enough paper and all three kinds of charcoal. Some weeks the morning easels will be facing a bowl of fruit, other weeks it's liable to be my daughter-in-law. It's very important not to be put off or overwhelmed by...your subject.' I would come to think she wanted to give that advice to her son. 'As you know, I'd been thinking of getting an assistant in for quite some time. I don't want you to think this is sympathy. Because of...'

'I won't. I don't. I promise.'

'I do need to looking into getting an online presence. Perhaps that can be your project. Everything until now has been through word of mouth. My husband Gerald and I were among the founder members of the gallery and when they bought the little place next door and made it into the members' area, it was a logical development. But I'm aware it is dependent on goodwill, and while we survived the credit crunch and what have you...'

'It wouldn't hurt to take advantage of free advertising.'

'What do you mean?'

'Instagram. I could take photos of you teaching the classes, get a few pictures of the gallery, and the club room.'

'Would they want that?'

'If we ask them they're likely to be delighted. I already follow them on Instagram and Twitter so can tag them in my own messages, thanking you for another great class, that kind of thing.'

'I'm sorry? And this is all free?'

She was thrilled at first, going through my account, but then when she saw the gallery's it was as if she'd caught her husband cheating on her. I didn't think anything of it at the time, just reassured her all businesses use social media these days, that there's nothing fake about reaching out and celebrating what you have.

'And you don't have a problem with this? That you're using your photography and your words to do this?'

'I don't think it's fake. I think it's absolutely true. Real. Perception, reality, art, life, why argue about the division of which is which when you could be celebrating what you care about, and letting others know it exists too?'

I'd moved around the desk to show her my phone, with my back to the window so was no longer blinded enough to miss that she looked unconvinced. Or unconvinced was how I read it then. Looking back, what she felt was betrayed. She hadn't wanted ideas to enter the modern world. She'd hadn't wanted an assistant to help with the business, she'd wanted a fan, to reassure her it didn't need to change. Someone who'd fallen in love with her little world and wanted to keep it small, keep it itself for as long as possible and keep whispering into her ear that nothing needed to change. That was the kind of gratitude, of love, she'd have understood. And I did the opposite from the moment I sat down with the light in my eyes.

Effie stood the other side of her desk with her back to the window; the one wall that wasn't comprised entirely of bookcase. Shelves poked from either side of what there was of the light, framing the view of Gerald's dark red car – something expensive, something that suggested pleasure in driving, I never paid attention to cars beyond their colour – in the driveway on the other side of the glass. I sat on the guest side of the desks, looking up into the eyes of my teacher, my mentor, the person I most wanted to please. It never occurred to me that she was seeing someone I didn't recognise, projecting a whole inner life so thickly she couldn't see my face under her own interpretation. The minute I told her what could be done more efficiently, the minute I stepped beyond the help I'd needed when I first arrived, it was all but over.

To be fair to my not-so-much-younger self, the dust would have been less thick then, less thick by five years. But it had already settled long before I came. That's true of a lot of things I didn't understand about this house. I remember pushing away the thought of whether she did it on purpose, make the books heavy and unreachable as a reason not to read. Hers was on the top shelf, a straight of burnt sienna, exactly the kind of colour she never wore – not that I suppose that meant anything, except that Effie had escaped the book that did so well and made her a future Booker prize expectation and reverted to painting, which she was a minor historical note for. 'I was twenty-one,' she said if anyone mentioned it. 'It took an art degree to leave it behind. Who wants to have to do three times what they never wanted to do in the first place? Who wants that sort of pressure?' She'd say in in front of students who wanted to be writers as much as they wanted to be painters, and she'd say it in front of painters who—

'It's a Kerry-Alice Day.'

Vincent is standing in the doorway, smiling at me directly for the first sentence and, I know before he does it, will drop his gaze like an anchor and look lost straight after. I offer a condolence and he waves it away. I don't ask how he is. I doubt he knows.

'What have you been up to?' he asks.

I realise he knew nothing about my life then and doesn't now. I might as well introduce myself. 'Living just outside London. There's a wood at the bottom of the garden. It's great for painting. And I sell a few, in local cafes. That sort of thing. I work on social media for a little gallery in the village.'

'Sounds wonderful.' The distraction is still there, and I wonder if he's inherited from Effie the quality of feeling other people talking about themselves is a sign of disrespect. But then he says, 'I remember how very talented you were, how resourceful. How many ideas...' He trails off. It's so unexpected I find myself waiting for more. Until I walked back in today I'd have given anything to stay as we were then, frozen in flight, stuck to the paper this room was; now I hear I was seen then, my wanting to help, to serve and feel my usefulness did not make me a monster. I would have done anything to make her happy, and that was the one thing she wouldn't allow. She refused to be loved. And if I know that, her sons must know it too.

'Oh well,' Vincent says in the silence. 'It doesn't matter.'

'Take care, Vincent,' I say.

We look at each other for too long as he replies, 'I will.' Then he leaves, instinctively closing the door, and I am alone with her absence again.

The door blows open.

I'd like to tell myself I looked up to see whether he'd come back. But of course that isn't true. I am looking to see if Effie has come back. It's been five years. I thought I'd stopped looking for Effie.

Alright, no, I hadn't. I never stopped looking Every escalator. Every stranger's house or every blind corner of every street or corridor. Calculations of how many degrees of separation each of us is from everyone else, from the places and people that through no intention or with no particular care landed in her life. Resenting every stranger taking up a space in my life, even an extra at the back of the shot that wasn't her. Who might be an extra, or a main character, in the life I was written out of. In which I was forbidden to appear. The mix of loyalty and love and injustice is almost as strong as it ever was for anyone I loved romantically. Worse, perhaps. I'd taken her as a better part of myself and that love is the evidence for how guilty of betrayal she had every right to decide I was. 'I tried to help you,' I told the empty room.

You tried to be me, the silence replied in her voice. I know I'm just talking to, listening to, the voices in my conscience that I brought here with me. But they are loud here, they are so loud.

I tried to help you, I tell her. Even if she's not Effie, but my own version. *That's what you couldn't forgive.*

Did she think I was in love with her? Did mentioning there had been women as well as men mean she thought that was *all* women and men? Did the one woman in my past who I knew saw her all the time say something that would rip all their lives apart faster than mine? Impossible. That's not who Veronica was.

All I ever did was worship you and that was stupid, Effie, but it wasn't unforgivable.

I just wanted to thank her by getting her to see who I saw, when she looked in the mirror. But she never did. She just smoothed that unflappable blonde hair that always made me feel more like a human birds' nest, and with a perfectly manicured hand, as rich in time as in money, turned the subject back to herself, where we both agreed it belonged. My self-esteem, like all mediocrity, knew nothing other than itself and was meekly, idiotically grateful.

They are *all* exactly as I left them. Her living people, her dead moths. Gerald's steps echo on the study ceiling, only one floor above me, two above the studio. It's all still here. All except her. Just the world that revolved around her. I listen to his steps as I stare into the picture I thought I was mad to imagine five years ago. Each at its own angle, caught like a well-chosen or lucky moment's photograph of flight. You could see that if you wanted to. Life, an open sky. But the only thing surprising about that was they didn't decay. Her world is still here and she didn't appreciate it then, and I feel a rush of anger that she's died without me being able to show her with the course of my life how wrong she was.

Adam walks back in, mercifully incurious as to why in a room of books that frame a square of wall around a desk with enormous comfortable chairs on either side I'm staring at the moth paper. He nods at the only actual photograph, standing as proud in its frame as the moth paper does on its own stand; the one photo of her the room contains. 'Willow took that,' Adam said. 'You never met Willow. She's Vincent's godmother. They formed the company together. Mum bought her out. I never knew what happened. Didn't ask.' He looks up, and down, towards and away from me, exactly as Vincent had. He stands beside me, and looks at the moth paper. 'It's almost beautiful, isn't it?'

'I always thought so.'

He thinks for a minute. 'Fucking hell. Was that always there? The same dead moths?'

I nod. 'I remember the... constellation.'

'You must think we're disgusting.'

I turn to look, to see if he's serious. There's something so fundamentally little-brother about Adam, even now he has his father's high forehead and hint of extremely premature balding, that makes me wish I had one. 'I don't think that at all,' I say.

Adam gives a single quiet laugh, turns his scarlet converse in small toecap circles on the carpet. 'Look, I'm stuck here for a while...' he trails off. 'I could use a drink. And I'd like to know... about the person you knew.'

I can't see her. Can't feel her presence. We are absolutely alone in this room that she, not I, chose to walk out of. She's not in this room unless it's through him or me. And right now, I don't choose that. 'A drink would be great,' I say.

Fire Pictures

[2023]

~

'There's only one James the Fourth.' Veronica gives that trademark, tight-lipped smile over her port glass. Her careless ringlets fall like purple rain over her mesh-covered shoulders and sequinned vest below, nails tapping at the glass, swirling the final inch of wine as she leans back in the antique dark brown armchair Vincent remembers climbing on and falling off with his brother on a million indistinguishable family holidays. She is too vivid, too real, as if he's looking at her through an Instagram filter. Her amused disgust marinating in a compliment is as familiar as the gesture, fingers gripping and tapping, making the digits look even longer. Vincent has never been able to picture his ex-wife's fingers without acknowledging how perfectly they fit around his cock, and gets the instant erection he always gets when she does this. He's never told her, but he assumes she knows.

'It's been a long time since I heard that,' he says. 'James the Fourth.'

'Not so very long.' The fire beside them glows warm on Veronica's face. The dark green carpet, glass-covered bookcases, grand piano and mahogany fittings, the faultlessly realistic fire in the grate in front of them, the whole thing is deafeningly romantic. The patterns from the low light of the lounge make everything stronger, truer, better and worse. The fact she arrived at the hotel with someone else, and this is not a family holiday but the base for his mother's funeral is, according to his erection, utterly irrelevant. According to his erection, everything is perfect. 'I said it during lockdown, didn't I? Gerald James the Fourth. Mainly to annoy your dad. I know he loves it really. You and him, all those generations, one name…'

'Lockdown,' he says. 'I miss lockdown.'

Her eyebrows seem to darken as they scrunch. 'Do you? Miss it?'

'No, of course not.' Yes, of course he does. At least things were clearer. The spirit of caution, the suspicion a stranger's breath could kill, was at least in the open. Everyone still sees the masks that are absent on the faces of others, as clearly as they saw them when they arrived; everyone left wondering how unsafe it is to hug a friend, to look at a stranger.

But it does mean the hotel is entirely theirs. He's never known it so empty, thanks to people still not quite believing they're allowed to book again. Which merely feeds the lifelong sensation this place is his, part of his family. Which he only realised recently it was, once, before his father sold it. He'd still rather have lockdown back than have his girlfriend – if that's what Amber is – and Veronica's sleeping in rooms almost exactly above them now. *Exactly* above this barroom, if he remembers the geography – which he does, as well as he knows his own house. Lives entangled and separate, remote and mysterious. 'It's good to see you, Vee,' he says.

'You haven't changed, James the Fourth,' she says again.

'Is that why you're leaving?' Veronica is either flirting because it's what he expects, or because she wants something. If she wants something, it can only be to check she's still got him if she wants him.

'I've left. Remember?'

'Barely a week. It's clear from Mum's note she hadn't even noticed you were gone. Fast work by the way.'

'Chloé's been on the scene for ages. I told you about Chloé.'

'Yes, yes.' Had she? Perhaps she had. 'And you came back.'

'For this? Of course I came back for my mother-in-law's funeral.'

'Of course you did.' They were never officially married. But Veronica had shrugged ostentatiously to all friends, "I had the wedding with my first wife, I had a marriage with Vincent. Which would you say is more real?" He doesn't care what's true, not really, never did, just that she was saying it for all to see and believe. What was more true that that? No, God damn it, he didn't *need* to care what was true. True didn't matter. He'd never asked for her mind. Just for a life that worked. And anyway, there was no need to know what was objectively true. No one could ever know that. He was more interested in knowing what she was going to do.

'You never said what did change,' he says.

'Didn't I?' She slides her non-wedding ring up and down her middle finger, where it seems to fit just as well as it ever did on the finger he put it on.

'You just started fading.'

'Fading?'

'I know *when* it was. It was the night Cauliflower died. And Kerry-Alice was fired.'

'Was it?' She sits back in the dark brown swivel armchair, the one he used to pretend to be a Bond villain on. Is it his imagination, or is she holding herself stronger, colder, trusting the chair beneath her less than a moment ago? Her face has not changed, but it's set. She wants to know what he knows, or what he's guessed. It's not the same as wanting to be known, for herself, the way every other woman he's ever met wants, but it's enough. She's here. They both are. Surely that in itself is enough of a call to action.

'Vee,' he says, 'did you ever meet Kerry-Alice?'

She looks up too fast, with too much interest. 'That's a strange question, isn't it?'

'You were already living with us when she started working for Mum, weren't you?'

She puts the port glass down carefully on the table, then lifts it up again almost immediately. 'That sounds about right.'

'And I suppose you were out a lot.'

'I suppose I was.'

'I can't remember you being home on a single Kerry-Alice Day.' He's looking at the fire as he says this, and for some reason he can't bring himself to look up, as if he knows that, if he isn't looking at the ever-changing pictures in the fire, he'll see something far more dangerous, and he won't be able to unsee it. 'Anyway, it doesn't matter...'

'I suppose it doesn't,' Veronica says sadly, smiling into the port glass. She goes on swirling with the lightness and control of a cigarette, and that's when he knew there was nothing more to say, or at least no real change to make on the other side of it. She was gone again.

'I did it for you,' he says. He's speaking to her smile, and not to the deed he's just admitted. Fucking someone else. Proving his love for her, proving his vows of infidelity. 'Amber. The kids. You told me you didn't care.'

'Didn't care?'

'Wanted me to have other things going on. Other people. No, wait, not just wanted. Told me to.'

'And that's what – I mean that's who – you picked. You had sex with a peroxide millionairess—'

'Actually she prefers millionaire…'

'Lived the *Hello!* magazine dream, *for me.*' She drains the glass as he bashes the table. 'Only you, James the Fourth.'

'No, Vee, only *you*! No one else in the world would I… Do you think I have so little self-esteem that I'd have just bumped along with that level of compromise for just anyone?'

'Compromise.' The convincingly flickering flames dance on, reflecting its unfathomable patterns on her face. 'I offered you the world, absolute freedom, and you called it a compromise.'

'I wanted…' An explanation is the closest thing he can bear to an apology. 'I wanted to want what you wanted.'

'And did you? Ever?'

There's a new reserve in her voice, it arrived when he asked her if she'd met Kerry-Alice. And Vincent already knows, because it's a fact in the world, that something has been unwrapped, has changed, he's seeing a more real expression on her face than anyone else has been treated to.

And he doesn't give a shit. Because he never needed to understand anyone. None of that nonsense has ever mattered to him. He just wanted what he wanted, to live an undisturbed life, not hurting and not being hurt. And nobody had ever managed to explain to him what was so wrong with that. He'd never seen a ghost and he never expected to, like his mother seemed to see in every bloody room, every conversation. But he saw what was real, what was in front of him. That was more than most people did. If he could find his way back to not having asked that question, he'd take that path. But now this expression is on Veronica's face and all the portraits who've looked down on every version of himself he's ever been, pushing and being pushed by Adam off the revolving armchair, hiding behind the curtains, revising for his GCSEs, A Levels and university finals, writing and deleting and rewriting texts to a plethora of pre-Veronicas, seem to be looking down on them, as if they can hear incidental music around this moment that he cannot, because he denies such moments exist. Moments when there's a choice to be made, a moment to decide who all those versions of him are in the end.

'No. Never,' he says. 'I couldn't.'

'No,' she agrees. 'Because what I wanted was not one person, whoever that person was. Because that's honest. And all you wanted was to be my husband. And that's beautiful, Vinnie, it really is…' She looks at him for longer than she has all night, as if trying to see him for the first time. 'You know, I've always observed it's the things we fall in love with in the first place that are the very things that drive us bloody mad in the end. That send us running for the hills when the end is signalled. It's not about choosing men or women. It's about choosing absolute honesty. Your whole self. That's the truest kind of marriage and the only kind I'd ever believe in.'

All he says is, 'I never signalled an end.'

'But I'm right, aren't I? You found it refreshing how little I demanded of the real you. Of your mind. Vinnie, does it bother you that we never knew each other? That neither of us has any idea who the person we're watching this fire with really is?'

He looks back at the ever-changing flames. 'I can honestly say it doesn't.' How could it? He loves her. All possible explanations of her.

'No?'

'I knew what I wanted.'

'But not *who* that was!'

'Do we ever, Vee?' He's begging her to agree with him, can hear the desperation in his voice. 'How do you know the person isn't lying to themselves, being who they think you want them to be? Could any of us be totally clear on the difference, even if we tried?'

She gets up from the armchair, and walks to the deserted bar, taking off her platform boots before swinging over to the other side. 'I used to watch the clouds with Meg,' she says.

What's left of his erection disappears. Meg. Always Meg.

Veronica stares, focused, at the various bottles of port, and selects one he knows will be not a favourite, rather whatever she hasn't yet tried yet. 'I'd try to work out what I thought she was seeing in the cloud pictures and pretend that was what I was seeing too.'

He still wanted to be her husband. It wasn't about possession, it was freedom, safety, soaring above the world. He didn't need to know what she saw in the clouds, or what pictures she saw now, looking into that fire. He just wanted to make, and be, that choice. He walks over to where she's climbing back over the bar. She doesn't need him to help her down, but he offers a hand and out of charity she accepts it, gripping it until she touches the ground and not a moment longer.

'So what's changed?' he asks as her feet touch the ground.

'Nothing,' she zips up one patent leather boot and then the next. 'I suppose. Except...'

Vincent follows her back to the armchairs.

Veronica as his wife was the sexiest thing he'd ever imagined. He'd always been so sure she'd never be, or stay, anywhere she didn't want to. A bit like the cats. Utterly authentic in their objectives but not wasting words on what actions could communicate so much better. 'Do you really miss lockdown?' she asks.

'Full weeks went by without a conversation that wasn't about groceries, Radio Four or gas bills.' He is as much in his family bubble in this enormous hotel as when there was a legal requirement to be locked in the house together. His girlfriend sleeping upstairs, Veronica's... they weren't as real as the first story. That's what his mother had tried to tell him. Characters were more real when you believed in them more. You got to choose who that was. It was terrifying because choice was terrifying. His mother hadn't ever tried to choose for him, and God damn it the tears in his eyes were because he was never going to be able to thank her for that now, for the fact that they are all in one place again. The normalcy of that thought is electricity inside him. Like the smell of fireworks on bonfire night, like the primary-coloured lights on the trees outside the house at the beginning of December. Since Veronica had left, he'd allowed the remaining cat to walk around the room as much as it liked. Nothing woke him up, he was cursed with the accusation of being an insensitive sleeper. Except Veronica finally sitting up too fast, screaming about the fucking cat. It was the most emotion he'd ever seen her show and it absolutely terrified and, almost as much, fascinated him too. He only realised because she was on the verge of tears that neither of them had seen the other one cry. Did that matter? Weren't you supposed to be able to, to want to, share all your feelings with your partner? 'No, not really.'

The look intensifies. It's somewhere between pity and *I told you so*, somewhere between longing and relief. Whatever it is, he wants to call her back from the flames. Humour that doesn't quite reach the surface. His human cat. 'I think I started to appreciate that, living with people you didn't have to understand.'

'Did what for me, exactly?' she says, before he can work out what to say. She hasn't been listening to a word he said and even that makes him love her more. 'You said you did it for me. Did what for me?'

Everything. 'Oh, you did hear me?'

'Yes.'

'Well. Told my parents, for one thing. That you were free to do what you wanted. That you never betrayed me. That that was how we were.'

Something he doesn't understand passes across her face. It's light but heavy, reminding him of the manatee they saw only as an underwater silhouette on their one and only holiday together, to Florida. What did any of this have to do with Kerry-Alice? Had his mother known something he didn't? Is that why his mother got rid of Kerry-Alice? Something to do with Veronica? He decides not to bring it up in case she asks him what reminded him, and he somehow makes it sound like her face reminds him of a manatee.

'Well, anyway, Kerry-Alice won't be there,' Veronica says in the end. It's such an obvious subject change, and yet no subject change at all, that it seems unkind almost not to allow it. Petty even, when the art was so well practised. 'At the church, tomorrow.'

'No. No, she won't be there.'

He wouldn't ask how she knew that. He wouldn't. They hadn't talked to anyone else about what was in the note, although his father would have shown it to the police before he'd shown it to either of his sons. His father hadn't risen so confidently to where he was artistically and personally without very careful housekeeping.

'Kerry-Alice always knew Effie better than she had any interest in knowing herself,' Veronica says to the fire.

'Right.' And there it was. The confession. Veronica did know Kerry-Alice, and knew her a lot better than the rest of them. More proof Veronica was closer to everyone in his life than he was. He'd never talked much to Kerry-Alice, sensed Mum didn't like it and never asked why.

'I'd imagine that's why she fired her.'

The silence goes on far too long. Impasse, or check mate? And who had lost? He's lost whatever plot he had a chance of understanding, and searches for a subject-change of his own. Another example of self-defeating cowardice.

'I did know her,' Veronica says. 'I didn't know her name. It was one afternoon. Just before things got…' He feels her look at him for confirmation. He keeps staring at the fire, and she continues. 'I met her in that café that used to be a church. We never saw each other again, it was just one afternoon, and she was just like you Vinnie, if any *one* would be enough for me… I've often wondered…' She sighs. 'She was staring into space, trying to find her way back into her sketchbook. I was too selfish to realise what she was looking for was someone like Effie, not someone like me. And I suppose eventually she looked for what she needed.'

The flames continue, not dying down, not repeating. 'Do you remember,' Vincent says, 'that ghastly carol concert?'

'She nods. 'The year Adam had his post-university mid-life crisis and joined the choir.'

'And that violinist going nuts over some irrelevant kindness I had done her when I brought the instruments in from the car. And you taking so much pleasure in laughing at that girl from your row behind her when you told me about it, and her major attack of mention-itis.'

'What? Oh, yes. Vaguely.' She rubs a hand across the edge of her face, careful not to smear her eyes. He never sees Veronica look in a mirror; she always knew how not to need to. 'Why?'

He didn't have enough energy for this. The truth is what it would have to be. 'I suppose I remember it because it showed you could be jealous.'

'You think I wasn't jealous?' Veronica shrugs. She looks at the fire. Her face is blank again and Vincent would pay real money just to know what that meant, what that's always meant. If he knew what that meant maybe he could read the map of them, find what she wanted and how they lost each other. 'I was jealous, Vinnie. All the time.'

'Of me?'

'Maybe that was the problem. You were so… corporeal.'

'What do you mean?'

'Wherever you were, that was your reality. Like Cauliflower or Aubergine, really.'

'I reminded you of a cat?'

She smiles, a normal, human, unhidden, imperfect smile. 'Yes, I suppose so.'

'That's very interesting.' He watches the flames crackle, then when he turns to look at her she's watching the flames too. Perhaps he was right that they deserve each other.

'A lot changes in five years,' she says. 'Perhaps things have changed for Kerry-Alice. Perhaps she's realises there's more to life than what other people do with it.'

He opens his mouth to ask what happened between them. Instead he says, 'Are you coming back, Vee?' He watches the flames instead of her perfect face, not to give himself dignity this time, but to give her space. He doesn't care that the way he's phrased it admits he'd have her again in a heartbeat if she agreed, pick up exactly where they left off in a house that had changed not one bit, except that they had outlived the person who kept them unchanging and he, in turn, had kept her living in a teenager's bedroom that had never evolved as his career had. When his mother was alive he had stayed for her, by the time there was no avoiding admitting that he had in fact stayed to begin with; now that Effie was dead he would stay for his father but somehow the house had already doubled in size, they gave each other space in a way that was suddenly uncomplicated, and there was no more emotional contact than there had been, but there was also no desperation for it.

'Your dad wants to bring her back as a PA. He says there's no one better for it and he's right.'

'Did she accept?'

The flames crackle in the silence like the shreds of wood are gossiping or trying to suppress their giggles. Even the fire is laughing at him.

Somewhere from behind, Vincent feels a real-life mirror of an ancestor – not his father or mother, but someone who might as well be – fire an accusing stare in the gilt mirror over the mantelpiece, above the flames. He's very conscious of the eyes of every painting in the room. Why couldn't they have stayed in a Premier Inn, for God's sake?

'I could have loved her you know,' Veronica says. 'But she was in too much of a hurry. Or it looked that way to me at the time. Maybe she'd have been in less of a hurry if I'd given her a sign there was something to wait for.' She looks up, too quick. Either the mask slipped then, or it's slipping now. 'Or maybe I wouldn't. And maybe it would have been kinder, or not. Because there were other things you could have been doing. I haven't kissed her for years, if that helps?'

'It doesn't matter.'

'What doesn't?'

The fire crackles and they both stare into it, and he'll never know if the patterns he sees in there are anything like those she sees, and he doesn't want to think about that because it does matter, it does matter, everything matters and there's nothing he can do about it. And she smiles, and he's lost the fight with himself. He knows how he can have the closest thing to everything he wants, and it's right in front of him.

That smile.

Vincent lunges to kiss her. It's not the first time he's done that, but it is the first time he's done it with both their current girlfriends literally above them. And it's the first time he's committed adultery, and at a funeral. And that purple lipstick tastes exactly like it smells, he'd half forgotten that. Her tongue presses, challenges, explores. His hand is on her neck, the scar he remembers her nail tracing on their first date, here, before his father sold the hotel, beside this same fireplace. His fingers press into every corner, every version of their story. He is greedy for skin, greedy for history. For his to be the true version of Veronica and hers to be him. And whether Kerry-Alice or Veronica or both or neither will ever be part of his family again, in this moment he feels more certainly than he has ever had the skill to feel anything that they are all connected, and they always will be, and he wouldn't untangle his life from all the other lives that ricocheted at and off it for as many billions of pounds. 'Marry me,' he says.

'We are married.'

'I know. But marry me. For real this time.'

She looks at him as if trying to see what is really there. Perhaps she succeeds. 'Alright, James the Fourth.'

'Alright what?'

'Maybe I will.'

There is no sound but the flames, and the occasional moth sizzling in the light.

Adam's Chip

[2014]

It's just gone eleven in the morning. The tube carriage is fairly empty. Adam's view of the young man in the advert, eating rustic oven chips from a bowl, is as uninterrupted as it is malevolent.

The man in the advert looks about twenty-five. He's dark-haired, with a casual smile and deliberate stubble. He's holding up one of the oven chips, but his mouth is shut and his eyes are wide and focused towards the camera, like he's listening to someone. A friend? A girl? Someone, Adam knows he is meant to assume, of equal attractiveness to the man. Someone worth delaying the first chip for. Basically, he is the guy Adam (and, if the advert has done its job, every other guy on the District line) likes to think he was, or will be, at that age.

The slogan is something about guilt.

Adam is picturing how this man would look with his girlfriend.

Adam wouldn't say the woman he's thinking about *is* his girlfriend, but he's thinking about her enough to resent how much better this advert guy fits the bill. Adam thinks, correctly, that the girl is still at their university and, equally correctly, that she could do better. She has her whole life to discover.

That's the reason he is not picking up her calls.

He sighs as the phone vibrates again, and pushes his hand into his jeans pocket, searching for the phone. The removal of the self-consciously old-fashioned Nokia – which his brother found on Etsy and bought him as a joke, and which for a bigger joke he replaced his iPhone with – from his jeans creates a process that's a bit too anatomical. It wins a look of concerned amusement from the old lady on the opposite seat, beneath the man with the oven chips. He is uncomfortable about how small the result appears for the fuss of getting it out.

Adam looks at the caller display, diverts the call and looks back at the poster. About twenty-five. Adam is *about twenty-five*. It had started at seventeen and he'd hoped to be more ready for it by now. Back when getting into bars without ID wasn't a problem because he was always subbing for someone (any questions were answered with 'A pint, thanks' and a wave of his guitar case), and once inside you still behaved like you thought real adults – the older musicians, the regulars, the owners – did with all the lack of self-consciousness you could manage. Then, he already knew perfectly well, one day you woke up as one of the adults, realised how much better at it the younger guys were at it. At being an adult, not at the guitar. He really must pick up the guitar again. Maybe.

About twenty-five. Whatever he's supposed to be doing, he's supposed to be doing it right now.

The phone vibrates again, and this time Adam finds himself looking down at his home number. He presses green and starts the banal answers about where he's going and where he's been, listens to the pre-recorded quality to his too-quiet answers. It's not like she's listening anyway.

Barely has his set piece ended and his mother's begun when he's contemplating his girlfriend (not that she *is* his girlfriend) and how not to encourage this unsought, unsuitable, un*dignified* love as he stares into the eyes of the advert.

Adam hates the man with the oven chips.

He hates his tidy stubble, his un-tired eyes and his years and years of unsoiled *time*. If Adam had what the man with the oven chips had, he wouldn't need to be indecisive about sex and music and CVs, he'd just—

His mother has asked him a question; he can tell by the lapse in sound. He's already given it too long to blame fluctuating reception. The last thing he had wanted was to give her anything to think about. This problem wasn't hers. Her brief was to *do*: tidy things, cook things, fill in forms, ensure he remembered and attended doctors' appointments however much he snapped; in return for which all he had to do was stay where he was. There was no reason to leave. The luxury of largeness and familiarity, a floor to himself: why leave? There was no reason to do anything, anything at all, but stay.

It was, in every sense, the least he could do.

Adam blames fluctuating reception. They part in platitudes. The call ends.

The phone buzzes again.

Adam wonders if he'll still be looking at the man with the chip and going up and down from Embankment to Richmond when he is an old, old man. Forty, maybe. Even his mother's age.

Without a glance at the display, Adam diverts the call.

Routes and Branches

[2022 & 2016]

∽

'They're getting rid of the clocks.'

When Adam comes back from taking his father's phone call, his face reminds Kerry-Alice more of Effie than either son ever has before. It's the same face, now she sees it expressionless, retreated into that familiar mask.

He sits back down opposite her, a shoulder against the stained-glass window. He puts his phone down in the middle of the table and stares at it for a while as if he's trying to identify it. She doesn't interrupt. 'They're taking all the clocks down,' he says in the end. 'All of them.'

'Oh.' She tries to imagine the hallway without the clocks and absolutely cannot. 'Well, I guess it makes sense to do it before the estate agents…'

'No, I mean now. Today.'

'Today? Now?'

Adam twists his glass one way and back again. 'I think,' he says, looking into it as if from far away, 'I'm angry.'

Kerry-Alice tries to see the hallway as they left it. Which is easy, because it still looks exactly how it looked when Veronica first unlocked the front door. And the same as it did that last day too, when she slammed it. And under it all, from the first moment to the last, the gentle cacophony of marked time. 'When I picture the hallway, all I think is "clock-coloured."'

'Me too.' Adam picks up the beer mat, lines it up with the edge of the table, flips it in the air and catches it between thumb and forefinger without really looking at it. 'If I try all I can come up with is…clocks.' He spins it in the air again. 'And I lived there all my life.'

'So did she, right?'

'Mum? Pretty much.' He nods, his back against the stained-glass window. That, too, is as it was when Effie sat in that same chair opposite. But with Effie there was blinding sunlight instead of dusk. And with Effie, this perfect table – the one Kerry-Alice always drew at because it gave the best of everything, all the light of the outside and all the security of a wall behind your back, the space and support to the spread, the mess of ideas – somehow became instantly imperfect under her eyes.

Until that one moment, of course. Not the food itself, or the neatness of the plate on which Effie saw her own creation, but her happiness and absolute presence in that moment between them. She doesn't tell Adam he's sitting in the exact seat his mother had occupied. It probably wouldn't affect him if she did, but she doesn't anyway.

Effie had been so dismissive of Café Sanctuary. She'd made comments about religion's place in life and art not being the same as commercialism's place. She didn't call the café in the ex-church heretical, or Kerry-Alice a heretic for loving it. A deconsecrated church simply had no business selling coffee. So it had been something other than kindness that led Kerry-Alice to go over and chat with the manager, something she'd never normally have presumed to do as a regular customer. Now she had a job to do, it didn't feel like courage anymore. He looked surprised, and happy, and when she made the request, he enjoyed the challenge. Her performative self was able to be so much more natural than her natural one. The performance made this stranger she saw every week into a friend. He had looked so pleased as he worked, impressed at the strangeness of tastes as he cut the cucumber slices, spread the cream cheese. She had watched him from the table over Effie's shoulder, as Effie dismissed every suggestion she made to make the business more visible; it seemed that, although she'd employed Kerry-Alice to help, she was going to fight every possible change.

The peanuts and cream cheese circles had arrived on a willow pattern plate. Even Effie couldn't find a way not to be touched by that. She stopped talking about the past, defending it against the future. Looking at the secret recipe she only made at home, in the dark, on a plate, in public. Rainbows of light fell on the circles through the stained glass.

'I've never seen them in the sun,' was all Effie had said. 'I only make them when everyone else is asleep.' And she'd smiled. 'I only mentioned them once. However did you remember?'

And even with what happened after, Kerry-Alice would always know she'd made her happy, at least for a moment.

'Bet she didn't say thank you,' says Adam.

Kerry-Alice looks up, from where her eyes have been fixed on the same table she'd been at half a decade before. Had Effie thanked her? Her face had. No, Effie didn't say thank you. She wouldn't be Effie if she had. Who needed manners with a face that eloquent? She shakes her head, picks up her coffee mug, watches the table where the rainbows of light had played, must play again once daylight returns.

The smile wasn't shared long. The absolute presence she'd never seen on Effie's face before had shifted to suspicion and anger. But still Kerry-Alice could not shift from the reality on her side of the table: everything was perfect – Effie, the business, the world beyond their window – or so obviously could have been that there was no real difference. She saw only how brilliant, how beautiful, how *possible* everything was. How she would show Effie how right she was to have chosen her, how they would make the world (alright, Richmond) see what Effie's classes brought to the lives of her students. After all, wasn't that what she was being paid for? To help? If Effie didn't like the café, surely she'd like the ideas? The offers of new routes to make her business a success? Treating Effie and her business like a chrysalis in the idiotic belief she was helping her to change into herself.

Beyond the glass, the sun kept beaming, spilling its colours over the table, encouraging her to share more and more ideas, as if the right one would make Effie come out from behind the cloud again. The day was spreading out, moving under them like sun on paving. She half-remembered a line from Prufrock and didn't say so. Any allusion to literature annoyed Effie. Even now, in the honeymoon period, Kerry-Alice had already worked that much out.

But just as an idea would burn through her hand to a clean page of her sketch book, she simply had to ask Effie about the possibility some of the students had suggested of classes in the garden.

'Suggested to you?' Effie's glare was the first expression to make it through the mask. 'Why not to me?'

'Well, they know I'm your assistant…' Effie didn't show favouritism so much as reliance, expectation. And Kerry-Alice was proud of that. She'd happily cut the grass, she said. The perfect house, the perfect setting. The whole Effie show. It was all part of the brand.

'Brand? Kerry-Alice, I am not a brand.'

'But you could be! Such a great setting too. If you aren't enjoying things at the gallery then aren't there ways we – I – could make teaching even easier, it all being at home?'

And that was when she saw the mask where the face had been.

'When I say home, Effie, I'm just thinking as the business. You. I didn't mean…'

But Effie was looking out of the window, the silence eloquent and unarguable. Every cucumber slice was gone. "Home" had changed everything. The cloud cover was instant, decisive. It never left Effie's face that day – and there would not be many more days. Perhaps Kerry-Alice already knew that. She fell silent, stopped trying to offer help. The happier Effie was in the moment, the harder she swung back. There'd been a million should-have-been examples. She knew rather than understood the enormous error she had made with the use of the word 'home'. She knew but did not understand why more than the mood of the day was at stake. She realised in a creeping physical realisation that that happiness made Effie believe she'd left herself fatally open.

'To what though?' Kerry-Alice wipes her face with the last of Adam's tissues. She whispers the next words to get them past her brain fast in the hope of not making the table wetter. 'I never knew.'

Adam doesn't answer. Not unkindly, just with the gentle shrug of someone who had stopped believing understanding helped anything long ago. 'I'm sorry,' she says to Adam again as he passes her another tissue.

'It's alright,' he says.

'I don't have the right to… she isn't… wasn't… my…'

'Mother?'

And now she really is crying, the inability to form words an eloquent confession. Whether he knows his mother's accusations or not, he knows the appalling truth. That Kerry-Alice had never been so happy as when she felt like a part of that house. And to tell Adam this would look like asking for something; it wouldn't be gratitude, like telling Effie how happy she was to be in the world that day wouldn't have come out like gratitude. All she'd ever wanted, was simply—

'She wanted what you wanted,' says Adam, reading her silence and getting it right. 'A daughter figure. She just didn't let herself want it. So she punished you for wanting it too.'

Kerry-Alice stares at Adam, where he sits so comfortably and effortlessly in Effie's chair. 'You know she always wanted me to be a girl?'

'What? Why? I mean… how do you know that?'

'One of each. I think if she'd let us all be friends then she would have had to realise how much she was grieving for… you not being hers. So we just hung around there. Like on the moth-paper.'

'Yes. Like art. Already framed.'

'I never saw a living moth,' Adam says conversationally. 'In the office. Just the dead ones. You think she liked them? Artistic value? She normally hated all that dead stuff. You know, Warhol… is he the dead stuff?'

'Hirst is the dead stuff. Warhol is the banana.'

'Right. Right.' She can practically see the information fall out of his head again as soon as it's in. Its unimportance is suddenly very refreshing. 'But art for, basically, art's sake.'

'Well, yes but…'

'Art's. Not for beauty's.' When she doesn't answer, he shrugs. 'Maybe it was for some other reason.'

Kerry-Alice nods, but she's lying, so she shakes her head straight after. 'I'm sure it's to do with the books. When she decided she didn't want to write anymore, I think she broke a contract… I think if anyone really thought they were more powerful than she was, they didn't stay in her life. People had to love her, but not too much.' They watched the flow of strangers past the window. There were as many stories and as many ghosts in all these connections and disconnections.

'I'm sorry, you're the last person I should be talking to—'

'She never said why she fired you.' Adam picks up the beermat again.

Kerry-Alice looks out of the window again. 'She said I was seducing one of you.'

'Which?'

'All three, I think. You. Vincent. Your dad.'

'Wow. God. I think I'd have noticed if you'd tried. Wouldn't I?'

'I'd imagine so. So would my boyfriend. And girlfriend.'

Adam opens his mouth with visibly no idea what is about to come out of it. Then they finally get served and Kerry-Alice asks about fruit ciders and they have a politeness stand-off about what to order and who's paying before they take the drinks back to the table.

'Ex-boyfriend,' she says. 'And girlfriend.'

Adam takes an extended gulp, puts the glass down on what's left of the beermat he's been spinning and says, as if to the mug, 'Yes'. He looks at her for a moment too long, then himself in the mirror behind the bar for even longer. Seeing them together is something he seems to like, and he looks away quickly in case she'd spotted him liking it. 'I followed you that day,' he says.

'Sorry, what?'

'This probably isn't the time to say it. But I wished I'd said it, all those years you were a ghost. For us. Gone, I mean. It was that day Cauliflower died. I saw you on Richmond Green. I knew it was a Kerry-Alice Day, but there you were. Alone. Walking. You went straight past me, just before the street where the Rabbit-Hole used to be. You looked as if you... weren't there. Paying a bit too little attention on corners. I walked behind you to your bus stop, just in case... I don't know. And then the bus came. And then I guess...'

'That was it.'

'I would have asked. Except, we never saw you again.'

She presses a palm to the stained glass, wonders when it was fitted, how many services and coffee orders, apparently important conversations have come and gone, people lived and died, the window remaining unchanged. 'I'm sorry, Adam.'

'What for?'

'I still don't know.'

Under the blazing sun on the other side of the window, lunch-hour traffic congealed on Richmond high street. A bus pulled up level with the window, and Effie looked at it for too long, some of her entrenched anger falling away from the wall on her face, giving way to present interest.

'It's one of those they hire for weddings,' she said, like Kerry-Alice was too young to know what a Routemaster was. 'I used to watch them when they were real buses, think about how many times I could see my past selves in every seat, standing at every point at every handle.'

A small boy in an uncomfortable suit pasted his face to one of the windows. He saw them looking, and looked back with the absolute lack of apology of a cat.

'I've been ten on that bus,' Effie says.

'Oh yes?' Kerry-Alice is grateful for the small-talk she's always been so bad at. At least it's talking.

'Yes. I used to look out from that window,' she pointed at his, 'to this one.' Her unvarnished nails and dry palm pressed the window. 'And I'd think about every time I went from the house to the town and back again, think how I was sitting next to ghosts of myself, the ghosts we're always going to become. And the journeys that have already ended.'

Kerry-Alice could already tell which today was, but was staring at it too hard to know how to change a thing.

'I always imagined taking a picture of myself in every seat on the bus, through the three years of travelling into university and out again, past the road I never saw, let alone knew was going to be mine. Every day. Well, almost every day. I moved out for a year. Then Gerald and I moved back.'

'I moved out for university,' said Kerry-Alice, and Effie got that look of inconvenience, of a liberty being taken. So Kerry-Alice drove her side of the conversation off the road and waited.

'I don't know,' Effie said after a while, eyes still on the bus in the traffic, 'but I think I believed I'd truly seen it at the time. The...'

'Ghosts?'

'Versions of myself.'

The ten-year-old on the private, ribboned Routemaster waved to them as the lights changed. Kerry-Alice waved back, and Effie's face grew its darker layer of being inconvenienced again.

'All the eras of a life,' she said. 'One bus. One road. Imagine if you could see them all at once.' She stood up. 'We have to go. I need to find an exact kind of tea before the shops shut.' She left too much cash on the table, snapped her fingers at Laurence, who looked up at Kerry-Alice with politely concealed humour as she apologised with her eyes, and left, Kerry-Alice running after her, as she would for as long as she was permitted. It came as no shock when Effie brought up the word "home" when she fired Kerry-Alice not so very many weeks later.

'I wanted to help. And I couldn't see anything else. Anyone can see the future, Adam. I couldn't see the present.' She shakes her head and doesn't look up.

'The cat liked you more than her,' he says.

She laughs, and it lets out the tears that have already formed, to stop any more from forming.

'The cat was never wrong about people. Mum often was.' She could hear the warmth in it. 'She never told us what happened,' he says after the next cider.

Kerry-Alice smiles at him, at his cider, at hers, scratches her nose. 'I can tell you what I think did.'

'No, it's alright,' says Adam. 'You'll just make it all your fault when clearly it wasn't, it was hers. She hated that about you.'

'What?'

'Kindness. If there was one thing to try and be then that was it. But you never had to try.

Kerry-Alice decides, entirely selfishly and unkindly, to tell him, the very moment before he asks the question.

'Tell me what happened. After the vet left.'

'This is not your home,' Effie said.

Kerry-Alice leaned against the edge of the counter, the kitchen that backed on to the painting studio on one side, the French windows to the garden on the other. Everything around her was entirely familiar and suddenly she was alone in it all. 'I never said it was.'

'You said it was! And now you're lying to my face about trying to make my life into yours!'

'Effie, I apologise for anything that's made you feel that's true.'

'Don't patronise me, Kerry-Alice.' She wished Effie wouldn't use her name anymore, the only person who said it like it was itself, and not two misfitting pieces of a name. The only person who made her feel seen hated what she saw. 'It's very clear I've been giving you quite the wrong messages. You are an employee. You are an employee of this family, of this house. You are not a member of this family.'

'I know that, Effie, I... I never thought anything different to that.'

'You didn't let me finish. Let me finish. You never let me finish.'

'I'm sorry, I thought you had...'

'Be quiet, Kerry-Alice. You might learn something. I had thought that was why you were here.'

'It is. I mean...'

'I had thought it was because you wanted a job. Or was I wrong?'

'You weren't wrong.'

'I know I said the intention was that you could work beside me, but your intention is obviously to take over the company, that is clear from how snugly you make yourself fit in with my husband and sons. You need a sense of propriety in dealing with men, and your elders, and you simply do not have it. I'm sorry I didn't make it clear.'

'Is this because of Cauliflower?'

'You will not!' She banged her fists on the table. 'Mention. A single. Member. Of this family. They are my sons. My husband. Mine.'

The sketchbook she banged down on the table opened at an angle. There was a dead moth pressed to it.

'You do not get...' Effie raised herself up to her full height, and even then a part of Kerry-Alice marvelled at the optical illusion, that Effie's height was really no more than confidence, '...to walk into my life and take it for yourself like scraps of meat. I've seen the way you and he look at each other—'

'What? Who?'

'How you find any little excuse to call Gerald down from his office.'

She could feel the shock on her face, feel Effie reading it as guilt. She'd never been so embarrassed by anything as she was by how much safer and happier she felt with a grandparent figure like Gerald.

'Vincent doesn't need his head turned again.'

And of course that made her face burn for a different reason. Veronica had not betrayed her. She'd always wondered if Effie knew why Veronica was always out on Kerry-Alice Days. All Kerry-Alice said was 'I got Gerald down once when the toaster caught fire. I didn't when Cauliflower was put to sleep. One time Gerald and I arrived at the kettle at the same time. At Christmas he saw how lost I felt and he talked about the cheese counter in the supermarket, told me he'd never felt richer than when choosing a cheese plate. Putting the tastes and shades together in his mind, developing the perfect colour scheme for his family and moods and how sorry he felt that you could never feel that happy.'

'You expect me to believe you talked to my husband about cheese?'

'You don't know anything about me.' And that was where she should have stopped. Except she didn't. 'Or him. You never wanted to.'

'Don't presume to tell me what I…'

You never wanted me to be anything but a blank canvas for you to imprint yourself on. Damaged and desperate for a repaint. And now you scream at me for seeing yourself when you look in your own mirror. Now, please decide if you're angry because I couldn't read your mind, or angry because I did. You're angry because I tried to help you, because everyone liked me, because I like you more than you know how to like yourself. Take your ghosts and your moths and please put today's fee as a tip to Natasha.'

'Natasha?'

'The vet!' It was the only time she'd raised her voice, and she only knew she'd slammed the door when she heard it.

Adam flicks the beer mat again. 'You were trying to help.'

'Thank you.' She isn't seeing Effie's ghost in Adam's seat. She wouldn't swap this familiar-but-new friend. Whatever power Effie had over either of them, it's become a choice now.

'You didn't just, you know, try less hard.'

'Like you all did.'

'Yeah.' A scattering of conversations overlap one another, over the beat of something Britpop she never liked yet instinctively knows the words to. A moth flutters briefly around a table lamp, thinks better of it and begins to throw itself at the smear of someone else's coffee at the bottom of the pane.

'How did it start?' she asks. 'The clock thing?'

Adam glares a little at his pile of beer mats. 'There was a new clock every Christmas. Usually more than one. Friends saw how many she had so thought she wanted more. She resented everyone for it. But never told them. Wouldn't let us tell them either. One year she just looked at me and said, "If they really liked me, they'd have known". Hey, you did it.' He congratulated her on the pile of beer mats she'd barely noticed herself flick.

'You taught me well.'

'Nah, it's all you. You observe, like an artist. Hey, in return for the beermats, do you think you could show me that fast-apply thing on LinkedIn? And all the other social media stuff? I'm not sure I want to live in the house forever.'

Kerry-Alice held her hand out, and he unlocked his phone. 'Effie didn't want to know about all this stuff.'

'But I do.'

Yes. Adam did want to know. Adam was a version of Effie that Effie had fought against, held back. From her husband, her sons, her would-be friends. From anything she didn't control. Which eventually meant her future. *Damn you, Effie*, Kerry-Alice thought. *You could have been sitting here. We could all have been so happy.*

'You're great at this stuff. No wonder she was threatened by it.'

'To anyone else it would have just been help… but not to Effie.'

'No.' Adam scratched the side of his nose again, and looked up and left the way Kerry-Alice had seen Gerald do a billion times. 'Not to Effie.'

'Did you call her that? Her first name? Not Mum, or anything else?'

Adam contemplates the window, the light flow of other people beyond the stained glass. 'I'm not sure I called her anything.'

They look back at the darkening street beyond the window. Outside, a bus pulls up in the traffic, and it's almost certainly the lack of light, but the silhouettes look for all the world like a thousand versions of Effie and herself. But she doesn't ask Adam what he sees and anyway, isn't that just what every other human being is? There are so many other stories to tell.

'What was the book about?' she says now.

'Sorry?' Adam asks.

'I never read it. Your mum's book. She kept all her copies on the top shelf. I knew she didn't want me to read it. Have you read it?'

'She didn't want me to. You?'

'I never did anything she didn't want me to. Not then.'

'Look, it's only those whose lives you take for granted whose details you don't care about. You know there *are* details, but only death or another pedestal elevates them from boring to need-to-know. My relationship with her was secure, a lifetime of entitlement, no thinking at all. And here we still are, existing in our own right, independent of her. You're who she wanted me to be. Of course she had to get rid of you. She could only control how much she loved us. So she controlled that.' Adam sits back against the cushions, with all the appearance of not having a care in the world. 'You don't need her permission.'

'For what?'

Adam smiles, but directs it at the lights beyond the window.

They talk more about the day that Cauliflower was put to sleep, how nice the vet was (Adam had met Natasha the second time, for Aubergine, when the time came). How Kerry-Alice's mother was as keen to call her Kerry as her father was to call her Alice, and that it told you everything about the passive-aggression of compromise that the answer was to do both; how she made a point of telling different teachers different names, even got a detention for lying when they didn't understand both were true. When they lived in different homes it became easier to have different names, but only with Effie and her family did it feel like an organic word, a concept that was herself for the first time. 'It was you all, not just her, who made me feel like me.'

'You are,' says Adam. 'We're all tangled at the roots. There's no untangling. We wouldn't know ourselves any other way.'

He holds up his glass and watches her comfort and amusement at the thought as she clinks her glass against his, the light bouncing off the connection of two identically made objects, in completely different colours and in all directions.

Effie walked ahead, too fast and too angry, playing the weather off against itself. They were overtaking the traffic, windows shining the street back at itself. Only Kerry-Alice looked up at the bus when it passed them. But she's absolutely sure that's only because Effie chose not to see.

Kerry-Alice's feet stopped of their own accord, before she had properly looked through the window.

As Effie ran too far ahead, Kerry-Alice saw: full versions of herself and Effie, and future possibilities. All together, one era on top of and beside another. A thousand different possible selves.

But Effie refused to look, and Kerry-Alice ran after her.

Nine Lives

[2023]

Megan still has the dream where she and Ian find that corpse of a fox in their garden. It's always Ian who buries the fox, because he's brave at things like that. In their conversation over the burial it becomes clear to Megan in exactly the same way, every night, that she isn't ready to acknowledge Ian's lack of bravery in other departments. 'What you have to understand about Geraldine…' begins Ian's every sentence about Ian's choices, and Megan tries to argue when, even in her dream, she knows she would be doing her sense of reality a bigger favour by noticing this instead of arguing with it. And she feels sorry for herself, in the dream, as she would for any other person in whose head she is a well-meaning but silent observer.

But the Megan inside the dream, like the Megan outside it, cannot see anything beyond the rich line of red pulsing over the lump on Ian's left temple where Geraldine had thrown his phone, cannot see beyond elementary good and evil: that bullies are baddies, that baddies must – will, if your heart is good and strong – be defeated.

The little idiot. She can't believe how recently she was her.

'You'll understand when we have children,' says the Ian in the dream, the way she heard him say when they lived together – like she was a child herself. As if reproduction was like reaching an important birthday. As if a woman without children was – like a pupil who might well be eighteen but hadn't finished sixth-form yet – a child, in the eyes of any real adult. 'Dennis is my child,' she replies in the dream, every time. Megan has never loved a man like this, and that love allowed her to want children in a way she never had before. But Dennis changed everything. Dennis was real in a way that nothing else was. When Geraldine had thrown Ian out of the flat they shared

– different bedrooms, Ian had sworn to her, in a way that let her kid herself that was ever the point – Dennis had come too, a pair of quiet green eyes, jet black fur and a face that read into your soul and selected you to become his…

'Monkey-butler,' she mutters as she wakes.

It wasn't her word. It was Ian's. Or rather his son's. The stepson Megan never had. She hasn't had the dream since the death of the child who didn't have a name, other than "Dennis's little brother or sister". It was around the same time the foxes started coming to the garden. She cannot look at a fox without thinking of her dead baby and ex-husband. So why had burying their cat alone – no, not alone, of course not alone: Seth was there, but "alone" was a word she had the right to, didn't she? The right to think of as meaning "without the man who'd asked to be my husband"? – why had that brought the dead fox right back?

'This, Dennis, is absolutely not…' Megan lifted her vase and swept a cloth across the kitchen table, '…by any stretch of the imagination…' she removed the faded irises and upended the dark water into the sink, '…a date.'

The water gurgled down the drain and she turned her attention to the rest of the room. The kitchen was starting to look like a kitchen. Like the one she half-remembered was presumably under there somewhere, beneath the piles of sketches and half-finished sewing or hemming of vintage dresses that made the place a recognisable reflection of her. It was even starting to shine, something she'd never done herself and didn't particularly see why a room had to. She wasn't keen to shine, but she supposed it didn't matter if the kitchen did. Maybe that was the safer way around. Just as she made costumes for other people and never for herself. But the tidiness and shine of the kitchen just made the echo of her voice alone in it all the more obvious. 'It's just a chat. And dinner. Dinner and a chat. About you, obviously.'

The pool of silence echoed around the words she'd dropped into it. Each word sent out a brief ripple, whose waves dissipated all too quickly.

'I should probably stop talking to you,' she said to the empty room. 'I mean, it wasn't even normal when you *were* here. Was it?'

As long as she'd known him, she'd told everything to Dennis. Even Seth, her best friend and glittery-jacketed all-but-brother since high school, didn't come close. There was only one Dennis.

The secret of why it had worked – and, Megan privately considered, the reason any successful friendship worked – was she didn't expect Dennis to fully understand. That was something she'd tried to pass on to partners, and had only really succeeded with her first, who'd dropped out of her life when Ian came along. Probably because they were friends, at their core. All the heartache, she was so sure, came from unrealistic expectations about subjective experience. There was no God, no objective truth, people didn't have to understand you or share your feelings about everything. Or anything. True friendship between human beings – true love, if she was honest – should mirror that between Megan and Dennis. Dennis was never bothered he didn't fully understand her. He fully listened when she talked to him, and let her find her own way through whatever the problem was. And only yelled at her if she was too busy sewing to remember it was time to eat or sleep.

A tear slipped past her defences, escaped the corner of her eye. Damn, she'd got lost in the story again. No point in that. She dabbed quickly, against the tear, against the bright summer greens and cold marble greys of the headstone that were as fresh in her memory as Seth's arm tight around her shoulders. 'I don't even believe you can hear me, Dennis. And I'm still talking. Isn't that the saddest thing?'

And if he was, she reflected, if Dennis were here – quiet green eyes shining with wisdom and patience, in that way that went beyond the need to say a word – she would never have been in this situation anyway.

With enough people – and cats were certainly people – packed into her life, today would not be necessary.

In fact, it was Dennis's lack of loyalty to her, like everyone else she'd ever cared about, that caused all this. Ronni had realised how driven and boring Megan was. Ian had realised she'd never push him to stay like Geraldine would, never convince him he didn't have a choice. Everyone had a choice, with Megan. And everyone chose to leave.

A beep sounded from everywhere and nowhere. After the microwave and the cooker and her phone and the smoke alarm, her own wrist was the last place she looked. 'Right, so the alarm works.' She pressed enough buttons that one of them made the sound stop. 'But it can't be time yet, can it, Dennis?'

It was. Five to seven, five minutes before her neighbour of nearly a decade, who she'd nodded or smiled at hundreds of times in passing and each time instantly forgotten, would cross the boundary from his driveway to hers. She'd mostly got the tray ready: avocado and tomato penne with dairy-free parmesan, a recipe she'd tried out a few times back when she and Ian first bought the place. There hadn't been much call for that recipe after they started making their meals separately. A life-long vegetarian, she'd tried so hard back then to get Ian excited about the tastes she loved. When Luke mentioned he was vegetarian too, the recipe had flashed into her mind and given her the courage to suggest all this. She'd never had the luxury of cooking for someone who wouldn't see her favourites as a compromise. It was good to have an excuse, after all this time. Still, she wished it was any other excuse than Dennis.

She'd only just slid a foot into the gap of the French windows when the buzz of the intercom filled the kitchen. She placed the tray on the patio table, and leapt back up into the kitchen and through the hallway. In her mind – only in her mind now – Dennis looked up with that soft glare of his in the direction of the outside world that had dared to interrupt. She smiled at the memory of him all the way to the door.

Behind the frosted glass, the shape of Luke's thick, dark hair was surprisingly near the top of the door. Had he really been that tall? She remembered confidence, but had been too nervous in their short conversation to record much else. In ten years, there had never been a reason to notice. She opened the door. There was the familiar stranger, looking down at the bottle of wine in his hands with a perplexed expression, like he wasn't expecting to see it there.

'Megan.' He smiled over the edge of his dark green glasses-frames, as if peering out from a place of safety. 'Hello.'

'Luke. Hi.' She opened the door wider. He stepped into the hall and looked around. 'So,' his voice was quiet, calm but full of friendly curiosity. 'This is where he called home.'

'Well, I'm sure he thought of your home that way too...' She turned her back, walking quickly to the kitchen to put their plates on the tray and collect her thoughts, which seemed to be only able to form themselves around questions. It wasn't just the clumsy way of immediately addressing what they were both here to talk about – Dennis's double life – but the embarrassment of it. She wanted to demand he hand over everything he knew about Dennis. Everything Dennis had seen, heard, done without her. She also, inexplicably, wanted to apologise. 'Do come through…'

She felt Luke move past her, through the gap in the French windows, and turned to watch him place the bottle he'd brought gently on the patio table.

'I'll bring the glasses out…' The blur of the short conversation on his doorstep was difficult to replay. She was surprised to find she'd forgotten how good looking he was. 'I wasn't sure if you'd want to see… it, first? Or eat first?'

'Let's go and say hello,' he said. 'Then we'll have plenty of time…' He seemed to look at her too long, catch himself off guard. As if he'd only just noticed her in her own light and not Dennis's reflection. 'Time to talk.'

'Of course.' She led him across the grass to the bottom of the garden.

The soil patch was a deep, earthy brown under the late afternoon sun.

'Hello, old friend.' Luke bent over the marble gravestone Seth's partner, a set designer for a tiny theatre above a pub they'd once taken her and Ian to, had sculpted for her in their workshop shed. She couldn't even remember the theatre's name. But there was the photo she'd chosen for the little frame. Dennis's bottle-green eyes and coal-black fur, the unapologetic gaze with which he seemed to read your soul stared out from under the words "In loving memory". They stood for a few moments and then, as one, made the silent decision to walk back up the garden to the patio table. She found herself talking about Seth's boyfriend's career in theatre, as if both to make herself sound interesting and, on ancient autopilot, to make it clear she were not the significant other in her significant other's life. She always had to tell people that, for some reason. She'd hoped it was to do with not giving the wrong impression, but she wasn't sure right now what the right impression was.

It wasn't even a date. The only person who'd used the word "date" was Seth, on the phone, and only after he'd checked out Luke's LinkedIn profile, and Instagram, and made sure he wasn't on TikTok because that would be too far. Seth, being an actor, was doing what he did best, living a vicarious imagined life through every conceivable character. But that was nothing to having a real double life, like Dennis had. Everyone lived vicariously except her. They all put their vicariousness into action too, leaving her far behind.

They started with the Instagram account Dennis had in his bigamous life as Lucky. That was run by Luke's daughter. She obviously had an eye as a photographer. Apparently, though, she got very angry if anyone said that. When Luke told Megan that, she caught herself thinking she'd just failed an audition as stepmother. Not a healthy thing to think twenty minutes into a first date – which obviously this wasn't anyway.

'Tell me about him.' Luke leaned his elbows on the table as she poured the wine. 'Tell me about his life.'

'Where to begin… Probably with Dennis's real dad, Ian. Not that you're not…'

Luke waved a dismissive hand. 'In here, I'm not. Tell me about his life as Dennis. I'd love to hear.'

So she told him. How Dennis had been Ian's cat really, not hers. As she did, for a moment she saw Dennis on the doorstep in Ian's arms, barely more than a kitten, Ian telling her how Geraldine had "thrown them out" as seemingly truthfully as he'd told her for the three years they'd been together that Geraldine didn't see herself as his partner, that they still shared the flat for financial reasons. Then he'd moved in, and moved out, and in again, until finally when he stopped coming back, or she stopped letting him – it had been hard to see the difference in the end – Dennis had stayed. She and Dennis were together longer than she'd been with any man. And she wasn't bringing that up with Luke either. Where, then, if not the beginning? She stared at Dennis's photo on the grave, those eyes, waiting and trusting her to work it out herself. 'I suppose I'd better begin with the funeral…'

'Do you want to… you know, say a few words?' Seth asked her quietly. His arm tightened around Megan's shoulders as she shook her head, a fast, small gesture that did nothing to shake the watery blur that was the warm greens of her spring garden and the grey, black and brown of the marble headstone and freshly dug earth.

'No.' Ian should have been the one to speak. But Ian, true to form, had a terribly good reason not to be there. When Megan first got together with Ian, one of the things she'd been most excited about was meeting his son. Then she'd learnt Greg didn't know she existed, hadn't known about any of the girlfriends Megan had known Ian with during their decades of friendship. All Megan ever knew of Greg was that he looked a lot like Ian and a lot like Geraldine and that he'd inexplicably named a kitten Dennis. She shook her head again. 'He knows. He always knew.'

Seth led her into the kitchen and made jasmine tea in the designated herbal teapot. There were eight teapots on the shelf and Seth always picked the right one. While the kettle boiled he looked from it to her, as quiet and patient as Dennis would have been.

If this was a delayed reaction to all the humans who had left her, that was a massive disservice to Dennis. Why should he be any kind of consolation prize when he'd been nothing but honest with her, valued his own space, never flattered or made false promises, truly never let things that didn't matter get in the way of what did – their life – from a haircut (he still recognised her, nothing important had changed) to a change in government. 'If cats' needs came first,' she said aloud, 'there'd be no threat of nuclear wars, no global warming or the need for things that cause it. We'd all sit on the sofa reading books and watching them wash their faces on the corners of the pages.'

'Yeah, I still think that was gross, the way he did that.'

'It was, kind of, wasn't it. Until you stopped noticing.' She remembered when he'd arrived and the first time he'd sat on her lap when she was reading, the way he'd lick the corner of the book, move the corner of his eye onto it and start scooping off the sleep. 'He was part of everything.' She wiped her eyes. 'In the best way. I know how soppy that sounds. I know every cat's special. But Dennis gave me so much. Not everyone gets that lucky, you know?' He reminded her to eat, even if it was just because that meant she sat on the sofa and he sat on her. He reminded her to sleep, even though it wasn't so he could sleep on her. But he only went to his special armchair in the bedroom when she went to bed. They had their own lives, but those lives worked in tandem. She would not change a thing. Except for Ruby-or-Richard, who she imagined in the spare bedroom, on the kitchen calendar, in all the space no one took up, in asterisks on calendars no one would ask about, even there had been anyone to ask. How old would Ruby-or-Richard be now? She didn't count so exactly these days. She used to know to the day without the calendar's help. But Dennis was real, he was real and straightforward in a way her secret life, the one only she could see, never would be. Even if it was truer than her real one.

'I know.' Seth brought the pot and mugs to the table, re-enveloped her in a hug and a familiar, safe cloud of aftershave, the same one he'd worn since school. Seth was not an animal person – so he frequently said – but as he sat down beside her at the table was she imagining the smallest tear-like splodge at the edge of his guyliner?

'For some people it's never like that. It wasn't with Percy, the one my parents got when I was at university, or even with Snowdrop when I was a kid. Or Sooty in the shared house. I loved them all, and it's different every time, but Dennis…' She wiped her eyes again. 'Dennis was…'

'Dennis was the one.' Seth smiled, in that way he had of making things totally un-embarrassing. Things made sense when Seth heard them.

Nodding was all she could manage. But she mentally blessed Seth for understanding.

'Thanks for giving him a good send-off with me.' She held up the mug of jasmine tea Seth had poured for her.

Seth held up his. 'To Dennis,' he said. 'I bet you made this the happiest of all his nine lives.'

'Thanks Seth.' She squeezed his hand. 'You're the best human friend a person could have.'

'I'm no Dennis.' He smiled over the lightly steaming mug.

'No.' She clinked hers against it. 'But you're the best a human could get.'

Spring was really making itself known when she said goodbye to Seth at the door. 'Sure you won't stay for a drink?'

'Not on a school night.' It was what he'd always say when he was teaching acting at the local high school the next day, but she could tell why he was really going. He wanted her to rip the plaster off, to learn as soon as possible that being in the house by herself was something she could do. He'd done the same thing when Ian left. As difficult as that was, it started a rush of anger now. Ian had chosen to go. Dennis hadn't.

Although it was nine thirty, it was as bright as an afternoon as Seth got onto his motorcycle and she waved goodbye. She couldn't help noticing the familiar shape of "lost" posters on trees and lampposts. Someone's beloved pet who hadn't come home. She hoped animal and humans found each other again. She closed the door.

Waking up the morning after the burial was the worst. She'd known it would be, but hadn't quite realised why. It wasn't because of remembering what had happened. Not really. The worst thing was the moment before you remembered. That bit where you still didn't know, with the return of consciousness, what you'd lost.

She pushed herself up from the pillow, eyes wandering to the gap in the curtain where there always used to be the possibility of a pair of green eyes looking back. Or, if not the eyes at the window, then a stalking black fluffy line moving around the grass below.

She pushed her legs over the edge of the bed. Everything felt too big. The bed, the rug, the dressing table. The space around her body. The gap on the surface of the vanity desk where he used to sit and watch his nemesis, next door's tabby, over the garden wall, tail flicking with controlled aggression. She moved from bedroom to kitchen without the pressure of hungry eyes boring into her back. She could still feel the way he used to stare at the kettle when she clicked it on in the morning.

But she had to go to work. Books didn't sell themselves. Especially these days.

She used to enjoy choosing coats from the stand, used to watch his ears flick at the sound of her keys falling into her pocket. Used to watch him stare her all the way to the door, in a way that felt for all the world like appreciation, like he wanted to remember every detail of her even though he knew she was coming back.

She walked down the driveway and turned into the street before she saw the posters again. Or not the posters themselves, but the one visible word in capital letters, visible all the way down the street. LOST. 'You don't have to tell me,' she muttered.

The tabby's owner was just coming out of the tabby's house, walking the opposite way to the way she was going. She nodded, and smiled, and so did he. Ludicrously, infuriatingly, the world went on.

LOST, proclaimed the next tree.

She was starting to suspect her subconscious was shouting something. She half knew what it was before she retraced her steps.

LOST, proclaimed another lamp post.

She retraced her steps a few paces, but all she saw was the familiar empty street. With a shrug, she turned back towards work.

She gasped. Every one of the six trees ahead, lining the street all the way up to the corner, had a picture of him. A cat that looked identical to Dennis was looking back at her from a white A4 piece of paper in a plastic file attached to every tree.

No, not a cat that looked identical to Dennis. Dennis. A photo of Dennis on each tree, each lamppost. Dennis's, looking up at her out at her from the past, from someone else's bottle-green sofa. "LOST," the poster screamed. "BELOVED FAMILY PET. ANSWERS TO LUCKY…"

'Meg,' Seth was using his teacher voice, calling her by the name she hadn't used since they were teenagers. It was the name he told her off in, the voice he'd used when he was head boy of their school and she was trying to argue extra time inside at lunch for sewing club, correctly suspecting that without him she'd be with Ronni on a roof somewhere. 'Don't do this. Dennis is gone. There's nothing to be done. So what if Dennis had a whole other life? That's over too. And you weren't part of it. Let this family grieve in their own way.'

Megan tried to focus on the book cover design on her computer screen, but was more concerned with whether the assistant whose desk faced her glass-walled office was looking over at her. She hadn't listened when Seth used that voice on her at school; she wasn't going to now. 'But that's what you don't understand.' She pushed her fingers against her temples, tapped a fingernail on the cold plastic of her wireless headphones and tried to keep her tone quiet and measured enough to sound like a work call. 'They can't. That's what I'm worried about. False hope is just the worst. You don't understand that living in hope, when I never knew when Ian was coming back or leaving, or the two days Dennis was gone before I checked under that hedge…' She stopped herself going any further. The words would be the pictures, and the pictures meant tears. You didn't let yourself cry like that in an office with glass walls.

'You can't know that.' Seth's voice was crackly over the mobile. It might have just been the reception.

'I can.' Her own voice was still low enough to blend with the bubbles of the water cooler between her office and Sophie's desk. But the assistant had definitely looked up. She could see the movement out of the corner of her eye. Stupid glass walls. She got up from the desk, went to look at a bookshelf, turned her back to the glass partition. 'I do. I know. It's him.'

'Did you take one of the posters?'

'What decade do you think this is, Seth? All I had to do was take a screenshot. Hang on.' She walked back to the computer, brought her photos up on the screen, signed into the messenger app and texted the picture of Dennis – or Lucky – to Seth.

A short beep sounded at the other end of the call. 'What I'm looking at,' said Seth, 'is a black cat.'

'You're looking at Dennis.'

'I'm looking at black cat. A black who lives with a local family…'

'Look at his left ear.'

The silence was longer this time. She tried to picture Seth's face as he zoomed in, recognised the little tear from that one round with the tabby five years ago. 'Oh.'

'Right.'

'So, Dennis had a secret identity.' The disbelief in his voice was totally new. A bit like the certainty in hers. 'A double life.'

'I know. Wait, hang on.'

Sophie was knocking at the door that was a full-length window. 'Sorry, Megan, is this a bad time?'

She softened when she saw Sophie's genuine worry. 'No, no of course not. I just…'

'I heard about your cat. I'm so sorry. I know it's awful when people say it gets better over time…'

'Yes.'

'I still think about mine. I know there's nothing I can do, but if there's anything you need…'

'Thank you, Sophie.' She smiled, and meant it, totally, for the first time since Dennis had died. She really was starting to feel less alone in her grief for Dennis. But it wasn't her assistant's words as much as that stranger's picture. Before she picked up the phone again, she knew exactly what she had to do. For some people who cared about Dennis, maybe people who cared about him as much as she did, the story wasn't over. And Dennis's story was her story too.

The plan did not involve going round there. Not immediately. The plan had involved a friendly but respectful note through the door. After that, it involved careful, well-planned and well-chosen words. Above all, it involved time. For the family to adjust to the probability Lucky wasn't coming back. For it not to be a total surprise to see a total stranger, looking sad, standing at the front door. They needed to have lost hope in a slower, kinder, sadder way. A normal way. Only then would it be even slightly okay to inform them of their cat's death and – Megan couldn't help thinking the word – bigamy.

What she absolutely hadn't planned to do on a Thursday evening, for goodness sake, was walk half way up her own driveway, turn round and march next door. The family might be eating. And who, Megan found herself asking for the twenty-seventh time as she walked up the mirror image of her own property, was she to knock brazenly on the door of the house right next to hers, when the five years since she and Ian had bought what they'd said would be their place forever hadn't involved so much as a note to say hello? In the plan, she'd put on enough make-up to look like a professional. This house – number twenty-seven – had the same reflected glass in its door as hers, which wasn't clear enough to check her fears about her post-rush-hour make-up, and she had no watch to check if it was as early in the evening as she'd assumed from the light, or whether they'd be eating. They had kids, didn't they?

But then the door opened, and she had to start talking before she had time to panic and apologise and leave. In the plan there'd have been no reason for the look of bafflement on the face of the suited man who answered the door, looking as harassed and baffled and unprepared as she felt. She was doing well until the silence. The silence was long enough to think, which meant it was long enough to worry. She didn't give herself long enough to read the man's expression, or guess the age of the children she saw drawing at the kitchen table beyond the hallway behind the man with the dark hair and the tired, confident, welcoming smile.

'I'm Megan. I live next door. I'm afraid I've got bad news…'

'And then what happened?' Seth gazed over the table at her, in what looked like a measure of being impressed somewhere under the disbelief.

'And then I told him.' Megan swirled the final inch of their traditional Friday lunchtime white wine at the bottom of her glass and scooped the remainder of the feta salad half onto her plate, half onto his. 'And it was horrible. The way he just kept asking, "Are you sure?" over and over, and not quite hearing what I said because… you could see him thinking, Seth. He knew I was right, that it was true. Or maybe it was just that my make-up was smeared from rush hour, so I looked more like I'd been crying. Actually, it's the first afternoon since it happened that I haven't been.'

'Good.' Seth reached for the bottle, chucked it gently onto the newspapers in the recycling bag. 'That is good, right?'

'Right…' The grave that had been such an active reminder had become a peaceful lunch companion. There was nothing sad in that, not sad in the throat-closing, world-swallowing way it had been. It was sad but it was life. She was starting to understand what death being a part of life really meant. Dennis's life had been a happy one. What more could anyone ask? 'Good. It'll certainly make tonight easier. Or, at least, I think it will.'

'What's so special about tonight?' Seth asked, sharply. She knew that tone of voice. Seth had an almost psychic ability to detect heterosexual relationships on the horizon, rather than anything more useful to him personally.

'He's coming round.'

'Who?'

'Luke.'

'Who's Luke?'

'Dennis's other dad. He's been Dennis's other dad all this time, it seems. Even when Ian was living here. We did the maths. Their kids, Andy and Rebecca, were already in bed. But Lottie was there. She's his ex-wife, lives down the road. He was sad for Dennis but he was sadder for what he was going to tell the kids. I made it really clear it was old age…'

'And it definitely was the same cat?'

'The dates match. Lucky – that's Dennis's name at number twenty-seven – appeared in their lives the week Ian and I moved in. You remember I told you how he disappeared for three days the first time he went out? After those first days under the wardrobe when we'd moved in? That's where he was. Curled up by the fire. Luke showed me photos. Bex even made Lucky his own Facebook page.'

'Bex?'

'Rebecca. Luke's daughter. She's going to be fourteen next Saturday.' She clingfilmed over the rest of the feta. 'That's why he's so sure he has to tell them now. While there's still some chance the events won't be linked in her head. Her birthday and her pet's death.'

Seth's eyes widened. 'Dennis had a Facebook page?'

'*Lucky* had a Facebook page. And Instagram. He even had a Twitter account. The works. I think he might be doing better on social media than my company. Anyway. That's what we're going to talk about.'

'His social media?'

'No. His life.'

'When? What do you mean you're going to talk about it?'

She lifted her empty wine glass from the table, peered in just in case she'd missed a bit. 'I just told you, Luke's coming round tonight.'

Seth's eyes widened even further. 'A date? You're actually having a first date with Dennis's other dad?'

'A second funeral is not a first date.'

'Are you getting booze in?'

'Of course not!' She toyed with the bottom of her glass.

'Why not?'

'Because Luke's bringing wine…'

'It was the idea of us being linked through him.' She could feel the tears in her eyes as she told him, but they didn't seem to matter anymore. 'That there were people to remember him with, who loved him as much as I did. Look.'

Megan held up her right hand, tilted the oval tigers-eye stone she always wore. 'Dennis used to love scratching his chin on the corner.'

'Like he did on books,' Luke said, watching the stone.

'Yes.' It glittered, black and red and gold, its own colours brightened by the surrounding light. 'You know how people say cats don't care who their staff are as long as the jobs are done? Feeding, stroking, changing their litter? When I came back from holiday, and he'd been looked after by friends, he always walked towards this ring for a chin-scratch. Even if it's self-indulgent, even if it's not the same as a human friend, it's still a one-off. We were still important to each other. I just wanted to hear about other lives he'd touched.'

The phone rang, and for once she ignored it. There had been a couple of texts too. Ian did this every so often: remind her how much he loved her, how if he was free he'd be there, and what she had to understand about Geraldine. And as she realised for the first time in her life that she could improvise, that she was free to make up the rules of what her life would be, it all seemed so absolutely obvious. From when she and Ronni were children, and Megan used Ronni to pull herself up, and the noise of Ronni's crying had scared her so much she'd toddled out of the room and never liked roller coasters, scary films or loud noises, it had been about what other people had thought and what other people might do. And maybe she had loved Ian for the reason that he made all her fears come true, made her believe that you had to be other people's version of you, and if you did that properly, if you made that as real as it could possibly be, then one day you'd be rewarded with the right to your own life. Well fuck that, maybe being Megan was enough. Maybe being Megan meant whatever she wanted it to mean. There would be no Geraldines for her, ever again.

'He had a third home, for a while,' Luke said. 'I never met them. He gave up on them when his stepbrother died, it turned out. A grey Persian. Extra-long hair. They must have spent all day brushing it. The youngest son is a friend of mine.'

She was looking into Luke's eyes as he said it. Even when she didn't say anything back, neither of them stopped looking.

'Well, you know what they say,' Luke said after a while. 'Nine lives.'

'Sorry?'

'Every cat has nine lives. You don't need to believe in reincarnation, just look at him and us. As Dennis he had you, Seth and Ian, and as Lucky he had me, Lottie, Bex and Andy. Nine lives. All his own.'

'You're right.' She smiled. 'He was surrounded by so many people who loved him so much. Lucky Dennis.'

'Yes. Lucky Dennis.'

She heard her smile echoed in Luke's voice, and followed his gaze to the sunset, beyond where the trees that backed off the end of her garden locked arms and touched fingers with the trees of his and, at the edges of both their gardens, with those of other strangers, a story that carried on through fences, branches and blades of grass in every possible direction. The sunset over all of this had more colours than she'd ever seen. 'And lucky us.'

'Yes. Lucky us.'

Twisted Branches

[2017]

The filter turns the branch a darker brown, shades the moss a deeper green. There's a richness, a chorus of textures, that Daniel would never have known was there without the filter. But Kerry-Alice must have seen it, its potential at least, to know which filter to use to bring it out.

'People think photography is straightforward, point and shoot, like aiming a gun,' he says, which isn't what he wants to say. But awe is such a turn-off to women.

Their steps are soft crunches on the woodland floor.

'You mean that's what you thought?' She's teasing him now.

'You have to have an eye. I don't have an eye.' Daniel has only ever seen what was in front of him. That's why he's been trying to stop himself saying things like "Was that really today?" or "I didn't notice that" as she flicks through her phone as they walk, and she's just nodding, never berating him, her polite silence and his unspoken thoughts roaring together over the crickets and birdsong. She'd never have taken the A-level without his encouragement, all that time ago. He hit the first domino. In that much, he helped create those images of those trees too. He has that much right to be proud of them.

'It's… it's like, narrowing the gap, between the thing in your head and the thing in the world. The thing the audience sees. Just like theatre.'

'Sure. Yeah.' Her mention of theatre is charity. Her world of photography and art is nothing like his. Drama isn't art like painting and photography are art. Drama requires an audience. Kerry-Alice only requires herself to make her work meaningful, real. Or she did, until recently. Something has changed, and he's as much in danger of asking what it was as asking whether she wants to break up.

A black-brown speckled streak of dark eyes and dull feathers shoots over the path and it brings him back for a moment, long enough to exchange a smile with his girlfriend. Kerry-Alice. An adult woman. And him an adult man. In a wood. In "her wood", because every house on that street backs on to a patch of wild. He feels real, scriptless, for the first time in his life. Is this really the day he sets her free?

'Sparrowhawk?' he asks.

'Kestrel.'

'Right.'

She starts walking again, and he falls in line. Nobody needs a permission note. That's all long gone. Neither of them are doing anything wrong. Yet that time feels very real today, very close. He keeps thinking of opening the conversation, the one he can feel they are going to have. Is it his job to release her? Or is that patronising? They are equal, aren't they? Both adults, now?

'We used to call them "wind-fuckers",' he says.

'Who's "we"?'

'Society. Elizabethans. Shakespeare would have called them "wind-fuckers".'

Why the fuck is he talking about Elizabethans? Why is he asking himself why he's talking about Elizabethans? Does everybody live in these onion layers of reality, or is he the only idiot?

'"Fuck" was a perfectly acceptable verb before it was elevated to a swearword,' he hears himself continue.

'Hmm.' She's lying too. Just like he is lying with trivia, she is lying with silence. She isn't really here today either, even if nobody else would know. She'd been a good actor, but it wasn't that actors make good liars. It was the opposite. You told the truth on stage. The hard thing was adjusting to the rules off it. You were supposed to work out the right layers of lying in every conversation, all the time. She could have been a wonderful actor. The truth came so naturally to her. If he asks her what's wrong she'll tell him. But he doesn't want to know. Because he's a coward.

They come to a stop, initiated by her, and he looks down to see why. It's a dead wood-pigeon, head pointing into the bracken so its features are invisible to them, fluffy and soft and new as a child's cuddly toy.

'It's so clean,' she says. Her fingers are still, not twitching over the camera as they would be if it were alive. 'So perfect. Kind of looks like it's just come out of the washing machine.'

'What a waste,' he agrees.

'Just shows. What you see as healthy and what is actually healthy are no guarantee of...' There are tears in her voice, and he looks up from the dead pigeon to see if he can spot them in her eyes. 'Danny?'

'Yeah?' He isn't really Danny. Never has been. Danny was a person he made up when he wanted to tell her not to call him Sir anymore. He invented the nickname on the spot, and she'd unknowingly and unthinkingly made it real. She hasn't commented on none of his friends calling him it. Not once. If she breaks up with him then that name, that side of him, will be dead.

'Something's happened.'

'What?' Here it comes. Neither of them has said this might be their last walk. What they had said was that it was New Year's Day and lovely – alright, bracing – weather and they might as well go into "her wood" as look through the window at it. 'What's going on?' This is it. It has to be. She's going to tell him who she's leaving him for.

'My boss.'

'You love her?' It comes out too fast, and she laughs through tears like he's made a joke. This doesn't feel like what he was waiting for. He wants an enemy to put the insecurity on.

'She hates me.' The tears are coming faster now. But actors know how to focus, to catch their attention on the fishhook of their objective, stay in the moment rather than let their brain drive off the road into the abyss – as he used to say to his classes, before the headteacher told him not to talk about the abyss anymore. But the hook was your boundary, as sure and real as the boards beneath your feet, supporting you. It was the greatest life lesson drama school, any school, had taught him. No awkward choice to be made about whether or not there is a floor; no choice about your focus either. It simply was. A boundary was not an opinion, it was a fact, leaving you to glide, confusion sliding like water off feathers, over the obstacles and forward towards the objective. Kerry-Alice had heard all this in his class but now it's fading in front of him, as he understands implicitly that he is the obstacle. So he doesn't take her hand. He keeps very still, the way he'd do with any child in his class, giving them the absolute focus that kept them talking and kept him distant, separate. Letting them listen to their story. It's easy, doing the right thing in this situation, like sliding into a familiar pair of slippers.

'I don't know what I'm doing wrong.'

'Who says you're doing something wrong?'

'She misread something,' she sniffs. 'Last Christmas. Cauliflower, the cat I got on with. He leapt on my lap on the sofa at the Christmas party, and I couldn't move. And her husband stayed and talked...' Her hair is falling over her eyes. She pushes it away but doesn't change her posture, so it just starts to fall forward again, identically. 'I saw her face, when she came in and saw us, laughing at a private joke, and I felt so guilty, and I saw her see guilt on my face... I thought he'd explain it away. I should have known she had written her own version in her head, she'd see disrespect and betrayal when it was all about love. Appreciation. His. Mine. For her.'

'Right,' he says. *Women*, he thinks. *Onion rings.*

'I tried to do everything she needed. I made that strategy plan, what kind of posts to make when, and every week she hasn't done them. And the more I suggest taking photos at the gallery, or at home... at her house... she gets this frozen look as if I'm overstepping.' But I'm doing what she wanted. I don't understand. She said she should have done all this years ago. What I'm trying to do for the business. I don't get it. It's like she hates me.'

'Of course she hates you.'

'What? Why?'

Daniel waves his arms at her, the wood, the dead pigeon, the world. He remembers that first year, how he'd shouted at her for not wanting to take her bra off. For not enjoying and being defensive about gifts his previous girlfriends hadn't had. Alright, he hadn't said that bit. But she's never got it, how beautiful she is. How much of a waste of energy she put into what other people – idiots like him – think of her. Sometimes Daniel has to leave the room rather than deal with how little she knows of how beautiful she is. 'You want to understand things. For them to be what they can. She just wants to tell them what they are. You made the plan she couldn't begin to make, showed her how to do exactly what on her own she'd call impossible. People like you, instantly. You understand them, appreciate them, and they shine.'

Kerry-Alice shakes her head, stares at the dead pigeon.

Most of him is in the old drama studio, the first time they played the Trust Game. She'd been in his class several weeks before they played, but the time Daniel thought of as when they met was when he put himself at the centre of the trust circle and said, 'The game doesn't work unless someone's willing to trust. And look how many of you there are. No one catches me alone, so as long as you all concentrate there's no danger." And didn't it just have to be at the one moment the least unfocused teenager in the room joked "Concen-what?", just as a reply to one of the other students, that they let him fall, nose first. It was exaggeration rather than lie, but it had hurt like buggery. And she'd been so apologetic, white with terror before he laughed it off and she changed to red with humiliation. But that was almost a decade ago, and she was scratching at the edges of being the kind of adult he had never had any interest in putting the work into becoming. The kind who believes in her own responsibility for how others throw themselves at the ground. He remembers the parents' evening, each parent calling her by a different name.

She'd asked him over and over again if he'd meant to fall. If the intention was to teach them something. "You'd never believe me if I say it was, you'll never believe me if I say it wasn't," he told her, over and over again. And she'd always look away, and he'd realise the reason she didn't believe him was he wouldn't know the truth of his own thoughts if it bit him on the arse. Other people's needs had always been far too real for that, his own not real enough. His daughter said something similar. She was convinced what he was doing was wrong, and the only thing he knew for sure was the vehemence he saw in her emotion. Maybe that was how the religion he still quietly missed worked on people too. Maybe that's what his ex-boss had meant in the pub, raising his glass to a relationship he was never supposed to know about, once A-Levels were over and everything else had begun.

She'd never even had the kind of what-does-everyone-think vibe he thought was in the contract for teenagers. Not back then. Weren't they supposed to obsess over who knew and what they thought? But on her results day all that happened was the rest of the drama group looked away if she hugged him a little longer. It was a year before they were out in the open, and he'd resigned from the school rather than put anyone in an embarrassing position. He ran into the head teacher in a bar years after, and the headteacher had asked entirely genuinely how Kerry-Alice was. He was so virtuous even the faculty he would otherwise have so embarrassed only felt sorry for him.

'You didn't do anything on school grounds. Did you?' was all he asked.

'Oh God no,' Daniel had said. 'The guilt was bad enough…'

'What were you guilty of?' his ex-boss asked.

'Falling in love. Leaving my daughter.'

'How old was your daughter then?'

'Twenty-eight. She lives in Tashkent. Why?'

And the headteacher had smiled to himself, raised his glass and said 'Enjoy your "guilt", young man. Do give my best to Kerry-Alice,' and walked off humming something Catholic and sad that Daniel half-remembered from his childhood. He was disappointed she didn't want to be an actress but could see – or, rather, couldn't see – what it was she saw in the leaves they were walking over. The things she looked at and truly saw.

He'd seen that boss of hers once. They'd stopped to say hello to her in Richmond, in all her Edwardian cut-glass glory, and what he remembered was how nervous she was, how brittle. Like she had to show up as the character she'd been told to play.

He'd also seen the girl Kerry-Alice met in the café. Whether that was the lover, or a friend who knew the lover, he'd instinctively known this was part of the secret life Kerry-Alice needed, the fuel for what she was missing out on by falling in love so early.

'Most people don't want to change,' he says. 'They want to be told they don't need to. If you want her to love you, to trust you, give up on her.'

'But that would be a really selfish love.'

'Most people only understand that kind. They don't recognise any other.'

She starts to look up from the pigeon. 'So she does hate me.'

'That's how some people do respect. And friendship.'

'I was so ready… to start sending off my pictures.'

'What does that have to do with anything?'

She looks up from the dead pigeon, meets his eyes. 'I don't know. I suppose I thought…'

'She was the gatekeeper? She owned art?'

'Perhaps.'

'Print five. I mean, I'm not telling you what to do. But if you print five, take them to the café on the High Street, offer a percentage on sales, he'll put them in the café, and then it'll be real, won't it?'

She's still looking at him. 'It's too near.'

'To her? Richmond existed before she did. So did you. Stop waiting for permission. You didn't need it from me, you don't need it from her.'

And when Kerry-Alice hugs him it is as the old friend, the mentor, he could have stayed if they'd taken the shallower path rather than, through no fault of their own, fallen in love and waited and done all the right things in the right order. 'If adulthood is anything, it's deciding who to be of your own free will, not letting your own ghosts be more real than the people standing in front of you, and who you have the chance to be.' And in the comparative silence of her wood he knows he was absolutely right to love her and would never stop for a second, even when he tried his hardest. Maybe this was the love of his life, and he hoped he could be proudest of it in letting it go; it was the least he could do if he wasn't ever going to let it in.

And he realises that he doesn't have to be noble. He's not ready. He's not letting go. He knows that too. If anything is going to change, it isn't now. It should be the end. But she doesn't want to blame. She wants to understand. Daniel wishes it was because she loved him. Really it's because she's a photographer.

They take each other's hand, again, at the same time, and he knows nothing is going to change today. It's nobody's fault. They've just grown that way, intertwined. It's not his fault. It's just nature. She is going to leave him. Or he is going to leave her. He's sure about that. But not yet. No one has to make a decision today.

Plastic Tree

[2016]

It was the moment Christmas needed nothing more from him, rather than Christmas itself, that Gerald always looked forward to. That was why the big party happened on Christmas Eve, so Christmas Day could be as much relief as joy. Just them. But first, everybody. He leaned back on his default side of the sofa that divided dining room from lounge, facing the ludicrously small television Effie refused to let him replace despite it predating half the generations in the room. Close family and distant relations moved through the mulled-wine-saturated air, talking above each other over the gentle music. There was a completeness to the house each Christmas Eve, contained and celebratory, colourful and busy as tropical fish in a tank.

The small girl by his feet was watching *Labyrinth* on the tiny television with the sound turned down, not that it particularly needed to be silent under the volume of conversations filling the room. One bejewelled, shiny black shoe rested against his loafer in unselfconscious comfort. Gerald wondered if his oldest son being the child's all-but-stepfather made him her all-but-grandfather, and wished Vincent had reminded him of her name. Either of their names. The mother was somewhere in the crowds behind them. Both had been strangers last Christmas Eve. Gerald looked briefly at the Christmas tree in the far corner, but that was a thought there was no use following. He looked away again, back to the screen.

The film had got to that bit Vincent and Adam used to demand to watch every night. Gerald hadn't seen it for decades, probably wouldn't remember the words even if they weren't muted, but the action was as familiar as any face in the room: Sarah did not believe in a way in. She shouted how unfair everything was, threw herself to the ground outside the maze, and stumbled into a friendly conversation with a caterpillar, who politely suggested not taking things for granted. Sarah lifted her hands to the apparent brick wall and found herself moving through it. The way in was wherever we needed it to be, and always was.

Of course, all the boys saw was the furry caterpillar.

'It's the worm bit.'

'Worm. Indeed. Not caterpillar.' Gerald looked up, smiled as his youngest son perched on the arm of the sofa. He did not remark on the traces of crisps in Adam's stubble. You didn't get to do that after a certain point.

'You used to say he was the most important character.' Adam nodded at the screen, unselfconsciously pushing the crisp crumbs from beard to carpet.

'For the young viewer, I'd say he is.' Gerald moved his leg ever so slightly; the child's foot followed without her eyes leaving the screen. 'By his own value system, he's absolutely right. And honest. But he also happens to be taking for granted himself, that she wants what he wants. To stay away from the castle, rather than to find the way in. All while telling her to take nothing for granted.'

'Deep,' Adam said, as if that were a criticism.

Gerald settled into their silence over the noise; himself, his son and his potential granddaughter, Sarah walking deeper into the maze, and the sense of all simultaneous years piled one upon another.

He followed his youngest son's line of vision to the mantelpiece, where Effie's cousin's nephew with the enormous cobalt mohawk and sparkling leather jacket (Seth, was it? Steve? Simon?) was positioning a mirror in the shape of a postage-stamp Queen. A strange gift, but perhaps no stranger than its neighbours. It was between Effie's teal ceramic clock and the ship in the bottle he'd had given her as an anniversary present some recent decade or other. Gerald's eyes ran along the mantelpiece: the Galileo thermometer he'd disliked so much when it arrived, the miniature Egyptian cat Vincent had fallen in love with in the British Museum gift shop that led almost directly to their buying the biological ones. His paintings on the walls beside his wife's. Those struck him afresh every Christmas Eve, when he put himself in the shoes of those for whom this was not so normal as to be invisible:

his and Effie's combination of contrasting styles, of creative successes, was the collaboration to be proudest of. He smiled at the girl at his feet, and she, sensing she was being looked at, turned to regard both of them.

'I like the worm best,' she said, and turned back to the screen.

On the screen, Sarah was listening once again to the advice of another well-meaning and overconfident man – this time in the shape of an angry troll – about how to get where he told her she shouldn't want to go. At least this one was rude enough that it was obvious he was wrong. 'Who else do you like?' Gerald asked.

'The doggy. But they don't find him yet. Mummy likes the man in the tights.'

Adam and Gerald smile at her, and then at each other. The men of the family never shared the contents of their mind aloud, but there was always plenty of evidence they didn't need to.

'There's Kerry-Alice,' Adam said, and Gerald looked not at his wife's assistant, but at his son's face. He'd already spotted Kerry-Alice, or at least her hair, over various shoulders in a gap between his and Effie's old university friends. Kerry-Alice was one of those people who enhanced a room. Knew how to ask questions. Genuinely interested in other people who were, of course, genuinely interested in themselves. Look for where the party was going best, where fewest people felt obliged to pull rank and show off, and there you would find Kerry-Alice, asking the right questions and listening to the answers. She would be such a good influence on his wife, if Effie didn't find a reason to get too angry with her first. Kerry-Alice was exactly the sort of person Gerald wished Adam would notice. 'She seems to like it here. Working for Mum. Doesn't she?'

'Yes. Yes, she seems to. Adam,' Gerald began.

'Hang on. Phone's ringing.' Adam retreated into his own head, clicking buttons on the Nokia Gerald had been so sure was a joke stocking filler when Vincent bought it. Adam was as addicted to that as Vincent was to his smartphone. Gerald looked over at the sofa, where Vincent and the mother of the child at their feet were engaged in parallel conversations with relatives even Vincent was unlikely to remember. The poor girl.

'Adam, have you spoken much to...?'

He looked from the girl to the mother, and watched Adam consider the question, which was as close to a request for an opinion on his older brother's choice of partner as family vocabulary allowed.

'No,' Adam said. His eyes moved to the Christmas tree. 'Has Mum noticed…'

'No.' Effie still hadn't spotted Veronica's best and final Christmas present to her former family. Even as they boys brought it down from the attic for its second year, Christmas Eve marking the anniversary since Vincent and Veronica – how instinctively Vincent-and-Veronica still tripped off the mental tongue – smuggled in the fake tree in and quietly decorated it from the usual boxes as if nothing had changed, before Effie could notice why the needles would never fall. The only reason needles never fell: because they weren't real. Effie was always so angry when the tree was removed and the needles stayed. And Veronica, who had been sensible enough to give up trying to help in any practical way with the things her mother-in-law loved to complain about, realised the only way to improve Effie's situation was not to be caught improving it.

'Who will Mum blame? If she does notice?' Adam asked.

Before Gerald could answer, an unrealistic laugh covered the length of the room. Vincent and Adam's Uncle Charles was an acquired taste, and Gerald was still working on it. Married to a distant cousin of either his or Effie's, he was not, Gerald thanked God, a biological uncle. But like the Galileo thermometer on the mantelpiece, the association was too longstanding to truly dislike. When feeling charitable, he reflected the man sounded like someone who had learnt laughing through observation, believed it started outside the body rather than in the mind. 'Does, um… need saving?'

'Amber, her name is.' Adam indicated Vincent's new girlfriend. 'And that's Jane.' He whispered the last bit, but the little girl looked up anyway and he smiled back, allowing himself for a moment to experiment with the idea of being someone else's memory. How many more of these Christmases would there be? Would Jane remember this when she was an adult? Would this sofa and this screen exist within her own layer upon layer of indistinguishable Christmases? Would she remember the old man on the sofa whose shoe she leaned against when she watched a film, itself older than her new father?

'Jane,' he said. 'And you said the mother is…?"

'Amber,' Adam repeated. He looked at the tree again, and at Vincent locked in a conversation next to Amber that didn't contain her, leaving her without escape routes from Charles and the laugh. If that had been Veronica, Vincent would only have been pretending not to listen to her conversation over his own. Even if it was with Charles. 'The important thing is to give it a shot, Dad.'

'Yes,' said Gerald, with the same regret he could hear in his son's voice. They had nothing against Amber, except for the entirely unavoidable fact of her not being Veronica. An invisible ball of string tightened itself lightly around his throat. Veronica had so *appreciated* Christmas. They did it all so much better, so much more truly, with her in the first row of the audience.

'I recognised my first wife in Effie's book,' Charles projected over the voices around him. Oh God, the book. Gerald did not need to look at his son to feel Adam roll his eyes and pick up his phone. 'She told me she'd written that before we met. I don't believe it for a second. She was right about it all too, no wonder it won every award—'

'Mum hates it when he tells this,' Adam hissed. 'Isn't this what they fell out over?'

'They didn't fall out.' Yes, it was exactly this they fell out over. 'Your mother just prefers the book to be less… present, than the art.'

'I know that, Dad.'

Charles's volume was growing. 'And why on earth she moved into painting I couldn't begin to—' Among his captive audience were both of the two artists present who were more famous than either Gerald or Effie, and Kerry-Alice, doing her best. The room was starting to smell more strongly of mince pies, so it was clear where Effie had been all this time. They were the usual ones she bought from Marks and Spencer, because she hated cooking but loved the ideal of cooking, hence whenever someone else offered something they could have prepared themselves, her mouth would set in a line. Gerald had never understood how the rest of the world managed to see as her real smile, when it was nothing – *nothing* – like it.

'You really must read the book, Kerry… Anne, was it?' Charles continued.

'Charles.' Effie was in the kitchen doorway, her smile a command.

'Dearest girl.'

Effie raised her eyebrows over her varifocals.

'Effie,' Kerry-Alice said. 'Would you like me to take the other plate?'

'I can manage, thank you, Kerry-Alice. Why don't you see who needs another drink.'

'Oh, no one, I assure you!' Charles draped a proprietorial arm over Kerry-Alice's shoulders and Gerald offered up a silent apology for his generation. 'Your assistant has been of excellent assistance, keeping me company and pretending to be interested in the ruminations of age.' He waited for contradiction. Effie glared not at him but at Kerry-Alice. 'Effie could have done whatever she wanted,' Charles projected for the benefit of the whole room. 'You know she was hot-tipped for a Nobel Prize for literature when she gave it all up?'

'I don't think it was the—' Kerry-Alice began.

'Wikipedia Man,' Adam muttered. 'Not all his citations are verified, but at the tap of a keyword all the information comes gushing out at whoever pressed the button, whether they meant to click or not.'

'Oh I don't know.'

'Oh come on, Dad—'

'Less like Wikipedia, more like watching an insect drowning in liquid… what's her name.'

'Amber.'

'Yes.' He felt Adam think for a moment. 'Actually, yeah.'

The falling out with Effie was decades before, when Charles was still a lecturer at their university. He'd wanted Effie to marry that hideous professor who ran out on her, his live-in-girlfriend and his job, and since being proved so wrong had never stopped trying to show how matey they were. He had also, before Gerald had become one, viewed all artists and bohemians as some kind of personal insult. Luckily, Charles' confidence meant you would be six hours into his acquaintance before you realised said confidence wasn't intelligence, and talking was not the same as having something to say. Gerald had the regular pang of guilt that he had never taken Charles aside to explain the rules. He still didn't know how he would, even if doing so didn't break them. It was always about the novel, too, the thing Effie least wanted talked about. But because they never spoke, and he never listened, nothing had ever changed.

'Now she's found you, Kerry-Alice, it's clear the business has a future. Will go on to great things, long after we…'

'Kerry-Alice,' Effie interrupted, 'would you see if Gerald or Adam needs another drink?'

'Of course.' She escaped towards the sofa.

'I thought she was here as a guest,' Gerald murmured as she moved towards them.

'She is,' said Adam.

Kerry-Alice aimed for the sofa beside Gerald and Adam. 'Do you…'

'We don't need anything,' Gerald said. 'Except, please, join us.'

'I'm not sure if…' The poor girl looked back over at Effie.

'It's not a Kerry-Alice Day, is it?' Adam asked.

Kerry-Alice turned back to them, the fear of displeasing Effie writ large. 'Right now, I'd have to say no.'

'In which case…' He moved along, so she had to sit beside Adam. Neither of the twenty-something children said a word to each other.

The imprint of paw on shoe made him look at the floor. 'Hello Cauliflower. He probably won't come up.'

The cat looked from him, to Adam, to Kerry-Alice, and leapt decisively onto her lap.

Adam gave him a look as if confirming his marbles were, finally, lost and rolling all over the floor for all to see.

'Has nobody opened the new monopoly set?' was all Kerry-Alice said.

'Not yet.' Gerald was fairly sure it would not be opened that day, and relegated to the games shelf; always so perfectly stacked, like a complex Jenga from which no one could bear to take any of the pieces from one Christmas Eve to the next. Except at his age, the possibility of something taking another year was more unsettling.

'Aubergine's outside.' Kerry-Alice was looking at the far side of the French windows. 'Does he want to come in?'

'Probably on his travels again. He'll be fine.' As if on cue, the green eyes were replaced by the grey-black tail, then absence. Aubergine would sometimes not be seen for weeks on end, but on Kerry-Alice Days he went to Effie's study, and sat just out of her reach, for as long as she stayed. He'd tried the same thing with Veronica, every so often. Veronica seemed to have such little time for cats. Or perhaps they just operated on even terms, regarded each other with a similar lack of expectation.

Beyond where Aubergine had disappeared, the children were playing giant-steps in imaginary snow. Another uncle was on boots and doormat duty, managing to vape and read the Financial Times in the glass doorway while smiling over the paper and returning encouraging and convincing comments whenever audience feedback was required. In another corner, Vincent and Amber had broken away from Charles' audience and become convincingly engrossed in one of the flimsier photo albums. If *she'd* asked to see it that meant one thing, but if *he'd* brought it out, the little girl would likely become a relation at some future point. The addition of two future daughters would be nice for Effie. Unless she found a reason to disapprove of Amber and Jane as much as she'd disapproved of Veronica.

'Does it change much?' Kerry-Alice asked. 'All this? Over the years?'

'No. Wonderfully, no.' Except how much quicker each year passed than the last. And he was so aware of Veronica's absence. He didn't claim to understand their relationship, sensed it wasn't... conventional? Was that word still allowed? But he did understand the way Vincent never met Amber's eye, as if his attention was on something just out of sight. Kerry-Alice's presence was welcome, Amber and her daughter's perhaps would be adjusted to in time – or it would fade, and either way would be as it was meant to be. In the middle of a conversation, he saw Vincent giving the tree a long look. The light frosted quality on his face was what Veronica called "not showing your working". It was a mannerism he had learnt from her. He had to admire her courage in standing up to him and Effie both, determined as they were (and how ridiculous that seemed already, a year and six hours down the road) that plastic was a worse idea than cut wood, but Effie's vehemence wasn't permanence; even if it had been, disapproval did not shift Veronica. Effie might as well have disapproved of the sky being blue. And far from looking fake, the tree Veronica had brought looked permanent in a way the mess of needles falling to the floor, making him worry unnecessarily but constantly about the cats' paws, never had. It had been so successful as to outlive her as a family member, perhaps, if today really was what the future looked like. He still hoped Effie would give herself the opportunity to enjoy these people in their lives. Everything was so temporary, after all.

'What's the music?' Kerry-Alice asked.

'I'm amazed you can hear any under all this.' He'd barely remembered it was there himself, under the buzz of voices. 'My favourite band, as it happens. Always a mention of tea, trains and Christmas – every album. They started as jazz, moved into prog rock, never fashionable but always recognisable. Always themselves.'

'Well, what I can hear is beautiful.'

The cousin with the jacket walked away from the mantelpiece, leaving the Queen mirror where it was. One of the children who had successfully got her boots off and left most of the snow behind was staring at the purple tinsel over the fireplace. On the other side of Charles, Effie had brought in other relatives and was holding court, her Edwardian flowing royal blue skirt fitting so well with the tree and the decorations, as if this world she resisted were made around her. As, indeed, it was. He felt such a jolt of pride when his eyes happened to fall on her, the centre of any world worth having, if she'd only let herself get on with being in it.

He jumped slightly as she looked up, saw his gaze, glared, and turned her attention instead to their son's face.

'Adam,' Effie called. 'Your turn on the mulled wine.' She glared at Kerry-Alice, beside Gerald on her side of the sofa. As she did, Cauliflower leapt on Kerry-Alice's lap in a way he never did Effie's. Gerald fancied he saw trouble ahead as Effie left the room.

'Right,' said Adam. 'My turn on the mulled wine.'

'Go, go by all means.' A shame. But there would be other chances to introduce them properly. And Effie wasn't doing this deliberately, Everybody over the age of eighteen took their turn. Even though not everybody drank it. No one was really in charge, but somehow it worked. And the flavour was less important than the continuity. He could take or leave the taste of his favourite smell. But he liked the buzz of conversation it created, the familiarity of the saucepans on the hob, of everyone taking turns to restock. A ritual if not a recipe everyone in the family knew, more invested in making than drinking.

Cauliflower got up from Kerry-Alice's lap, and sat in the gap between them, filling the gap with fur. Kerry-Alice tickled the nearer ear. Cauliflower flattened it in sleepy acceptance.

'You're a cat whisperer,' Gerald said.

Kerry-Alice smiled down at the self-involved little demon. 'He's lovely.'

'He's not,' said Geralld. 'at least, not to everyone.'

Cauliflower looked with challenging disinterest, curled his feet under his face and fell diplomatically asleep. She stroked the cat, and looked around the room. 'It's lovely.' No, Kerry-Alice made people lovely because she saw them that way. An ability that, now he thought about it, was bound to infuriate his wife sooner or later.

'Yes,' he said, returning safely to her earlier question. 'It is. Always different, always the same.'

'Sounds... happy.'

'Happy. Yes.' He watched his wife's back, deliberately turned.

She saw him looking at Effie, and in her gaze he became aware of the sadness that passed his face. 'Constructing the cheese plate is my contribution,' he said. Just to say something. To get the children to join in with him, and then perhaps each other. 'The element of creative flair I exercise on the food side of things. It's very satisfying. Colours of grape, cracker. The mixing of textures. Hard, soft.'

Kerry-Alice looks charmed though. 'Designing the cheese platter is one of the great joys. It's the conversations in the supermarket. The passion and knowledge they always have at the counter. I only wish Effie enjoyed things as much as that. But you need to understand it's no one's fault if she doesn't.'

'I'll do everything I can, Gerald.'

He turned back to her, saw her understanding the worry in his eyes, not realising it was for her. 'I know you will.' And God help her, she would. No filter, no off-switch. Just wanting to help. What could she possibly be so grateful to Effie for that she let herself be resented like this?

'It's not going to snow again, is it?' Kerry-Alice asked.

'Probably not.' They watched the children's rising breath through the glass, white on navy over the frozen grasses in the winter night.

On the tiny television, Jane had pressed pause on the ball scene, a close-up of Sarah realising she's trapped in a bubble of fantasy. The little girl stood up, brushed off her purple leggings with the dignity of a matriarch, and climbed onto the sofa to sit next to Kerry-Alice... or, more accurately, next to Cauliflower. 'Why's he called Cauliflower?' the girl asked Kerry-Alice. Kerry-Alice looked at Gerald.

'You'll have to ask your…' Father?

'Uncle Vinnie?'

'Your Uncle Vinnie, yes. The boys named them. Adam and your Uncle Vinnie.'

'Mummy and Uncle Vinnie were naked when they met,' the child said conversationally. 'They were dancing. In a field. They were allowed to keep their shoes on so they wouldn't get athlete's foot. That's when your foot goes mouldy.' She trailed off, clearly able to tell from the way everyone looked at her that that was the wrong thing to say, but unable to work out why. 'They went to a place where everybody dances and it was Mummy's first time and Uncle Vinnie's second. Mummy likes taking photos. Do you like taking photos?'

'I do,' said Kerry-Alice. Vincent came over.

'Sorry about that,' said Vincent. 'All okay, Jane?'

'I was talking about dancing.'

'Right,' he said. Then, 'Well, it doesn't matter.'

'Is your… are you all staying, Vincent?' Gerald asked.

'No. I forget why.' He looked at the Christmas tree again, briefly, then followed Jane towards Amber.

Gerald and Kerry-Alice's eyes returned to the cat. 'I wonder how he sleeps through all this,' she said after a while.

'Probably because he knows it doesn't involve him.'

'Yes.' Kerry-Alice stared into the cat's fur. 'I sometimes wonder if the things that bother us would still bother us if we didn't take them personally.'

'Up to and including loud noise.' Should he try to talk to her about Effie? Should he warn her? And of what? If only Adam would—

'You have no idea how… Sorry, that sounds… sorry. But things at home with my… and his family…' She trailed off, looked around like a child seeing inside a storybook, no words for the wonder of normality. 'You know what? It's enough that everything is happening somewhere. Someone has a proper… a family that looks like a family. That's safe. I used to look at other places and… that had to be enough. That people were just like the trees in my wood. We are part of every tangle.'

'You have a wood?'

'Just a small one. Every house on our road has a bit we're responsible for.'

'How wonderful.' But what was touching to Gerald, he knew would be cloying to Effie. She hated to hear of other people's lives, heard only competition, not the gift such information was trying to be. But it was a language he spoke, and maybe he could give her what she needed even if she'd rather have it from Effie. 'What's Effie told you about my first wife?'

'Effie doesn't talk about...'

'Well. Her name was May. She ran the local record shop. I'd see her behind that counter every week in my early-to-mid teens. I was always plucking up the courage to buy something, and planning my outfits and purchases around what I thought would impress her. Eventually, something did. She scribbled her number on my receipt. Six months later I'd picked a deep enough hole in my relationship with my father to be desperate for somewhere to live. Not on purpose...'

'Of course not.' Kerry-Alice smiled the smile of the co-conspirator.

'I felt honoured to be picked. And I wanted to learn about... life. Which it always looks like others know about. The way when you know so little you believe the paths are laid out. We saw something in each other, right aesthetic, right time... I do absolutely believe in love at first sight, but what happened, just as I was buying a record she told me was going to be terrible, was that someone came in with a gun. It was all very polite and she leant one knee on the emergency button and looked into his eyes until the police arrived. It was the most beautiful thing I ever saw. It made me feel astoundingly... safe. Her name was the shop's name. May Records. The problem was, I fell in love with a grown-up. When I thought those were real things. May set me the example of how important confidence was when she found out I'd started a drawing group with two friends in a pub, sneered at my sketchbooks and said "I'm a better artist than any of you", the same way she'd impressed me by telling me the record I was buying was going to be terrible. She wanted to be my inspiration, but she also wanted to be better than me at painting. It was all a competition. And I was younger, and it was my job to lose the competition.'

'As if someone else being better is a reason not to paint!'

'She was wrong about trying to control me. And she was wrong about being a better artist. But mainly she was wrong about inspiration. If there's one thing guaranteed to irritate me, or anyone with the strength to turn up at a desk and treat this thing they claim to love like the job of work it is, it's people bleating on about inspiration. Looking soulful and misunderstood is easy to cultivate. The confidence that comes with practice… May could have been an artist. She had enough education and intelligence that had she added the slightest ounce of courage to her habits she could have been great. But she didn't *know* she'd be great. She didn't *know* she'd be better than other people. So she didn't try at all. And if not being sure you'll win is a reason not to play…' He trailed off.

'Go on.'

'Anger is so easy. Listening is much harder. And you know that. Because you don't resort to anger.' He sighed. 'I tried being angry. I'd planned to be furious with the café that eventually replaced the record shop, but went there years later on my own, to meet a friend. I sat in what I remembered as the jazz section, picked a coffee, something strange and modern called a flat white, and didn't realise until after we left that, other than thinking "I'm sitting in the jazz section", I hadn't felt anything. Until of course she came in, didn't she. Just like me, to meet someone. And I talked to her adult to adult, and I saw how very small and disappointed she was, and I wondered if she'd hit anybody else half her age…'

'She hit you?'

'…and I pitied whoever was in her immediate life, and because it was all as true as anything could be I didn't need to say any of it. I didn't tell her I was a member of the Royal Academy. I didn't tell her I was married to someone I loved, that I had two wonderful children…'

'And two wonderful cats.'

'And two wonderful…yes.' And two wonderful would-be daughters, who Effie would do all she could to make enemies. 'But you need to understand that if it's ever about a person…Be careful. With Effie.'

'Gerald, I… it's not…'

'Oh, I know. I know it's not that kind of love. But love is, as I've heard said, love. And there are always other kinds.' Other needs unmet, other calls not answered. For whatever reasons she had, Kerry-Alice adored Effie, and Effie had never known how to be adored. And Gerald did not want to lose another not-quite-daughter this year.

'It's hard to imagine you… not knowing all this was coming. Was waiting for you.'

'But I didn't, you see. This is what's impossible to understand when you're still young enough. The future isn't a dart board you aim for with absolute clarity. I didn't have any prior awareness of Gerald James RA when I dropped out of sixth-form and married a twenty-eight year-old record store manager. I didn't even think of Gerald as my name. If you'd asked me who Gerald James was, I'd have told you that was my father.'

He watched her look around again, saw her imagine a Gerald who didn't know this house existed. Who didn't know Effie's family would risk losing it and he would buy it back and gift it to her. He barely knew it himself now. The house knew Effie, revolved around Effie. But just because it and he did, it did not mean he would let Kerry-Alice do the same.

'The way there's part of you and part of her and the boys everywhere you look. The way everything fits.' Gerald suppressed the smile that Kerry-Alice, closer in age to their sons than to them, called them what Effie called them, *the boys*, bracketed them in the vocabulary of children. 'It's beautiful.'

'It's also messy, at times.'

She stared into Cauliflower's fur.

'Look, the way I made this work was not to seem to need to. I held back. I gave her the love she was ready for. And I have May to thank for knowing how to do that. What people would say is that I was a child. Legally, I wasn't. Emotionally perhaps we all are, no matter how old. But she was a friend, and an influence, and a very beautiful woman who ran a record shop. And I was an eighteen year-old…'

'Man?'

'Boy. It doesn't change, Kerry-Alice. All that changes is you understand you're not a grown-up and neither is anyone else. May also set me the example of how important confidence was. I'm sorry you never met Veronica, Vincent's wife. Ex-wife. She rather brought things together.'

Something he didn't understand crossed Kerry-Alice's face. 'She sounds like a good friend to have.'

'May? Or Veronica?'

Kerry-Alice looked at where Cauliflower was asleep, ignoring the music under the conversations as much as the blanket of voices having them. 'Do you think they wonder about us? Do humans seem to have their own inner lives or are we just tin-openers? Just monkey-butlers?'

'As adults are to children.'

'As they're supposed to be.'

'And they're not wrong, children have that biological truth on their side, that we do exist for their needs.' Was this it? Was this what Kerry-Alice wanted from Effie? Exactly what Effie wanted: a daughter? Which Gerald had so nearly given her, for the forty-eight precious hours she lived? 'Or we should. That's why there's nothing so horrific as bad parenting, and I'm sorry you had it.'

'Not bad, just… distracted. 'The reason my name is double-barrelled is my parents gave me different names. They divorced before I had any conscious memory of being a single unit. Mum always called me Kerry, Dad always called me Alice. They'd do it in front of each other, and I'd answer to both. It wasn't exactly that I didn't know this was all part of their argument, I suppose I thought if I showed them it didn't matter to me than there wouldn't be anything to argue about. I didn't understand that the argument was the point, not whatever they found to argue about. So it didn't work, and I just took both as my name.'

'And you never wanted to make it your decision?'

'That's probably exactly it. Not making a decision is, in all the ways that count, making a decision. I didn't choose between them. They called me by different names. By the time I was born they were still arguing over whether I'd be a Kerry or whether I'd be an Alice, one was a family name and one was the polar opposite of both their family names. It was so important to be right that they never agreed.'

'You don't know your legal name?'

'I think it's in this order. Or I assumed. Which is the opposite of thinking, really, isn't it.'

'You could have chosen yourself.'

'Dad said that. That it meant I didn't know who I was. He was wrong. It was the opposite. How many other Kerry-Alices do you know?'

He smiled. 'You are unique. But you're right. I suppose what I attribute to May is bad parenting. Not that I'd have admitted it. Neither of us would. But every partner is parent and child and everything else at one point or another.'

'Have you googled her? I mean, you must have done.'

'The internet is a wonderful thing, isn't it?' It was an obvious non-answer and he was vaguely touched and equally vaguely insulted she let him get away with it. 'When I was at university we only just had mobile phones by the skin of our teeth. The lecturer Effie was seeing when we first moved in together had one of those tiny Nokias that look like Star Trek communicators.'

She smiled, said gently, 'You were talking about May.'

'Yes, I suppose I was.' He sighed. Telling the truth felt so like cheating. It was so comfortable and so interesting to hear himself say it all. 'I wanted two things: to be a painter, and not to live with my parents. But being a painter and painting are two sides of a coin I hadn't quite acquired. I painted her, but I learnt nothing. And with every painting I was trying harder to capture a feeling, not on the page but in myself, the feeling I'd had when I first saw and experienced her. Before I saw everything else she wanted to be: the one with the power.' Instinctively he pulled his sleeve a little lower on the arm whose cigarette burn had faded before this girl was born.

'What changed?' she asked.

'The only thing that needs to. My self-esteem. Or failing that, my patience. I had missed out on UCAS again as we walked back into her flat, and I'd said something similar and she'd jumped down my throat for it. "Do you know how much of a teenager you sound?" and then I said something that changed everything.'

'What was that?'

'"I am a teenager,"' The words drop into their silence, over the voices, over the music. 'It's the silence I remember,' he said. 'She didn't apologise, I don't remember what came after the silence at all. But in that silence was a crack of light, I could see her acknowledging I was right, that there was a limit to her knowledge and, perhaps, a beginning to mine. I don't know if she felt caught out, or revealed, or if I'd given her the permission to give me up on me. To stop being her fan. I've met fans since. My own, other people's. Fans want to tell you about the person you are to them. They're not at all interested in the person you are.' He didn't give her long enough to work out why he thought this was relevant before he said, 'Be careful of Effie, Kerry-Alice.'

'What do you mean?'

'You could be so good for my wife,' he said, taking and squeezing her hand. 'If she let you. You have to understand how hard she makes things. She paints what she can't see. You're doing nothing wrong. Keep trying. Maybe we could get you an extra day here? As my assistant?'

And that, of course, was when Effie turned around.

Kerry-Alice pulled back from Gerald's hand.

And Gerald saw Effie look at the picture of the husband and the protegee, the cat between them, the one squeezing the other's hand; saw how clearly misunderstood the smile that passed between them, because she couldn't believe that she was loved that much. That two people cared about her enough for the secret that passed between them to be harmless. It was less of a reach to look at that picture and see betrayal.

And everything that was going to end, would end because of that.

Not for him. He would always be on that sofa, in the house he'd bought to return to her. One year would pile on top of the other, too established to rock even slightly, because she knew, didn't she, there was no betrayal? But about the one whose hand was squeezed, not the one who did the squeezing, Gerald knew Effie would be merciless. It was his fault. But all Gerald could do was change the subject, because to talk to her about what he'd read into her expression was impossible.

Gerald watched Kerry-Alice open her mouth to say it wasn't about managing, that she only wanted to help, but either through his advice or fear or despair, she sensibly closed it again. They continued watching as nothing continued to happen.

He could have told her. He could have explained the screaming alarm that went off when someone was being a fan not a player, preoccupied with telling you the person that you are to them, rather than asking questions about who you are. Effie never had the courage or the interest to do it herself. Effie did not like people helping her, or wanting to help her. It would probably be alright as long as Kerry-Alice didn't witness any kind of vulnerability, but you didn't get to spend time in someone's home and not have that happen. But he couldn't say that.'

Jane was back, walking towards them arm outstretched, camera in hand. 'Will you take a photo of all of us?' she asked.

Kerry-Alice took the camera.

Effie turned back, and Gerald was watching over the heads Kerry-Alice was organising into perfect height order, every face visible to the camera and no loss of atmosphere as Kerry-Alice kept the focus of the bossy, smiled at the shy, laughed or commiserated with the more and less enthusiastic. Gerald watched Effie pause in the doorway, run a cuff over her pale hair, her expression an articulate blank.

'Oh, Effie!' In her love of art, Kerry-Alice had already forgotten the possibility of Effie making up a story that had overtaken her. 'Will you come into the middle?'

Effie came back into the room; there were too many eyes on her to not.

'Gerald, will you stand next to her? In the middle?'

'They won't have put the clingfilm on the cheeseboard, I just know it,' Effie said at his elbow, as Kerry-Alice was passing round glasses of mulled wine, preparing her subjects for the photo.

'Well,' said Gerald, his fingers encircling his wife's as Kerry-Alice lifted the camera to her appreciative eyes, 'a new year is coming.'

'It always is,' Effie snapped, quietly enough for his ears only. 'This should be just family,' she hissed as Gerald put his arm around her.

'Amber and Jane might be family. Veronica was.' It was the wrong thing to say, but it was the truth. So surely not truly wrong? Effie must have known these things took root, grew together. You couldn't extract them all at once simply because they used to not be there, or because they might not always remain.

'Just move a little further left everybody, get the Christmas tree right in the middle...'

'I heard how you were talking to her,' his wife whispered from under his arm. 'I saw you holding her hand.'

'Okay and everybody facing forward, if you can't see the camera it can't see you...'

'She's grateful, Effie. She wants you to be happy,' he whispered. Their eyes didn't move from the camera, his in obedience, hers in defense. 'You must know I could never look at her, look at anyone, like I look at you?'

'You know nothing about people,' she hissed back. 'You know nothing about anything.'

Kerry-Alice held up the camera, her smile bright beneath it. And Gerald knew it was the version of them in that picture that would outlive any more subjective truth, that the camera would see what Effie refused to. Gerald gently clasped his wife's shoulder to his and he smiled.

Acknowledgements

Thank you to my friends and family for being such brilliant sounding boards and research assistants, including Amy Banks, Lucy Coleshill, Alex Davis, Colin Dunlop, Sophie Hannah, Sean Hogan, Marianne Izen, Neil Mason, Marc Morris, Jackie Naffah, Ben Reed, Lynda E. Rucker, Steve J. Shaw, Robert Shearman, Vanessa Thompsett, The Writers' Gym podcast guests and everyone who has joined me in the Writing Room. Special thanks to Professor Michael Dobson for "windfucker", Liss Macklin for "monkey-butler" and Kate Shenton for "my wood". Any factual inaccuracies, deliberate or otherwise, are my own.

Dr. Rachel Knightley is a fiction and non-fiction author, lecturer and writing and confidence coach. Her first short story collection, *Beyond Glass*, was published in 2021 by Black Shuck Books. Her non-fiction includes WJEC/Eduqas's *GCSE Drama Study and Revision Guide* (Illuminate/Hodder) and *Your Creative Writing Toolkit*. Her stories appear in *Great British Horror 5: Midsummer Eve*, British-Fantasy-Award-nominated *Dreamland* (both Black Shuck Books), and *Uncertainties vol. 3* (Swan River Press). She writes and presents features for film release companies including Indicator Films, Second Sight, Starburst and Severin Films, and for magazines including *Writing Magazine, Jewish Renaissance, The Dark Side, Starburst* and *Fangoria*).

www.rachelknightley.com

Milton Keynes UK
Ingram Content Group UK Ltd.
UKHW010828201223
434702UK00001B/50